SOUTH TO TH

*

Gareth Owen was born in Ainsdale, Lancashire. He was educated at Christ Church Secondary and Merchant Taylors School, Crosby. After leaving school at sixteen, he served for four years in the Merchant Navy. He then did various jobs including factory work, market gardening and bookselling, before qualifying as a teacher from Bretton Hall College, Wakefield. He taught English and Drama at Downshall Secondary School, Ilford for four years before becoming a lecturer at Bordesley College of Education in Birmingham.

A prize-winning poet, he has published five collections of verse as well as five novels and books for children. He has also written numerous plays, four of which have been broadcast by the BBC. For a number of years he presented the BBC's long-running *Poetry Please!* He has won both the John Tripp and the national Speak a Poem awards for spoken poetry.

For a time he managed the career of soul singer, Ruby Turner and ran his own record company.

He now lives in Ludlow where he occasionally performs his own songs in the guise of Country singer, Virg Clenthills.

*

South to that dark sun

Gareth Owen

Matador
5 Weir Road
Kibworth Beauchamp
Leicester LE8 0LQ, UK
Tel: (+44) 116 279 2299
Fax: (+44) 116 279 2277
Email: books@troubador.co.uk
Web: www.troubador.co.uk/matador

ISBN 978 1848763 944

British Library Cataloguing in Publication Data.
A catalogue record for this book is available from the British Library.

Typeset in 11pt Garamond by Troubador Publishing Ltd, Leicester, UK

Matador is an imprint of Troubador Publishing Ltd

Printed in Great Britain by the MPG Books Group, Bodmin and King's Lynn

For Jacquie

Preface

I feel I ought to explain why the early stories in this collection appear to be written by a young Italian woman and have Italian settings.

If I am known at all, it is as a writer of poetry and fiction for children, but I always had it in mind one day to try my hand at adult fiction. However, I found the required change of gear, psychologically intimidating. I was blocked.

Then one evening, everything suddenly changed. At the time I was attending Italian classes. Our spirited and talented teacher, Manuela, would intersperse her excellent lessons with various amusing anecdotes about her friends and relatives; all of them of course set in Italy. One evening I found myself, as it were, pretending to be her and working one of those scraps of anecdotes into a full-blown tale. In terms of style it was immensely liberating. It was a sort of acting job.

However, after the initial surge of delight I felt at writing those early *Italian* stories, I did wonder whether I was going to be stuck with being a young Italian woman for the remainder of my writing life; would this sudden rush of creative confidence disappear as suddenly as it had appeared, when I reverted to my own sex and nationality?

Confidence is a fragile commodity.

Happily, the new-found confidence and energy seems to me to have survived the change and the later stories are uncompromisingly English in mood and setting.

But, as always, it is for the reader to make the final judgement.

Gareth Owen. December 2009

Contents

*

Driving with my baby, driving South to that dark sun
Driving with my baby, yeah South to that dark sun
See Robert Johnson at the crossroads
With a guitar and a gun.

The Blues is a highway and the Blues can set you free
Yeah the Blues is a highway and the Blues can set you free
See Robert Johnson at the crossroads
And he's awaiting there for me.

Blues for Robert Johnson.
©Virg Clenthills

Zia Teresa

My brothers and sisters knew her as Zia Teresa: Aunt Teresa. She was my mother's older sister. 'Come era bella! - How beautiful she was,' my mother was always telling me. It was a special kind of beauty that induced in the susceptible young men of our little Italian town, not mere sexual excitement but a sense of awe that was almost religious. They trembled tongue-tied in her presence, wondering how best they might conspicuously lay down their lives for her. There was something haunting about her. A soulful and sensitive intelligence seemed to shine from those limpid and sensitive eyes.

And yet, all this was sadly illusory.

My mother, in talking of her would describe a circle with her thumb and forefinger: the empty space between the two digits serving to denote what she considered to be the miniscule dimension of Zia Teresa's brain. 'And yet when we were young, how I envied her beauty. But you know I was proud too. When we walked down Via Santa Agatha to do the family shopping or went to the little local cinema – even the old men would turn and stare at her as though they had seen a vision. Even Father Cavalcanti himself!'

Father Cavalcanti was the eighty-five-year old priest, whose reputation for piety was universally acknowledged throughout the Abruzzo. Yet, even he, in Teresa's presence, would tremble, spilling the sacramental wine, as he gazed upon her with an undisguised wonderment quite inappropriate to his age and calling.

'As for me,' my mother confided regretfully, 'men were hardly aware of my existence. It wasn't that I was excessively plain. It was just that next to her I sort of disappeared; like a glass bead next to a diamond.'

And yet strangely, Zia Teresa seemed unaware of the power that the genetic accident of her beauty had conferred upon her. In her sixth year, an incongruous piety took possession of her. This was not unconnected with the continuous pain she suffered at the loss of her first set of teeth, which were in contrast to the rest of her person, something less than perfect, being discoloured and randomly uneven.

Her piety grew, my mother thought, out of a fellow feeling, she developed with a little known saint: Santa Appollonia. Santa Appollonia is the patron saint of all those who suffer from the toothache. My grandmother, while shopping one Saturday morning in Piazza Mollinuto Market, had spotted a framed, rather sentimentally painted portrait of the Saint. She was shown hovering on a bank of white cloud, a pair of forceps in her hand, gazing down with infinite compassion upon an unhappy cowhand who was fingering a mouthful of decaying teeth. My grandmother was immediately struck by the uncanny resemblance the Saint bore to her little Teresa. She bought the picture and gave it to her daughter as a birthday gift. It hung next to a small mirror at the turning of the stair in my grandmother's house in Porto Salva. From the moment she first saw it, Teresa seemed entranced by the picture and the character of the Saint. On the wooden step beneath it she placed a crude, wooden shelf as a kind of offertory. On it she would place wild flowers, small guttering candles and, now and again, whichever misshapen tooth had happened to detach itself from her gum that particular morning. For sometimes half an hour at a time, she would stand transfixed upon the stairs, her gaze shifting continuously back and forth between the sentimental depiction of the saint and her own, entranced six-year-old face, that stared back at her from the mirror. It may be, that with time, a certain confusion developed in her mind as to her true identity. Who knows? According to my superstitious grandmother, her prayers and her attachment to the Saint did produce one happy result. As Zia Teresa's second set of teeth began to make their appearance, they proved to be quite perfect in every way. My grandmother was overjoyed. 'Un miracolo! Veramente un miracolo!' she would exclaim offering up prayers of thanks to the little Saint upon the stair. From thenceforth, until she became ill some years later, every year on the occasion of Teresa's birthday, she would plant a fresh olive sapling in the stony, sloping garden at the back of the house, to each one of which was attached a picture of the Saint. And whenever relations, visitors or tradesman called, Teresa would be summoned to show herself and her new teeth. 'Smile, smile cara for the ladies and gentlemen,' her mother would instruct her. And as her little Teresa smiled her most dazzling smile, her mother would cross herself and beam with pride.

In fact Zia Teresa was a kindly, sentimental young woman who was content to stay at home and tend her mother, my grandmother, through her final illness, while *my* mother was studying fine art at Bologna University. Yet she evinced not a trace of malice or envy.

Naturally, her beauty led to several nervous proposals of marriage; all of which she turned down. For this, her attachment to Santa Apollonia was partially to blame. Because of her dedication to the Saint, she at one time harboured a secret ambition to be a dentist. But when it became clear that she lacked the brain power to pass the necessary exams, she elected instead to become the next best thing: the wife of a dentist. 'I shall wait for my dentist to sweep me off my feet,' she would murmur, her dark eyes agleam with dreams. It seemed unlikely, since within living memory, there had not been one dentist among our extensive range of acquaintances.

'You'll go to your grave a virgin,' my grandmother warned; a fate that did not appear to worry Teresa unduly.

She had a firm, if sentimental belief in destiny.

*

And then one evening, fate rapped upon her door. Or rather, it pressed the bell on the pizza take away café where she was working.

Her life changed for ever.

She was approaching forty at the time, though still beautiful, serving behind the counter at *Da Giulio*: a small pizza parlour and takeaway on the corner of Via della Lupa and Vicolo del Oro, owned by two of her uncles. As she was about to lock up for the night a large black Mercedes limousine drew up at the pavement and a stoutish, middle-aged gentleman in an expensive-looking grey suit rang the bell.

Zia Teresa mouthed the words 'Closed' through the window but he continued to knock and gesture for her to let him in. It was almost midnight. She had been on her feet for eight hours. She was tired. However, her uncles had always impressed upon her the age-old shopkeepers' principle of the customer always being right; so, she unlocked the door and opened it. 'I'm sorry sir. Mi dispiace, but we're closed,' she said smiling guardedly. 'The ovens have been turned off. The cook has gone home. There is nothing to eat. Niente. Niente. Mi dispiace ma...' And she shrugged prettily and smiled that smile of hers that years of practice had perfected.

But when she attempted to close the door she found an expensive looking black brogue in the way. She glanced nervously up and down the lamp lit street. It was deserted.

'Signore, please!'

But the man wouldn't move. He stared fixedly at her. 'Again,' he whispered. 'Please do it again.'

Teresa frowned. 'What? I don't understand. Do what again?'

And the man in the doorway clasped his hands together. 'Smiiile,' he implored her.

'Smile?'

'Vi prego signora. For me eh? Smile. Please.'

And Zia Teresa - who throughout her life had become accustomed to smiling to order - smiled.

A groan emerged from somewhere deep in the man's being. 'Oh grazie Signorina, grazie. May our Blessed Lady visit her joys upon you. '

Zia Teresa watched the rise and fall of his Adam's apple as he struggled to give voice to his feelings.

'Signorina, your smile…' he thumped his fist lightly against his heart. 'Please we must talk.'

'But…'

'We must.' His vehemence startled her. From a brown leather wallet, engraved with his initials, he produced a gold embossed card and pressed it into her hand. She recognised the name from somewhere but she couldn't be sure where. And then a single word leapt out at her - *Dentist*.

She looked up at him. Her face was radiant. She smiled again.

'Oh God,' he murmured weakly.

She took his hand. 'Come,' she said.

She locked the door and flicked the *Closed* sign round. They sat down opposite one another at a square plastic table. 'I wish to show you something,' he said leaning forward.

'Anything,' she whispered.

From his jacket pocket he took a small leather case and placed it between them on the table. He pressed a button and the case sprang open. Within, encased in red velvet, lay a toothbrush. With delicate reverence he removed it from the case and held it up to the light. 'Take it,' he whispered.

She hesitated.

'Go on take it.'

She took it from him.

He leaned forward. 'The future of dental hygiene lies in your hand. After this, the act of brushing will never be the same again.'

And with infinite delicacy he raised her hand so that the toothbrush almost touched her red, full lips.

'Now,' he said, - 'Smile.'

And in that humid, midnight café with its greasy plastic tables, the air heavy with the aroma of ten varieties of cheese - an advertising legend was born.

Six months later Zia Teresa's face, toothbrush in hand, could be seen smiling from hoardings up and down the country. Magazine editors pursued her. She was interviewed on television. She met the Pope and made him a gift of the patented *Apollonia Wonder Brush* in a special case, on which was an inscription alluding to the indissoluble union between Cleanliness and Godliness. Three months later she married her dentist.

Her life was transformed.

With her new-found wealth she induced her husband to buy a large but rather ugly villa on the banks of Lake Maggiore. And yet she never lost her simplicity or, what her detractors might have called, her vulgarity. Although she could now afford to visit the most exotic resorts on God's Earth, she contented herself with staying at popular destinations such as Sorrento and Viareggio where she sat amongst crowds of holiday makers, eating ice cream.

There was not an ounce of snobbery in her.

And after every holiday, she would pull up at our door in her chauffeur-driven limousine, her now more ample figure squeezed into an expensive little silk number. We always knew it was her by the tinkling of her jewellery, as she tottered up our uneven path on her spike-heeled sandals, her bosom bouncing amiably. And on every visit, she presented my mother with a tissue-wrapped gift. Despite her wealth it was as if she still needed my mother's approval in some odd way. The gift, no matter where she had been, was always the same: a coloured plastic Madonna filled to the brim with Holy Water. Underneath would be written - *A Gift from Viareggio* or *Sorrento* or wherever it was that she had last visited. My mother's sense of taste was extraordinarily well-developed and these vulgar, sloshing Madonnas induced in her a revulsion that was almost physical. Yet she was sensible of Zia Teresa's feelings and so, disguised her disgust with a constrained smile saying. 'Ah another Madonna. How lovely! Darling Teresa you are generous.' And Zia Teresa, whose ingenuousness rendered her blind to the most blatant hypocrisy, would smile the smile that in the past had sold a million Apollonia tooth brushes (patent pending) and be happy.

As soon as she had left though, my mother, unable to bear having them in the same room with her, would consign the Madonnas to the outer reaches of the attic or the cellar or some other distant location where they could no longer offend her sensibilities.

Then, whenever we got word that Zia Teresa was about to

make another visit, we would spend hours desperately hunting them down before lining them up on a chest of drawers, for all the world like some odd religious ladies' football team.

And then suddenly there were no more Madonnas. Zia Teresa had succumbed to a sudden heart attack while lying beside a crowded hotel swimming pool, one hot August afternoon; an ice cream cornet melting in her hand.

After the funeral we returned home and drank a toast to her memory. When the guests had left we sat down at the kitchen table; my mother, father, my other sister and my younger brother and looked at one another. We each of us knew what the other was thinking.

The Madonnas; what were we going to do with them all?

'Let's find them first,' said my mother.

Three hours later, nine of them stood side by side on the table. My mother gazed at them with revulsion. 'My sister!' she said. 'She was such a stupid woman.' And quite silently, she began to cry.

'But surely there were ten.' my sister said.

She was right.

My mother wiped her eyes. 'We have to find it: the missing Madonna. I can't tell why but it's really important to me.'

But a further rigorous search brought nothing to light.

'Never mind,' my mother said. 'I know what we can do with them,'

We marched out into the back garden and quietly and ceremoniously emptied the holy water onto the roots of the ten olives that my grandmother had planted on Zia Teresa's birthdays so many years ago. Finally the empty Madonnas were piled unceremoniously into the rubbish bin.

There was a limit to my mother's sentiment.

Sitting on the sofa beside the fire that evening, something pressed into my leg. I lifted the cushion. The bland face of a Madonna in pink plastic stared up at me reprovingly. I was about to dump it with the others when my mother took it from me. She gazed at it for a moment. 'Serves me right,' she said. 'I'll put it here where it will always remind me.' And she placed the Madonna on the mantel shelf, between a copy of a Picasso print (blue period), and a reproduction of a smooth white head from the Cyclades.

She stood back to admire her handiwork. She looked at us all.

'In spite of everything, she had a sort of goodness about her,' she said.

Made in Heaven

I

As her latest client left the office, Anna Livia briefly inspected the cheque she had given her, before slipping it into the drawer where it joined all the others. Stretching her slim arms to the ceiling she spun her chair in a circle, smiling contentedly. 'I am happy,' she said to herself. 'On this day on the twenty-fifth of July at 3 o'clock in the afternoon I am happy. And I was happy yesterday too. And the chances are I will be happy tomorrow.' And in order that she might remain on the sunny side of fate, she touched her lips to the topknot of the small plaster effigy of Saint Anthony that stood on her desk.

The light flashed on her intercom.

Her secretary's voice said, 'There's a Signorina Sandra Torielli to see you.'

'Ah yes,' Anna Livia said, bringing the new client's name up on her screen. 'She's a little on the early side. Ask her if she wouldn't mind waiting just a few more minutes. Offer her a coffee. Oh and talking of which, I'll have mine now.'

As usual she drank her coffee standing at the second story window that looked out onto the streets of Turin. She enjoyed observing the passers by; the women in particular. Very occasionally she would recognise someone she knew: someone she had helped in the past. And then again she would study the faces of those legions of anonymous women of whom she knew nothing: each of whom with a singular life, that stretched back to a misty hinterland of joy and sorrow and mundanity that was entirely separate from hers. The thought made her dizzy. But then her practical side reasserted itself and she couldn't help speculating, how perhaps one day in the near future, one or two of these hitherto unknown women might knock upon her office door and she would learn something of their lives: their heartsickness, their long-deferred dreams, their disappointments; and she would help them. It had become her vocation. The thought brought her immense satisfaction. The fact that it also brought her a not inconsiderable income, in no way served to detract from that pleasure.

Was there, she wondered sipping her coffee, anything in the world to equal being an independent, healthy, intelligent, young woman who was happy in her work? She decided there was not. And not for the first time she wondered at the change that had come about in her life over the last year or so.

When had it begun? When?

The phone call from Sylvia? Yes, that had probably been the start of it.

And yet at the time, how resentful she had been. Perhaps resentful was too strong a word. It was more that she felt ill-used. By any of the normal standards of friendship Sylvia's behaviour had been unforgivable.

They had met at University as eighteen year olds, where in

truth, Anna had considered Sylvia to be more an acquaintance than a true friend; but following her graduation, when she discovered they were working and living in the same city, sometimes feeling rather isolated, she had willingly allowed Sylvia to, as it were, heat the temperature of their relationship. They lunched together at least once a week; stayed over at each other's apartments; went to the same parties; shared acquaintances, secrets and even on one occasion their boy friends - though not, I may add, at the same time. In short they became inseparable. Anna, who was less naturally gregarious than Sylvia, had always felt that it had been Sylvia and not she who had made most of the running in the cultivation of their friendship. There was, she felt, a rather light-headed, selfish side to Sylvia, together with a sentimental and rather superstitious religiosity that deep down irritated her. But she learned to suppress her feelings. That was her way. There had always been a chameleon element in Anna Livia's make-up that enabled her to accommodate herself comfortably to what she considered to be, the more vexatious aspects of her acquaintances. And anyway, she concluded, when had friendship ever been based on moral considerations? Naturally there was a distaff side to all this: mainly the necessity Anna felt, out of consideration for Sylvia, to suppress certain essential traits in her own personality; in particular her intellectual seriousness and ambition. It irked her somewhat, but she considered it to be but a small sacrifice; and in the long run, the social and emotional gains brought by Sylvia's lively and impetuous companionship far outweighed the losses.

And so it came as an unpleasant shock when Sylvia dropped her. The lengthy, breathless, giggly phone calls dwindled; the gossipy lunches and the shared holidays became a thing of the past. It was a disturbing and unexpected development. Anna Livia was a proud and independent young woman and it pained her not a little to admit that Sylvia's withdrawal left a considerable hole in her life. Her chagrin was further exacerbated in that the schism disturbed a conviction she had hitherto always held: that it was Sylvia who needed her much more than she needed Sylvia. This sudden reversal of roles somewhat dented her self-esteem. However it wasn't in her nature to display neediness; to make the running; and so she swallowed her pride and, under the pretence of a touching concern for Sylvia's well-being, plied her with solicitous notes and left countless messages on her answer phone. But the notes remained unanswered and shortly afterwards a message from the telephone company informed her that the number she required had been changed. She understood immediately what this meant and resigned herself, with not a little sadness and pain, to the fact that their friendship had run its course. She did wonder what might have occasioned the break. Had *she* done something wrong? Mentally she trawled through all their recent conversations and encounters but recalled nothing that might have occasioned the rift. And so, after making a number of discrete enquiries she learned it was the old, old story: *cherchez l'homme!* A good-looking, well-connected partner in a large accountancy firm had walked into Sylvia's life one day and swept her off her elegantly shod little feet. Three months later Anna Livia read of her marriage in *La Stampa*.

She studied the accompanying photograph with a mixture of mild bitterness and sadness and her tears splashed onto the image of bride and groom that smiled out at her from the newspaper. She read through the names on the guest list; a list from which hers was conspicuously absent. Then in an unusual fit of temper, she tore the announcement into tiny shreds and flung it into the waste paper basket. For a certain time she wore the bruise of her rejection like a badge; but then after a few weeks, as was her way, she mentally shrugged her shoulders and decided that life was something that just had to be got on with.

In an attempt to distract herself from the *longeurs* and the empty diary occasioned by Sylvia's absence, she turned to her work at the Publishers for distraction, only to realise sadly, that her job no longer gave her any satisfaction. She was in a rut. The break with Sylvia made even more clear, what she had half suspected for a number of years now: that her job no longer stretched her. Sadly she recalled how excited she had been, when as a fresh-faced, ambitious twenty-one-year-old, Zwingler and Sons had offered her her first job. Granted she was the firm's dogsbody: reading unsolicited manuscripts; working her way laboriously through, what is known in the publishing world as the 'slush pile'. It was the lowest step on the ladder. But it was a beginning; her foot was firmly in the door. And she had sufficient belief in her own abilities and intelligence to believe that it could only be a matter of time before her talents were recognised and her climb up that ladder would begin in earnest. She had always dreamed of being an innovative and celebrated editor at the cutting edge of the publishing world. Yet here she was, her thirtieth birthday about to heave itself lugubriously over the horizon, still occupying the same dusty basement: listening to the hurrying footsteps of the passers-by on Via Pietro Mica above her head; footsteps that seemed to her, in her depressed state, to be going somewhere; footsteps, whose hurrying sense of purpose seemed derisively to mock her own inertia.

Yes, she was in a rut. And worst of all it was a rut, which with each passing year, infected her with a kind of creeping complacency. The once sharp edge of her ambition had grown blunt. And as she gazed at the piles of as yet unread manuscripts, she began to accept the fact that this dull work-a-day existence was how things were likely to be for the remainder of her life. It was growing too late to change.

It was not so much that she was in a rut, she concluded. It was worse than that. The rut was in her.

And then, out of the blue, that phone call had come.

'Anna Livia?'

'Who is this?'

'It's me.'

'I'm sorry.'

'Sylvia.'

'Sylvia?'

Recognition slowly crept over her. That Sylvia! The silence had lasted three years. She tried to think of something to say: something that was distant but at the same time not too obviously churlish; something that made clear her cool disapproval but at the same time revealed subtly that she was not the type to bear a grudge.

But nothing appropriate came to mind.

'Oh,' she said rather lamely. 'It's you.'

She could hear Sylvia breathing at the other end. To her disbelief she heard her say, 'Cara, I need you to do me a favour.'

The naked effrontery astonished her. My God the bitch, she thought. Three years of silence and then she rings me demanding a favour! That's so typical of her. Who does she think she is?

And so she told her:

'My God who do you think you are? You drop me out of your life without a word of explanation and then after three years' silence, you phone me out of the blue and on top of that have the cheek to ask me to do you a favour.'

But Sylvia, as was her way when in pursuit of her own ends, blandly ignored the savage reproof and came to the point: her point. 'Is it true you are going to Padua?'

'What!'

'Padua. I heard you were going there.'

'How did you know I was going?'

'Oh your father mentioned it.'

'My father?'

'Yes I ran into him in town. He said you would be going to visit your aunt in Padua.'

'Is there anything you don't know?'

'He told me your mother used to visit her there. But now, well...' She left the sentence hanging.

Anna Livia said, 'Did he tell you mamma died?'

'Yes. I'm sorry.' She paused hardly at all. 'So do you think you could do this for me?'

Anna Livia took a deep breath. 'Sylvia, have you any sense of how badly you treated me? Have you?'

'Oh darling I know, but this is important to me. Look, why don't we meet for a coffee and I'll explain everything? Honestly.'

With Sylvia all ills were cured over a cup of coffee.

'No!' Anna said vehemently.

'Anna Livia. Please! If you knew what it means to me.'

'Sylvia, you hurt me badly. I honestly never want to see you again. Ever. I'm afraid that's final. Do you understand?' She was shouting now down the mouthpiece. 'Do you?'

II

Typically Sylvia was late for the appointment. Anna Livia was about to leave when she saw her enter with a flourish, looking about her with that utter unselfconsciousness that was so characteristic of her. Anna noted, with not a little chagrin, that if anything, she looked even younger; the picture of health and vitality. But there was a pallid sense of preoccupation about her that was untypical. Sylvia, suddenly spotting her, waved theatrically and hurried across. Anna Livia composed her expression to one of cold disapproval. She wasn't going to make this easy for her.

Sylvia kissed her extravagantly on both cheeks. 'It's lovely to see you. Darling am I late? The traffic was absolutely fearful. Have you ordered? Waiter, I'll have a bicerin,' She studied Anna Livia. 'Darling, you look older. It's probably because of your mother dying and everything. I'm so sorry.'

'You mean you're sorry about my mother or because I look older?'

Sylvia frowned. 'Oh Anna darling don't say you're still cross with me are you?'

Anna Livia bridled. She didn't enjoy having her righteous anger reduced to mere crossness; as though somehow it was her normal state. In order to recompose herself she sipped her macchiato, then wiping her lips with the napkin said, 'I am not, as you put it, cross. I am angry. After the appalling way you behaved, d'you find that strange?'

'Darling let's not be like this. It wasn't my fault. Honestly.'

Anna Livia frowned. 'Not your fault. I see. Then whose was fault was it exactly? Mine I suppose. Oh yes of course, I'd forgotten how you were never to blame for anything. Silly of me. It was me who didn't answer your letters or telephone calls wasn't it? Me, who didn't invite you to *my* wedding? And I suppose it was me who rang you after a three years' silence, begging for a favour?'

Oh God, she thought to herself, now I'm sounding sarcastic as well as cross. It wasn't what she had planned. She must have raised her voice. The middle-aged couple at the next table stared straight ahead of them transfixed with interest. Anna Livia decided it was probably a good time to leave. She was gathering up her things and pushing her chair back when she noticed there were tears in Sylvia's eyes and that she was trembling. Slowly she sat down again.

Sylvia said brokenly. 'Oh Anna darling don't talk about faults. Nobody's to blame.'

'Nobody? How very convenient.'

'Well I suppose it was him.'

'Him?'

'Davide. My husband. Well not any more. He walked out three months ago. Three months and three days actually. And I'm on my own and I can't stand it. That's why I rang you, you see.'

Anna Livia found it difficult to retain her aloofness in the face of Sylvia's dejection; those tears. 'Darling I'm so sorry. Tell me about it.'

The couple at the next table ordered another coffee. They were settling down for Act 2.

'Where shall I begin? Well of course he loved me. And I loved him. He seemed so kind. And tremendously good-looking in a rather dark way. I've always gone for that dark assertive type. You know, I'd always wanted to be married ever since I was a little girl. I was the one who was always playing at weddings. And now it was happening. I couldn't believe how happy I was. And, as I said, he was so kind and attentive. He couldn't have done more for me. Well, to begin with anyhow. And then one afternoon, I started making a list of my guests for the wedding; your name was at the top of the list of course. So I told him all about you: what good friends we were. Everything. Then I noticed such an odd expression on his face; as if he were thinking of something else. I didn't think much of it at the time. I knew he had a lot on his mind. I'd gone out of the room for some reason I can't remember what and when I came back I noticed something funny. Every name on the list had a line through it. And well, I couldn't believe it. So I asked him about it. I could do that then. And he took me in his arms and kissed me and said he loved me. Then he held me by the shoulders and looked into my face and said very seriously, "But do you love me?" I told him of course I did. But he shook his head and said, "I don't think so. Because you see, if you really loved me, you'd forget about everyone who was important to you in your life before." '

'You mean. He was jealous? Of me?'

'Of everybody Anna. Of everybody. It wasn't just boyfriends; it was my whole past. Everything. He wanted me as if I had just been born on the day we met.'

'But that's crazy.'

'I know. But - and I know this sounds silly - but the way he explained it, he sort of convinced me, you know, that it was a proof of our love and everything; and because I loved him and I was so frightened of losing him and everything, it sort of came to sound reasonable. So I did what he asked. We got married and to start with everything was fine. And then one day the oddest thing happened. I was coming home from somewhere or other, I don't know where and anyway I went upstairs and there was a large black bin bag in the corner of the bedroom. On the dressing table was a pair of kitchen scissors. Well I didn't think too much about it. I thought, you know, he was getting some of his old clothes together or something. And I was just going out when I noticed a piece of dark paper on the carpet. When I picked it up, I saw it was a photograph: a photograph of you and me. It was when we'd gone to Taormina on holiday. You remember. And it had been cut in half with these scissors. And when I went to the bin bag, it was full of all my photographs. Everything from when I was a little girl: pictures of my mother and father, my grandmother, even Mimi the little dog I had. He'd cut up my whole past. Everything. And then, I heard his footsteps on the stairs and for the first time I was frightened. When he came into the room, I was still holding the piece of the photograph. I looked at him. But the funny thing was he didn't say anything. He just talked to me as if everything was quite normal. And I got angry and asked him why he'd done it. "Done what?" he said. So I got hold of the bag and tipped all the scraps of photographs out onto the carpet. "You cut them," I said. "Why did you cut up all my photos? Why?"

'And he sort of smiled and said, "We've talked about this before. I thought you understood. Don't tell me you're too stupid to understand?" He picked up the scissors off the dressing table. Large scissors. He walked over towards me opening and closing the scissors. He held them against my face. He said, "They had to go. Don't you understand? I can't have things like that in my house because it makes me think you don't love me you see. So I cut them up. Snip, snip, snip." And he did that with the scissors. Snip, snip, snip. His face was so cold but at the same time sort of angry. And I was so scared. Really scared. I thought he was going to stab me. I stepped back and I think I must have screamed because I fell over the bag of photographs. I fell onto the floor hiding my face and there was blood on it where one of the blades had scratched me. Then he bent down towards me with the scissors still in his hand. I thought he was going to kill me, so I covered my face. But he just picked me up and held me very tight. Very tight in his arms. "You understand don't you," he said. "You understand it had to be done." And he kissed me very softly. Then he said very calmly, as if he were suggesting some kind of outing or something, "Come on, let's tidy this up." So we picked up all the scraps of photos and put them back in the bag. He put it over his shoulder and said, "Now you know what we have to do don't you?"

'And I didn't know really but I said, yes. We went down into the garden and he piled all the photos in a corner. Then he got a tin of petrol and poured it over them. He struck a match and I was looking at all the bits of my photographs: my father and mother, me with my sister. All my past. And suddenly he shook the match out and I thought, Oh he realises the terrible thing he's doing. He's going to say how sorry he is. Everything's going to be alright again; like it was before. But he wasn't sorry. He wasn't at all sorry. He handed me the box of matches. "You do it," he said. And I couldn't. I couldn't do it. And he looked at me and his face wasn't angry. It was just sad. So sad as if I'd let him down. "So," he said, "you don't love me after all."

'I said, "Of course I love you. Of course I do."

"Then burn them," he said. "Burn them all. For me. For us."

'And I did.'

Anna Livia put her arm about her. 'But he's mad. Why didn't you tell somebody?'

'I couldn't. I still loved him.' She closed her eyes. 'I know don't ask me. And I was frightened. But I thought it would change.'

'Did he ever hit you?'

'Oh yes,' Sylvia said matter of factly. 'If we were at a café like this, he would go very quiet and I'd know something was wrong. When we got home he'd accuse me of looking at some man in the café. Or smiling at the waiter and then he'd start hitting me; calling me awful names and saying, "If you really loved me you wouldn't need to look at other men." '

'But *he* left *you*.'

'Yes in the end. Three months ago.'

'That must have been a relief.'

Sylvia hesitated. She looked out across the café. 'In a way. I went to see my father and mother. For a few days. I had to get away. But then, and I know this sounds funny, I started to miss him. I'd got used to living in the same house with somebody. With him. So I went back. But the apartment door was locked and the key wouldn't fit. I looked through one of the windows and it was empty. Everything had been taken. Everything. The lady from the upstairs apartment must have heard me. I was crying. She came down and gave me a letter. It was a five page, typed letter from him. The first three pages made clear everything that was wrong with me. And I sort of believed it all. The rest was made up of columns of figures explaining why I would get next to nothing from the divorce. That I'd signed something, I don't know. And if I chose to fight the settlement, I'd get even less. As for the locked apartment, it had been bought in his name and there was nothing I could do about it. I sat on the doorstep and read it all. He said he'd met somebody else. That he'd been sleeping with her for some months. She was younger. She understood him better than I did. She was able to truly love him; something I didn't seem capable of. He didn't even sign it. It was horrible. But you know, Anna, I still miss him. In spite of everything I want him back. I...'

She couldn't go on. Her eyes squeezed tears. She dabbed at them with a small handkerchief and blew her nose. Anna Livia got up and sat beside her, putting her arms about her. The couple on the next table watched now with undisguised interest. Anna Livia turned on them and said caustically, 'Why don't you get a life of your own?' And then she pointedly turned her back on them.

They got up muttering and left.

Sylvia gathered herself together. 'I'm making a fool of myself aren't I?' She attempted to smile but her eyes still glistened. 'You see,' she said, 'I was married for three years and I just got used to it. It's as if I'd always been married. All my life somehow. When I go home now it's so empty and quiet. I just hate it. And then lying in bed on my own. It drives me crazy sometimes. I want him back you see. I desperately want him back. But I didn't know how. So that's why I rang you.'

'Why me? Naturally I'm pleased to see you. I can understand now what happened. But honestly I don't think you should take him back. He sounds half-mad to me and the half that's not mad sounds plain brutal. And suppose I do bring him back, which God forbid, suppose he starts knocking you about: I'm going to feel terrible. Those sorts of men can't change. So please Sylvia don't ask me.'

Sylvia shook her head. 'Oh I don't want you to ask him Anna. I wouldn't dream of it. No I want you to ask Saint Anthony.'

'Saint Anthony?'

'He's always been my favourite saint. His shrine's at Padua. Of course you know that. That's why I thought of you.'

'But what's Saint Anthony got to do with it?'

'Well, he's the saint of lost things. He helped me once when I was a little girl. I had a pet rabbit and it ran away. So my mother lit a candle for him and prayed to Saint Anthony to find him and the next day there he was.'

Anna Livia frowned perplexedly. 'There's a bit of a difference between finding a rabbit and a runaway husband.'

'I know that of course. But you see, it's not just making him come back. There'd be no point in that. That's why *you* couldn't do it, Anna. And anyway there's this other girl who's younger, probably prettier than me. No I want him to *want* to come back. That's what St Anthony can do. I'm sure of it.' She grasped both of Anna Livia's hands tightly in hers. 'So that's the favour I wanted to ask. It's not much really. When you're in Padua say a prayer and light a candle for me. Help me get him back. Oh Anna Livia please!'

Anna was perplexed. 'But why me? You could do it yourself. You believe in all that kind of thing. If you're short of money, I could lend you the fare.'

Sylvia shook her head. 'Oh no it wouldn't be the same. If

you ask things for yourself, St Anthony won't listen. I know he won't. You see, it was my mother who prayed not me. That's why my rabbit came back.' She squeezed Anna Livia's hand firmly. 'But if *you* asked, Anna. If *you* asked.'

Anna Livia looked her full in the eyes. 'You know I don't believe in any of that mumbo jumbo don't you? I'm practically an atheist. D'you think the Saint's going to listen to me? An unbeliever?'

'Saint Anthony is a great saint. He'll understand. He's the most understanding saint. That's why I love him. And you will learn to love him too Anna. Honestly you will. Are you married?'

Anna shook her head.

'Then you could ask him too.'

'Ask him?'

'To bring *you* a husband.'

'No thank you,' Anna said rather shortly. Then she was serious once more. She spelled out the difficulties. 'Number one, I don't think you should want this man back. He's wrong for you. The whole thing's wrong. And I don't think you want him back for the right reasons. Second - I don't really want to go round lighting candles and saying prayers. It's just not my style.'

Sylvia released her hand and her face fell. She stared at the floor. Anna Livia had never been able to deal happily with the disappointment of others. Against her better judgement she began to relent. 'Look,' she said, 'the best I'll do is this: I'll go to the Cathedral and I'll think about it. I can't say more than that can I?'

'Oh thank you. Thank you,' Sylvia said impetuously flinging her arms about Anna Livia. The coffee cup spilled its contents across the white table cloth. 'Saint Anthony will listen to you. He always listens. You'll see, you'll see.'

They walked out of the café arm in arm. It had begun to rain. Anna called a cab for Sylvia and then made her way back to her basement office on foot.

All the way back to her apartment Sylvia sat staring out of the cab window at the rain. Now and then she smiled.

It was something she hadn't done for some time.

III

Anna Livia had never really cared much for her old Aunt Julia but there was that promise she had made to her mother - so she made a point of visiting her once a month. Aunt Julia was by turns dependent and demanding; an irritating combination. In addition she was almost completely deaf and like many deaf people she shouted. As a result, her most innocent requests - for her keys, her slippers, a piece of cake, that the door be shut or opened or left ajar – came across as though she were attempting to make herself heard above a force ten gale. And Anna, because of her aunt's deafness, was compelled to shout back - so that any passing listener would have been forced to conclude that a life and death argument was in progress which could only be resolved by the violent death of one or the other of the parties. The result was, that after four hours of fetching and carrying and shouting, and suffering unrelenting criticism,

Anna was not only exhausted and irritated but was beginning to lose her voice. In the end she resorted to writing whatever she wished to say on a pad of paper. This in itself was a lengthy process, because Aunt Julia as well as being deaf was practically blind; so the writing had to be extremely large. Thus the simplest request not only covered several sheets of A4 paper but also took several minutes to write. However it saved what remained of Anna's voice.

Remembering her promise to Sylvia, and as much to pass the time as anything, she asked her aunt for directions to the Basilica of Saint Anthony.

'Why it's off Piazza del Santo of course,' Auntie Julia shouted, managing somehow to imply that this was a piece of universally understood knowledge denied only to the most stupid of people among whom she numbered her niece. 'What d'you want to go there for?'

Anna had no wish to share Sylvia's secret with her aunt. 'I'm interested in the architecture,' she wrote.

'Humph!' snorted Aunt Julia disparagingly and then launched into a rambling reminiscence of her lengthy relationship with the Saint: how forty years earlier she had misplaced her purse and had pinned a request on the Saint's shrine that he help her find it. And then weeks later it had turned up in the pocket of an overcoat that she had been on the point of throwing away. And she crossed herself several times, closing her eyes and offering up, in the general direction of heaven, a murmured prayer of thanks to the Blessed Saint.

IV

Later, standing amongst the shifting crowd of pilgrims that thronged about the Saint's shrine, Anna Livia noticed that many of the scrawled prayers pinned to his tomb were for the recovery of just such mundane articles as Auntie Julia's purse:

Blessed Saint Anthony my father before he died hid all his savings books about the house and now he is dead we are unable to find them. Please Saint Anthony help to lift the suffering of my widowed mother and my brothers and sisters and myself by telling us where he has put them...

Blessed Saint Anthony I have just lost my job after twenty years and I am having difficulty finding another at a good salary. I have an interview at a Bank on Monday. Please find it in your heart to let these new employers look kindly on my request for work...

Blessed Saint Anthony look kindly on one who loves you. Last Saturday my wife misplaced my car keys. It is an old Fiat and the manufacturers no longer stock the key in question. Without my car I can't get to work unless I beg a lift from my neighbour who I don't like very much. Also my wife and me, because I think it was her fault that she lost it, are arguing all the time and our marriage is in danger. Please Saint Anthony out of your great wisdom and mercy...

Anna Livia shook her head in bewilderment. The Basilica, she thought, amounted to little more than a sanctified Lost Property

Department. But then she noticed a small, misspelled almost illiterate request and as she read…

Blessed St Anthony. Our little girl Louisa is gone and we cannot find her. We are so afraid for her. Don't let her die or be bad. Hear our prayer and bring our darling daughter back to us…

…her eyes filled with tears.

Some deep need, she concluded, was being fulfilled here.

But what of Sylvia?

She bought a candle and knelt beside the great shrine. She took out the notes that she had made on the train begging Saint Anthony to bring Sylvia's husband back to her; but only of course if he returned of his own volition. She sellotaped the prayer to the stone shrine amongst all the others then, rather embarrassed, rose swiftly to her feet and walked away.

It was done. Over. It was up to the Saint now. But as she hurried past the pews, the pillars, the reliquary containing the Saint's tongue, the great gloomy paintings of Our Lady, her doubts turned to anger. What was she doing playing a part in this absurd charade? It was utterly mad. She was ashamed of herself. And suppose, just suppose, by some miracle it worked: that this malicious, neurotic husband of Sylvia's came back, it was bound to turn out for the worse. Sylvia was a naïve, silly superstitious child in many ways. But she was a friend. She had a loving heart and much to give the right man. But the right man wasn't this one. She deserved better.

A guide approached down the central aisle, a raised umbrella in his hand. About him clustered a crowd of German tourists.

'Oh fuck it!' Anna said aloud.

She turned and hurried back to the shrine and tore her request from the wall. One or two nearby petitioner's stared at her in astonishment. She smiled at them. To cover her embarrassment she pretended she was re-writing a message of her own to the Saint. As she did so, her eye caught a neatly written prayer. Anna leaned forward and read the message. It was written on a piece of headed, rather expensive-looking paper, from which the address had been neatly torn. It read like a letter to the Saint:

Dear Saint Anthony,

Really I feel a bit of a fraud writing this. Although I was brought up a good Catholic I haven't even been in a church for fifteen years. I'm not sure what I believe. But really I'm like a man dying of cancer who in the last resort will try anything. Or an atheist, who on his death bed, takes up the old religion just to hedge his bets; any port in a storm. I have no wish to demesne you, as I'm sure you were one of the best of men. The point is Saint Anthony, my dear wife died a year ago now and I've become a bit of a recluse: gone into my shell as it were. I'd like to marry again, you see but well I've lost the habit of how to go about it. Yes I know dear Saint Anthony you'll probably advise me to join a Drama Society or go to Night School but it's just not me somehow. I'm not too outward going. I don't make a good impression. But if I could just have a chance I think I improve with familiarity. Well that's what my wife used to say. Well, I just thought I'd give it a try. I hope you understand. I won't leave my name if you don't mind as someone might know me but if you are there, you'll know who I am. Saint Anthony if you can help me with this I'd be eternally grateful. And I mean that. Thank you

Anna was intrigued. She read the petition three times. There was something about the formal, educated hand and the natural simplicity of the request that touched her. Wouldn't this rather hesitant wife-seeker be a better bet than Sylvia's brute of a husband?

She peered closer; part of the address remained. She scrutinised it carefully but all it contained were the last three letters. There were however, what looked like four digits of a telephone number. She looked about her and surreptitiously unglued the letter and popped it into her handbag then hurried out of the Basilica and sat down amongst the statuary in Piazza del Santo. She glanced at her watch. Her train left in half an hour. There was no area code with the number. She wondered if the writer lived in Padua. It was worth trying. She took out her mobile and dialled the number. She had no idea what she would say. How should she address this stranger? - *I read your letter on the Saint's tomb and I thought I'd give you a call.*

It was unfamiliar territory.

But when she had finished dialling there was merely a silence. She pushed the redial button. More silence. It was hopeless. Who knew where he lived? It could be anywhere in Italy. She counted the numbers. There were four. She took out her notebook and checked her aunt's Padua number. There were five! She glanced back at the letter. The final number was torn off. She decided to add a different number by turn. It was a one in nine chance. She glanced at her watch once more. There was time. Just. She decided to begin by adding one to the numbers and then work her way through methodically to nine.

She dialled.

At the other end she heard the phone ringing. She was relieved about that. A woman's voice said rather abruptly, 'Yes?'

Anna hadn't thought of a woman answering.

'Oh er hello,' she said uncertainly.

'Is that you?' the woman asked abruptly.'

Anna wasn't quite sure what to say. 'Well yes. But I wanted...'

'Lucia?'

'No, I'm afraid not. You don't know me but...

'What d'you want I'm busy.'

'Ah yes sorry.' She was confused. Stupidly she said, 'Is there a man there? I mean living there?'

'Man? What is this some kind of a wind up?'

'No. No you see it's about a letter.'

'Letter? What letter?'

'It's about a letter to St Anthony. You know the shrine. And I wondered...'

'Porco Dio!' the woman swore and slammed the phone down.

Anna stared at the phone for a moment and sighed. Then she added a two to the numbers.

A gruff voice answered. At least it's a man this time, Anna thought. She'd worked out her approach this time.

'Oh good afternoon,' she said with the confident air of someone selling double glazing to a complete stranger. 'I wondered if you could help me. This sounds an odd question I know, but could you tell me if your wife died about a year ago?'

'My wife?'

Anna heard a woman's voice in the background. She heard the man say:

'Some woman on the phone wants to know if you're dead.' Then the man said to Anna. 'She says she's not dead yet. Is that alright? Anything else you want to know?'

Anna apologised and rang off.

The next man who answered, worked in reptile house at a zoo and the fourth was a car showroom service department. The fifth was at a private art gallery.

'I'm looking for a man?' Anna said.

'Aren't we all dear,' the man said.

Then there was another woman and then a man who breathed heavily and asked her what she was wearing.

She began to despair; but then the eighth to answer sounded more promising. Familiarity mixed with the anonymity of the telephone was beginning to make Anna feel more at ease with her strange request.

'Hello,' said a man's voice.

'I was wondering,' Anna said almost casually, 'if you had ever by chance written a letter to Saint Anthony.'

There was a lengthy pause. Then suspiciously: 'Why are you asking?'

Good question, Anna thought. 'It's just that I read it and thought I'd call you and find out what you were like. If it is you that is.'

There was a silence. Then: 'How did you find me?'

'Ah so it is you.'

'Possibly. What did you want?'

'It's a long story.' She hesitated. 'It is you isn't it?'

There was an even longer silence. The man cleared his throat. 'Yes it's me.'

It's him, Anna thought. She wondered what to say next. It was difficult and delicate. After a pause she said, 'It's just that, well, I liked your letter.'

'You did?'

'Yes. I thought it was quite touching actually. Perhaps, I don't know, perhaps could you tell me how old you are?'

'Thirty-two.'

'Oh that's fine. I mean, you know, it's a nice age thirty-two. Well I think so anyway. Perhaps we could meet. Sometime. Somewhere. That is if you want to.'

For the first time the man's hesitancy left him. 'Oh no,' he said,' I don't think that would be a good idea.'

'But I thought that's what you wanted.'

'Yes. Yes I do. But not now.'

'Oh I understand. You're busy.'

'No, it's not that.'

'When then?'

'Perhaps we could do this for a bit.'

'Do what?'

'Talk like this. On the phone. Or perhaps I could write.'

'Write?'

'Yes. Letters. That way we could get to know one another.

You see if I met you and didn't like you I...' he hesitated.

'You wouldn't know how to get rid of me?'

'Well...'

''No I understand. So we should write, you think. At first anyway. Is that what you mean?''

'Is that all right?''

'I think so,' said Anna.

'And you might send a photo?'

Anna Livia had plenty of photographs of Sylvia. 'All right,' she said. There was another silence. Anna Livia said, 'So what is it?'

'What's what?'

'Your address.'

'Ah yes.'

He dictated it and Anna scribbled it down in her notebook.

'And yours is?' he asked.

She realised she didn't know Sylvia's address. She hesitated.

'You do have an address?'

'Oh yes. But it's just that...well, I don't want to sound critical but I don't know anything about you. You might be...'

'An axe murderer?'

'Well not exactly but...'

'You could write to me with a poste restante address. Then you'd be quite safe.'

'That should work. I'd feel safer then.'

'I understand,' the voice on the other end of the 'phone said, 'Of course *you* might turn out to be an axe murderer. But I'm prepared to take the risk.'

'I know what you mean.'

Anna Livia thought of Sylvia's insatiably romantic nature. There must be another way. What was she to do with all these letters? The *other way* suddenly came to her. 'I've got a better idea,' she said warming to her role. 'Why don't I write to you giving you the address of a café in Torino that I know? I'll give you the date and the time and I'll tell you what I look like and where I'll be sitting and everything. And then if it suits you, you could sort of turn up. Then you could take a look at me and if I wasn't your type you could just creep off. But if you sort of liked the look of me, you could start a conversation. We could pretend we met just by accident. It will be more romantic. As if Saint Anthony had listened to my…our prayers.' She hesitated. 'What do you think?' There was a lengthy pause. 'Hello. Are you still there?'

'Yes. Yes I'm here.'

'Is Torino too far? We could meet somewhere else if you like.'

'No that's fine. It's just that I'm thinking.'

'Thinking?'

'About it.'

Anna glanced at her watch. 'How long d'you think that will take? I don't want to hurry you. It's just that I have a train to catch.'

'No. No. I think that sounds alright to me.'

'You do? Oh good. Oh and there's something else I'd like you to…well to suggest. If you don't mind.'

'Yes?'

'I just think it would be sort of better somehow if we didn't mention this phone call or the letters or anything ever again. Just pretend it never happened. Do you think I'm being silly?'

'Not at all. As far as I'm concerned this phone call never happened.'

'Oh good.'

'Can I ask you something?'

'Absolutely.'

'What do you look like? You know roughly. You see I'd need to know.'

'Oh yes of course.' She summoned up a picture of Sylvia in her mind. 'Well I'm pretty tall. Sort of blonde hair. Quite good legs. Exceptionally good teeth. I did an advert once. I'm pretty good really. Good sense of humour and all that. Oh and I'm a bit superstitious and religious too.' She stopped. She was beginning to lose her voice altogether. 'Is that alright?' she managed to say hoarsely.

'Sounds fine to me.'

'Oh good. What about you?'

'Me. Oh I'm just ordinary.'

'Not er disfigured or anything?'

'Not that you'd notice.'

'Oh that's good. Not that there's anything wrong with being disfigured. And you're fairly sort of kind?'

'Not for me to say really. I think so.'

She looked at her watch once more. She had ten minutes. She'd have to take a cab. She was about to say goodbye when she remembered something. 'But I don't know your name.' she said.

'It's Gianni,' he said.

'Gianni.'

'Yes.'

'Good. Look I'm sorry but I have to catch a train now. So goodbye. I mean for the time being.'

'Wait!'

'What?'

'You haven't told me your name.'

'Oh no. Of course.'

'So d'you want to give it to me? I would like to know your name if that's alright with you.'

Anna paused. 'It's A...It's er Sylvia.'

'Sylvia?'

'Yes.'

'It's just that you don't sound too sure.'

'Oh I'm sure all right.'

'Nice name. It suits you.'

'D'you think so? Oh good.'

'Yes really.'

She glanced at her watch once again. 'I have to go I'm afraid. The train and everything.'

'Of course. Yes. Well Goodbye. Sylvia.'

'Goodbye.'

And she switched off the phone and hurried away to catch her train.

V

'So would you say you were happy?'

They were sitting in the same café three months later.

'Oh yes,' Sylvia said. She put her hand over Anna's and leaned forward. 'And it's all because of you.'

'Not me really. It was Saint Anthony.'

'Well both of you. You make a good team. But it was your prayers that did it. It has to be the right person you see or he won't listen.'

'He?'

'Saint Anthony.'

'Ah yes, of course.'

Sylvia leaned forward. 'Anna I'm terribly curious. What did you actually say?'

'Say?'

'I mean in your prayer to Saint Anthony.'

'Oh this and that,' said Anna vaguely. 'I can't really remember.'

'Well what ever you said. It worked. Saint Anthony was listening. It was just amazing. I was sitting right here and he came over and asked if he could join me.'

'Amazing!'

'And can I tell you something truly amazing? He'd written to Saint Anthony as well. Isn't that incredible?'

'Incredible.,'

She changed the subject. 'But tell me Sylvia what's he like?'

'Widow.'

'Really?'

'Yes. His wife died about a year ago or more. He's shy actually.'

'Shy?'

'I've never been with a shy man before. It's a novelty. I've always gone for the assertive type. Mistake. They all went wrong. I think shy's better don't you?'

'Oh every time,' Anna agreed. 'Although on second thoughts I quite like a touch of assertiveness now and then. At the right time of course.'

'Oh yes. And that side of it's good too,' Sylvia murmured with a louche glance from beneath her long eyelashes.

Anna laughed. 'And what does he think of you?'

'Naturally he thinks I'm wonderful. And I can't help agreeing with him,' Sylvia remarked with an amiable leer. 'Do you know what he likes?'

'What?'

'My voice.'

'Really?'

'Yes isn't that strange. No one's ever said that to me before. He said when he first noticed me he thought I'd have a huskier sort of voice. Like somebody who'd been shouting a lot.'

'That's nice,' said Anna. She changed the subject once more. 'What about Davide?'

'Who's he?' Sylvia said dismissively.

As they walked to the cash desk and Sylvia paid the bill, Anna said, 'Have you told anybody else?'

'Told them what darling?'

'I mean how you met and everything?'

'Yes of course. Just my girl friends, you know. Why not?'

'I don't know, some people would be embarrassed.'

'Embarrassed? Why?'

'Oh you know meeting in that way.'

'Oh I don't mind at all. I tell them it was all down to you and Saint Anthony and prayer. They all loved it. I think it makes it even more romantic don't you?'

'Maybe,' said Anna. 'Maybe.'

VI

When Anna got home the phone was ringing. A girl's voice she didn't recognize said, 'Could I speak to Signorina Anna Livia Mazzoni please?'

'Speaking.'

'Oh my name's Antonella. I don't think you know me but I'm a friend of Sylvia's. Sylvia Bertonelli.'

'Yes?'

'I just wanted to ask you something. I hope you don't mind. Have you got a minute?'

'Please go ahead.'

'Well it was just that Sylvia mentioned you would be going to Padua next week.'

'Yes I am. I go to see my aunt.'

'That's what Sylvia said. I just wondered if you might be going to visit the shrine of St Anthony and if you are I have a small favour to ask...'

VII

Anna sipped the last of her coffee and moved away from the window. She pressed the buzzer on her intercom. 'Rosa could you take my coffee away now please. Oh, and is the lady still waiting?'

'Yes.'

'Tell her,' she glanced at her screen. 'Tell Signorina Torielli that I'll see her now.'

When the well-dressed woman, whom she judged to be in her late thirties, entered, Anna rose smiling to shake her hand. She showed her to an easy chair beside the window and sat down opposite her. She had always made a point of not sitting behind her desk when talking to prospective clients. After the initial, brief formalities had been concluded she asked the client, as she always did, to talk as openly as possible about her life in general and then moved on to ask her to talk in more detail about the kind of relationship she was seeking. Most of the time she spent listening. She was a good listener. It was probably the secret of her success. Secure in the trust that Anna generated in that small, cosy room, clients found themselves talking about aspects of their private lives that they had not revealed even to their most intimate friends.

The interview lasted almost an hour.

When it was concluded Anna Livia asked Signorina Torielli, as she always did, if there was anything that she wished to ask her in her turn. 'Anything,' she said spreading her hands. 'Anything at all. Feel completely free.'

'No,' the woman said, 'I think we've covered everything, honestly.' She laughed shyly playing with her hair. 'I must say though, although nothing's er happened yet, I must say I feel better all ready. Better than I've felt for ages. I feel I'm doing something. You know, taking charge of my own life somehow.'

'Good. That's very good,' said Anna. She rose and kissed the happy client on both cheeks. She was laughing. 'That's what we're here for, Sandra: to make people happier. And by and large I can honestly say we succeed.'

She accompanied her to the door. 'So there's nothing else then? Sometimes when people get home they think, Oh I wished I'd asked her about this or that or the other. It often happens. Well don't hesitate. You have my number. Ask for me personally and I'll be happy to talk to you about anything. Anytime.'

The woman frowned and put her finger to her lip. 'Well there was something. Nothing to do with me actually. Quite a silly thing really.'

'If there's something you wish to ask then it's never silly. Tell me.'

'Well, I was just curious that's all. About the name.'

'Name?'

'Of your agency. You know it's a marriage agency. And most of them have names like *Hearts Together* or *Soul Mates* or something. So it just struck me as strange.'

'Strange? How?'

'Well, I was just wondering why you called it *Made in Heaven* and why you have a picture of Saint Anthony on all your correspondence.'

'Ah,' said Anna, 'It's rather a long story.' She opened the door. 'But if you're really interested I'll be happy to tell it some time.'

Faith

I

On the day his mother died, somewhere between his twelfth and thirteenth birthday, Roberto Amoretti lost his faith. All night he had prayed at her bedside but as the sky lightened beyond the curtain he saw that she had fallen silent for ever. Roberto took it personally. His knees stiff from kneeling and his young voice hoarse from prayer, he began to think that God was probably too busy with somebody else's prayers: somebody wealthier or more influential than himself. He was still only a child but suddenly the whole nature of belief struck him as being ridiculous. How many people in the world had died that night; many of them at the same hour? Thousands. Possibly millions. How could God possibly give his full and undivided attention to each and every one? Unless it was a cursory nod of salvation. But a million nods! How long could that take? And what if he did save them all, as a forgiving god should? That would mean that nobody would die; ever. Think of the overcrowding that would result!

Later, he would tell anybody who was interested, that deep in his soul he had *never* in fact been a believer. He'd merely gone through the ritual motions out of a kind of deference to communal practice. In the same way he'd became a Juventus supporter; though that habit, unlike his Catholicism, would last a lifetime.

While studying dentistry at Pisa, he became a convinced humanist and wrote several articles for the student paper which were scornfully dismissive of the Catholic Church and indeed of religious faith in general. Perhaps months of staring into mouths full of decaying teeth makes one sceptical of the promise of Eternal Bliss.

And then there were the numbers. Where did God keep them all?

It was absurd.

'When I die,' he would say, 'I believe my body will serve to nourish a few worms and plants and that will be the end of the matter. Well, the end of my matter. Paradise - what an absurd notion! Everlasting life is nothing more than a species of sentimental wish-fulfilment. I'd sooner live with a discomfiting truth than with a cosy and sentimental lie. 'And confession,' he would say getting into his stride, 'being forgiven by celibate old men in black frocks for sexual peccadilloes they know nothing about and probably secretly wished in their shallow hearts they had themselves committed. What's all that about for God's sake? If you're guilty - you're guilty and you should bear the consequences and there's an end of it. Speaking for myself I'm glad to be rid of the whole rotten business.'

And yet we deceive ourselves if we imagine old habits can be jettisoned quite so easily. Sometimes, with a kind of atavism, they have a habit of reappearing just when we least expect it: like those mysterious streams that seemingly disappear underground, only to re-emerge once more, hundreds of miles away from their sources.

And indeed that's how it happened with Roberto.

As the years passed, he mellowed and settled for the comfortable life. His easy sarcasm and passion left him and he dedicated his social life to getting on with everybody he met. He detested any kind of confrontation and for the most part, unless amongst close friends whom he knew agreed with him, kept any provocative thoughts to himself. He would often say, 'The only people you can profitably argue with are those who agree with you.' He ceased proselytising his once passionately held humanistic beliefs and joined the golf club. Politically he proclaimed himself to be a man of the Left, but in truth he was emotionally of the Right: for he liked to keep things as they had always been. Experience had taught him that change only tended to make things worse. Deep down, although he would never consciously admit it to himself, he didn't believe in anything very much; unless it was the getting of his own way. If he had formed any political affiliation it would have been called the - *Leave me alone to live my own very nice middle of the road life thank you very much Party.*

In his own way, he was good natured and popular and women warmed to him as a friend because he was, up to a point, kind, thoughtful and unthreatening. He made them laugh. He listened to what they had to say and he flattered them. 'Quite frankly, I like the company of women,' he would proclaim to his cronies as if he were voicing some rather daring and radical notion which drew on vast experience. But by women he generally meant girls with long blonde hair who had not yet reached thirty. 'Quite frankly' was a phrase often on his lips. He said it with a kind of forced defiance as though prefacing some challenging and dangerous opinion, which in fact turned out to be the merest bromide. Sex fascinated him, though prior to his marriage he was almost entirely without experience. It was something to be talked about amongst other male friends, rather than enjoyed. Deep within him there was a stultifying lack of confidence that subtly communicated itself to prospective girl friends and made them wary. Hardly any of these encounters reached any kind of satisfactory fulfilment.

So, he was strangely surprised at the age of twenty eight, to find himself married to a long-legged ex-dancer he had met while attending a conference on *New Developments in Isotopic Sealing during Root Canal Procedures* at the University of Turin. Frederica was an over-indulged, only child of working class parents. During early adolescence she had contracted tuberculosis and for a time there were fears that she might die or at least become a permanent invalid. But her mother had devoted her life to nursing her through the crisis, for which Frederica was suitably grateful. However it left her with a deep-seated inclination to dependency which her mother emotionally exploited to the full. Roberto recognised this trait in her and progressively, if subconsciously, gradually weaned her away from her over-protective mother. There was a deep animosity between them and at one point Roberto had quite seriously contemplated the notion of slowly poisoning her, but common sense eventually prevailed. With time, Frederica transferred her dependence to her new husband.

He found something transcendently feminine about her: or what he, given his relative lack of experience in these matters, considered to be feminine. There was a whimsicality, an innate goodness and spontaneity in her personality that utterly beguiled him, mainly because they were qualities conspicuously absent in himself. They saw each other almost everyday for some six months but he was wary of permanence.

And then, one late December afternoon while walking in Parco Sempione, he surprised even himself by proposing. It had suddenly begun to snow quite heavily. He turned up his collar, promising himself to consult the weather forecast when he got home. She, on the other hand, had begun running in large overlapping circles through the falling snow, her arms held wide, singing aloud for pure pleasure. This display of uninhibited *joi de vivre* caused him some embarrassment. He gave his characteristic little dry cough and gazed about him, fearful that someone he knew might be observing them. And yet the thought was accompanied by a warm and insistent appreciation of how spontaneously and genuinely good she was.

When she finally returned to him, breathless and pink, plunging her arm beneath his and pressing her body to his side as if she craved to enter him, an immense warmth and affection, that was quite new in his experience, flooded through him. Then she placed herself before him, planting her small feet on his large boots and stretching her face up to his. Her nose was pleasingly cold and at its touch he felt a sudden turmoil between his groin and his heart that convinced him: *this sensation it must be love. Mustn't it?'*

But he said nothing.

And she, looking about her, gave a sudden cry that startled him. 'Oh look!' she shouted. 'My tree! My beautiful tree!'

It was a young, spreading oak that stood patrician and isolated at the summit of a small mound of grass. And she ran from him towards it. He was once more moved by the sight of the unfolding pattern of her tiny footsteps in the snow. It signified something but he wasn't quite sure what. So he set his large boot against her smaller print and mentally calculated the difference. How tiny her feet are, he said to himself. And the words 'tiny' and 'feet' induced in him a surge of protectiveness. When he reached her, she had flattened herself against the trunk of the oak and flung both arms about it in a warm embrace. She was quite out of breath. 'This has been my tree since I was a little girl. It is me. Once it almost blew down in the gale and I was so sad because I thought it would die. But she's still here you see. She's still here.'

He had never thought of a tree as being a 'she' before. How typical, how charming, he thought.

She pressed herself harder against the trunk. 'Oh my darling tree. I'm so glad to see you well again. Promise me you'll never die.'

He said, 'The Latin name is Quercus from which of course we get our Italian name. It's said that the roots draw up over 50 gallons of water a day.' He began to calculate. 'Now how many would that be in a year?'

But she didn't seem to hear him. Her face shone with happiness and laughter. She turned to him. 'Please tell her you love her too,' she begged, her eyes sparkling.

And he, glanced nervously round once more, but the park, through its white bead curtain of falling snow, was empty. He did his best to join in the game but whimsicality did not sit well with him. He coughed almost apologetically. 'I er love you tree,' he mumbled.

Frederica laughed. 'She knows you do. I can feel it. You do it too, tesoro.'

'Do?' He frowned. 'Do what?'

'Put your arms about her so that she knows you love her too.'

And Roberto glanced at his watch. 'We should be getting home don't you think. I don't want you catching a chill.'

And Frederica, pouting, had stamped her foot in mock anger. But her eyes were smiling. 'Please?' she implored, pretending to sulk. 'Or my tree will be unhappy.'

But what he did was to press his body hard against her back and buttocks and extend his arms so that they embraced her. His arms, longer than hers, he flattened against the gnarled snow-flecked bark. He heard a voice that did not sound like his, saying with distracted longing, 'Oh Frederica, Frederica. Please marry me.'

And she had turned herself about, her eyes filled with tears, and pressed her snow-cold lips to his mouth with a passion that took him aback.

II

Later that year they married. And for a time they were happy.

Roberto enjoyed being a husband. He found it gave him

pleasure, when in the company of his friends, or even male strangers that he met or the patients at his clinic, to talk of Frederica as being *my wife*. It even gave him pleasure to mockingly deprecate what he saw as her stereotypically female habits and girlish self-indulgences. 'Oh my wife was at the sales all day yesterday. You should have seen the mountain of clothes she brought home. Quite frankly, we shall have to buy another wardrobe. Ah women!' he would say shaking his head in bewilderment, 'Women! But we love them don't we?'

In a strange way, he had always felt himself to be an outsider. He had played at conviviality like an accomplished actor till the role became him. But now for the first time in his life, he felt at last that he truly belonged. He had joined the great club of humanity. And Frederica, as the years passed, grew ever more dependent on *him*. It was *he* who made all the decisions: decided what car they should have; which apartment they should buy; where they should go for their holidays. And his role as the decision-maker, pleased him. It was part of the reason why he loved her. And he did love her; he was sure of that. When he was away sometimes at conferences or on courses, he would lie on his hotel bed and think about her. He loved her innate sense of virtue. I'm happy, he would say to himself. I have a home and a wife. And I'm truly happy.

But as the novelty of his new status lost something of its freshness, her fragility seemed to grow and her dependent whimsicality lost something of its charm. The illness that had so blighted her youth had left a mental, as well as a physical legacy; like a scar tissue on her mind. And over the years it perniciously spread until it became an intrinsic and recognisable part of her personality. She suffered a kidney disorder that may well have been psychosomatic. The most ordinary and everyday tasks became immensely complex. She could not perform the simplest journey: to the shops or to the school where she taught dance once a week, without taking a complete change of clothes with her. The steroids in the drugs her doctor gave her, made her body swell and the tranquillisers made her weary, so that when she turned away from him in the night with a sigh of regret, he found her determined yet affectionate rejection of him, strangely relieving. Yet he still treasured her and knew himself to be fortunate to be married to a woman of such goodness and generosity. Her fragility and dependence were a burden he embraced willingly. He knew he could never do anything to hurt her. The thought of being unfaithful or of seeking sexual solace with other women scarcely occurred to him; although latterly, he found that his eyes lingered longer on the shapely figures of the young women whose pictures he studied in magazines or on the laughing girls who thronged the streets as he drove back and forth from his clinic each day.

Curiously, it was Frederica who encouraged his first act of infidelity. They had been invited to a party by a colleague of hers at the school. She could not face the journey or the effort of being sociable. 'I'm just too tired, darling. You know how I get. I think I'll have a bath and go to bed early. You don't mind do you?' Then, as she was leaving the room: 'Look why don't *you* go? I won't mind. You'd enjoy it. I'm sorry to be such a drag.'

The idea vaguely attracted him but out of habit and loyalty

he demurred. He didn't know anybody. He'd feel like a fish out of water. 'I tell you what,' she said taking his arm, 'I'll ring Maria. You remember her. We get on so well at school. I'll tell her I'm not feeling well and that she's to look after you.' She looked up at him affectionately, stroking his cheek softly with the palm of her hand.

And so he had gone to the party and was surprised to realise that he was enjoying himself. There was something oddly liberating about meeting strangers who knew nothing about him. And they all seemed so healthy and energetic, so that he found his own spirits reviving. A weight lifted from him when he found himself talking and laughing with Maria, who, in contrast with Frederica, shone with health and vitality. She seemed to like him for himself, not just because she was a friend of Frederica. She laughed uproariously at his jokes. And what is more he laughed at hers. He felt like someone released from a prison sentence; although it was a prison that, in a sense, he felt comfortable in; a prison he knew he would always willingly go back to. But it was still a prison. And when he decided it was time to go home, the dark-haired Maria accompanied him to his car and, to his great surprise, kissed him. He found it surprising and pleasant but decided not to kiss her back. He started the car. She made a sign for him to open the window. She handed him a piece of paper. 'You ring me,' she said. 'That's how it's done.'

He studied the number foolishly. He was an uncomfortable Lothario. His first thought was of the danger of being caught out. 'What about your husband?' he said.

'What husband?' she said bitterly, her eyes flashing. 'My husband left me last week for a girl who serves behind the counter of a cake shop in Treviso. Ciao marito! Good riddance!' She pulled a face and slapped her hands together roughly as though her errant husband had somehow been turned to powder between her palms and deserved no better fate than to be spread across the gutter. 'I have no husband.'

'He left *you*?' he murmured. 'He must be mad.' It wasn't the kind of thing he said. He'd heard it in a film once and it seemed appropriate. Maria leaned her head through the car window and took his hand. She stroked his palm gently and then lifted it, cupping it against the softness of her breast. 'I think so too,' she said.

He had gone through two sets of traffic lights before his erection finally subsided.

At home as he slipped discretely between the sheets Frederica turned and looked at him with bleary eyes. The fungoid scent of the drugs she was taking was on her breath. 'Oh it's you,' she said.

'It had better be.' It was another line from a film he'd heard somewhere. Frederica was too tired to see the joke. She ran her hand through her hair and rubbed her eyes. 'I couldn't sleep,' she said. 'Did you have a nice time?'

'Alright,' he said. 'You know me. Not a party animal.'

'Mmh. How was Maria? Did she look after you?'

'Maria? Oh I hardly spoke to her.'

'She's sad I think.'

'Sad?'

'Her husband left her. She came home from school one night and he wasn't there. There was a note. He just went. Puff! Like that.'

He remembered the touch of Maria's lips on his.

'Really? I didn't know that.'

'She'll soon find somebody else. She's attractive don't you think?'

'Is she? Yes I suppose so. I didn't really notice.'

He ran the tips of his fingers over the palm of his hand: the hand that had cupped Maria's breast. He sighed at the memory. Frederica was aware of his rising excitement. With a mixture of sorrow, guilt, pity and affection he reached out and put his arms about her. The love making was swift and perfunctory on his part. When he was done, she began to cry and he told her he was sorry.

She ran her finger down his nose and pouted. 'I'm sorry too, tesoro. I've taken this sleeping pill.' She kissed him gently on the nose and then turned away. 'And these anti-depressants just leave me drained. They play havoc with my kidneys. I'm going to have to see the doctor about…'

She was suddenly silent in mid-sentence. He wanted to do something for her. Something that would seriously inconvenience him; a little sacrifice that he knew would make him feel better. 'I'll make an appointment for you. I'll take you there if you like.'

And then he thought he would tell her. Confess all. After all nothing had really happened. It had all been Maria's doing. Hadn't it? There was a way of explaining things.

'Frederica?'

But she was already asleep.

As he lay wide awake, his hands behind his neck, staring at the lights that played on the ceiling, he could hear the restless snores rising from her.

III

Adultery he found surprisingly easy. He decided not to ring Maria. Instead he ran his fingers down the phone book, searching for her address. Of course, she was entered under her husband's name but he knew it was her by comparing the number to the one scrawled on the paper. He stared at the configuration of the letters of her name for quite a time. He thought, *That is her name. This is where she lives. In that address she goes to bed. She lies there. Perhaps thinking of me. As I now am thinking of her.* Then he turned to the scrap of paper she had given him. He ran his finger tips over the telephone number she had hastily scrawled. He thought of the pen in her hand. How she had written those numbers with him in her thoughts. He discovered he was standing rigid with concentration, his eyes closed.

When she opened her door he hardly recognised her. She was wearing an almost white raincoat. She looked at him as if he were a stranger. 'Yes?'

It wasn't the welcome he had anticipated. He wondered how he should behave. His face went searching unsuccessfully for the appropriate expression: it hovered between prurient complicity and evasive detachment; managing somehow to frown and smile uncertainly, all at the same time. He sensed that he might be beginning to look ridiculous. He began to sweat. He felt the need to say something but his brain was a blank, so he said the first thing that came into his head. 'I've come,' he blurted out suddenly and immediately wished he'd said something else.

Maria frowned. 'Sorry?'

It wasn't going as he had planned. He almost turned and walked away. Back to Frederica who understood him; reliable, dependent, valetudinarian Frederica with her pills and her familiar neuroses.

'Who is it?'

A voice within the house. And then Maria was standing at the door.

'Ah Roberto,' she said with something almost like a song in her voice. 'Come in. Come in.'

He stepped into the hallway. She put her arm round the other woman. 'You've met my sister then?'

Her sister! Oh God. What if he had called her Maria? Kissed her even? He sought to cover up the gaff he had almost made. 'Yes of course, your sister. I was just about to say how alike you are.'

'Are we?' the sister said. 'No one's ever said that before. Have they Maria?'

He coughed. 'Well er, the eyes.' He gestured vaguely. 'The eyes are the same.' And even as he said it, he realised their eyes were of an entirely different shape and colour. The two women looked at each other, their eyebrows raised, mouths sceptically

turned down. He shuffled. 'Well, I mean not, you know the...
er...colour of course. The colour's entirely different. I mean
the er... well the sort of shape. You know the shape.'

Inwardly he cursed himself for not ringing Maria first, as
she had suggested. He'd behaved clumsily. He wondered how
much the sister knew. Had they spoken of him? Women did
that sort of thing. Didn't they? And Maria? Was she annoyed
with him for giving the game away? He improvised an alibi.

'I was just passing,' he said, with what he hoped was
professional *élan*. He handed Maria an appointment card that
happened to be in his pocket. She studied it blankly. 'I er
wanted to let you know that we had to change your appointment.
You know for that...er... molar.'

'Molar?'

'Yes the one that's been giving you trouble.' He tapped his
own tooth to give the lie credence. She stared at him blankly.
'So,' he said with inappropriate enthusiasm clapping his hands
together, 'what about Wednesday?'

'Wednesday?'

He took her questioning repetition for disagreement and
shifted ground with needless alacrity. 'Yes. Well, we *could* make it
Thursday.' He clutched a number out of the air. 'Say er four
o'clock? Unless of course that's impossible for you. In which
case Friday. Would Friday at 2.30 suit you?'

His galloping invention was taking on a reality of its own.

She said nothing.

'Two thirty then.' And to his infinite horror he found his
right eye closing in what could only be described as a wink.

The sister tied the belt of her raincoat. 'I have to go,' she said. She extended her hand to him. He shook it. He wondered if she noticed how his palms were sweating. 'Nice to have met you,' she said. She kissed her sister on both cheeks and walked out into the street. Roberto observed her. He couldn't help remarking how slim her waist was and how enticingly her hips rolled as she walked. He mused on which of the two sisters was the prettier.

'Come on in,' Maria said. She closed the door and he followed her into a small living room.

'What was all that about an appointment?'

She sat at one end of the sofa. He heard the electric whisper of nylon as she crossed her long legs.

He looked at her. He wasn't sure how to progress to the next stage. The thought crossed his mind that he may have misconstrued her motives after the party. But then, he thought, she did kiss me. He wondered if it was up to him to make the first move.

Maria had one hand behind her neck. 'Friday 2.30!' she said. She clicked her tongue mockingly.

He shrugged. How he regretted the wink. He thought of her, talking to her friends; laughing together at his maladroitness. *And then can you believe? He actually winked at me!*

He shrugged. 'Perhaps I'd better go.'

Now he just wanted to be out of that room. In the warmth of his car; the radio playing.

He turned and made for the door.

She said, 'As a matter of fact, I have been having a little pain with one of my teeth. I wonder if you'd mind awfully having a look at it.'

He walked across the room and drew up a chair beside her. She tapped a long fingernail on a tooth at the back of her pink mouth. He was aware of her perfume and the sweetness of her breath.

'Let me see,' he said, automatically assuming a professional air.

And as he leaned forward, he felt a cool hand at the nape of his neck drawing his mouth down towards her scarlet lips, while the other probed gently but insistently along his thigh.

IV

As he parked his car at the clinic, his appointments' clerk was on the pavement waiting for him. 'Thank God you've come,' she said. 'It's your wife. She's been taken to hospital'

At San Paulo hospital, the incredibly young looking doctor told him Frederica had had a miscarriage.

'What was it?' he asked needlessly.

'A boy,' said the doctor.

'I didn't even know she was pregnant,' he said. He thought about his lost son. He saw them playing beside a swing in his garden; going to a football match together. He felt he might cry. He said, 'She's not going to die is she?'

The doctor held out his hands, palms up and shrugged. 'I don't think so.'

'You don't think so?'

'It's too early to say. Recovery rates are normally very good with such cases. But your wife, as I'm sure you know, isn't a well woman.'

She was sleeping as he sat beside the bed and he took her hand. The nurse smiled sympathetically. 'Frederica,' he said. She didn't move. 'What are all these tubes for?' he said to the nurse.

'Don't worry. They're to help make her better,' the nurse said.

She spoke to him as if he were a child. 'Well I didn't think they were there to kill her.'

'We're all doing our best for her,' the nurse snapped.

'I know,' he said. 'I know. I'm sorry.'

Later she awoke and pressed his hand. 'I'm sorry,' she said with real sympathy. He felt an overwhelming desire to lie on the bed with her and take her in his arms.

'I called you. You weren't at the clinic. I was alone. There was blood everywhere. I was so frightened.'

He was thinking: *For a month or so I was a father and I knew nothing about it.*

He said, 'I was called out on a case.' It was a ridiculous excuse. He *never* went out to see patients. But she seemed to accept it. He thought about where he had been. What he had been doing. He needed to tell her. The guilt was like a wound. Only the telling would seal it. Somehow he couldn't help himself. He looked at her drawn face on the pillow; the silk night dress stitched with blue flowers.

'Actually it was Maria,' he said.

'Maria?'

He laughed. 'Yes funny isn't it. She called me. She was having terrible trouble with one of her teeth. So I went over there. Her sister was there.' He wondered why he needed to include this detail. He put his other hand on hers. He said, 'Frederica you know I love you don't you? You know that don't you?'

'Yes I know,' she said. And her trust made something break in him.

'I need you to know that. I'm so sorry.'

'What are you sorry for?'

He drew a deep breath and put his head on the pillow beside hers. 'I have to tell you. I have to.'

But the doctor came in. Roberto sat upright. The doctor said, 'I think you should leave her for a while. She needs to sleep.'

He sat in a crowded canteen amongst other visitors and drank a cup of lukewarm coffee, then walked out in the street. He didn't know why he entered the church. It had been over twenty years. The echoing footfalls, the sunlight transformed to rose as it beamed through the windows, the scent of incense – were all immediately familiar to him. He sat down in a pew and put his head in his hands. He groaned aloud. His guilt was like a stone on his conscience.

'Is there anything I can do?'

He looked up at the priest who stood staring compassionately down at him.

Roberto stood up. 'Yes,' he said. 'There is.'

'Come,' said the priest. He walked towards the confessional

and entered. Roberto sat down in the latticed darkness. He inhaled the familiar scent

'How long since your last confession?'

He ignored the age old question. 'I have to tell you something,' he said. 'I have to tell somebody. It's eating away at me.'

'Yes.'

Roberto thought of Frederica in her hospital bed. What had this unknown priest to do with her? He stood up suddenly. 'I've changed my mind,' he said suddenly and walked across the church floor; across the rain-wet street and back to the hospital.

She was sleeping. He asked the nurse to leave. He watched her until the door closed behind her. He flexed his fingers until the knuckles cracked. His hands clasped behind his back, he stood before the window staring out. His eyes took in the rain-swept car park and the tall grey buildings opposite. He licked his lips and coughed. Then he told her where he had been that afternoon and what he had done. Naturally, he left out the more physical details but he omitted nothing that might in any way exonerate him. With each sentence, he felt the weight of his guilt leaving him and a great tranquillity settling upon him like the held chord of a church organ. When he had finished, he stood still for a full minute his head bowed. He heard the voice of the nurse. But when he turned, the room was empty except for himself and Frederica. It was she who had spoken. Her eyes were open and were fixed on him.

'Frederica,' he said. 'Were you awake? Did you hear?'

Her eyes suddenly brimmed with tears which overflowed and ran down her face and into her mouth.

'She's my best friend,' she sobbed.

He knelt by her side, his head on her breast. He felt her hand in his hair. He didn't speak. There was nothing more to say.

He found himself smiling contentedly.

V

And so a pattern was set. Maria was merely the first in a long line of Roberto's adventures. Frederica recovered but the miscarriage had left her weaker and even more dependent on her Roberto. She deprecated his almost compulsive acts of infidelity but somehow she grew to tolerate them. On one occasion she even, howsomever reluctantly, allowed him to take a young rather pretty if empty-headed, clinical assistant from Bari on holiday with him. He told Frederica that they were attending a conference together; that he would be staying with her family. He'd be saving on hotel bills. He understood that they both knew that it was a lie. With the money saved, he told her, he'd be able to buy her that antique necklace she'd coveted for so long.

But usually his liaisons were with married women. Married women caused him less trouble because it seemed to him that it was *they* who were transgressing; married women could not lay claims on him for any kind of permanent liaison. If they began to cling he could tell them: I really think it would be better for us both if you went back to your husband. I mean, you have to admit, there isn't really any future in this for us. And you know my wife is sick. I really don't know how much longer she's going to be with us. I *should* spend more time with her while she's still alive. You do understand don't you?

And his confessions to Frederica followed a pattern. At first he would be vague, littering his conversation with indeterminate clues. He had just been out; he would tell her at the outset. Nothing had happened. But gradually he would allow her to worm something like the truth out of him. It seemed to suit him well. He felt cleansed afterwards. But it was never the whole truth. He allowed her a space where she could wrap herself in comforting delusion; where she could convince herself that nothing had really happened. They even joked about it. Well, at least he did. Things weren't perfect. But marriage is a game where every household plays by different rules. And the odd rules by which Roberto and Frederica lived enabled them to satisfy the two criteria by which a marriage may be judged to be successful: they were, as far as it went, kind to one another. And the union lasted.

Lasted, that is, until one bright Sunday morning ten years later when, as the bells pealed and the birds sang, Roberto was awakened by a strange smell in the bedroom. Frederica's head was turned away from him and there was vomit on the sheet. Her eyes were open but unseeing and the throb of her pulse was now still for ever.

The pain he felt at her death surprised everybody who knew him. It surprised him too. For the first time he understood what the term 'bursting into tears' meant. He wept like a child. He found himself howling at his terrible loss. He buried his face in the cushion on the sofa, sobbing out her name for sometimes an hour together. And it would happen without any warning: as he was shaving before the mirror; while he was driving his car so that he was forced to stop because the tears blinded him so; while somebody was serving him in a shop. Once while he was attending to a patient, a vision of the pattern of her tiny footsteps in the snow suddenly came into his head and he broke down so uncontrollably that the patient had to call the nurse. Somebody drove him home and the doctor was called. For a week he stayed in his bed with all the curtains closed. His friends and colleagues became seriously concerned for his welfare and even for his sanity. And as he lay there, for the most part sleepless, he had a feeling that he might never recover; that this is what the days and nights would be like for the remainder of his life. He closed his eyes and tried to will himself to die; to sleep and never to wake up. But he always did wake up. And as he blearily opened his eyes, Frederica and her death were always the first things that stepped into his mind. He never answered the ring at his door; the phone calls remained unanswered.

One afternoon however, a colleague's persistent knocking forced him to open the door. They sat opposite one another in his darkened living room, for the most part in silence. Occasionally, in the face of persistent enquiries and questions, he would give terse and for the most part non-committal replies. When the colleague left he discovered that his bathroom cabinet had been emptied of pills. Strangely this did something to revive him. From that moment he began slowly, to live in the world once more. However it was a dream world: somehow at one remove from his real self.

On the day he returned to his clinic, the staff gathered on the threshold to welcome him. They clapped with restrained enthusiasm as he emerged from his car. He was unaccustomed to such shows of affection. He wondered, could it be that they liked him? Gradually his life returned to something like normality, though he found going home to his empty house difficult. After work he developed the habit of going to a small bar near his clinic, where he would sit drinking endless cups of coffee until it was dark. The coffee often kept him awake at night but he didn't mind unduly.

One evening, staring into the mirror at his own reflection he became aware of the eyes of a woman watching him with some curiosity. He felt he knew her but couldn't find a context in his memory for the face. It worried him. Mentally he ran through the faces of the women he had known since his marriage? How many had there been? Fifteen? Twenty? But this particular face he couldn't place. When he slowly turned to look at her, she smiled and came over to him. 'You don't remember me do you?'

He shook his head.

'Maria?'

'Ah,' he said but he still wasn't sure. 'Maria?' he said doubtfully.

'Her sister. I opened the door to you. You thought I was her.'

'You noticed?'

'Of course I noticed.'

He remembered admiring the slimness of her waist as she had walked away. Surreptitiously he tried to judge if she had thickened over the years but she was wearing a heavy tweed coat. It was difficult to tell. He bought her a glass of white wine. They talked of Maria and of Frederica and her death. Was it sympathy or affection that made her rest her hand on his arm? Perhaps both. He was happy with both. His own house, he knew, wore an air of neglect since Frederica had died. There was something sepulchral in the dust that hovered in the airless, overheated rooms. And Frederica's spirit was everywhere.

So when she invited him back to her apartment, he readily agreed.

VI

It was nearly dawn when he turned the key in his front door. The silence was stultifying. He walked from room to room as if he might find Frederica. She seemed omnipresent. But at the same time her absence was terrible. There were photographs of her everywhere. He gazed at each one in turn, as if trying to discern some fugitive secret concerning her life and his. He gathered them all together and set them in a small circle in the hallway, facing inward. Then he set himself in the centre of the circle and gazed at her several faces as they smiled at him. Maria's sister's perfume still clung to him. Maria's sister. He realised he didn't even know her name. The scent of her filled him with revulsion. There was a taste of bile in his throat. He ran up the stairs to the bathroom pulling his clothes from him as he went, leaving them littering the stairway.

In the bath he scrubbed every inch of his body with a stiff brush till his flesh was red. Then, naked, he returned to the hallway. He lit a candle and sat cross-legged in the centre of the circle of photographs. Frederica's eyes stared at him but there was no forgiveness in them. They did not speak to him. Deep in the pit of his stomach was a painful knot of unease, of betrayal. He had a feeling that it wouldn't go away. Ever. He closed his eyes and spoke into the air, begging her to forgive him. He confessed, as he had always confessed, but the knot in his stomach remained hard and unrelenting. He cried out aloud but to no avail: 'Why did you have to go and die?' he screamed. Then naked as he was, he lay on his side and fell into a deep sleep.

He was awakened by the shrill ring of the telephone. It was the clinic. The pain in his stomach, he noted, was still there. If anything, worse than ever. He told his secretary that he was not feeling well; that he wouldn't be in that day. He put on his dressing gown, took two sleeping pills and lay on his bed.

It was three in the afternoon when he awoke. The pain in his stomach was now so acute that he thought it might be something purely physical. It began to frighten him. He knew what the possibilities were. He could scarce walk upright. He wondered if he should consult a doctor friend of his. Probably it would be wise. He picked up the phone to make an appointment and in answer to the doctor's questions inexplicably found himself saying, 'It's Frederica' - and thought that he was somehow right to give this awful pain, her name. He hadn't said who he was and so put the phone down suddenly. He thought, perhaps he would drive out to see the doctor. Leave it to chance. If he was in and could se him: well and good. If not...

He wasn't quite sure what followed 'if not'. The house oppressed him. He climbed into his car and drove through the afternoon traffic to the outskirts of the city. As he stopped at some traffic lights, the pain became so severe it made him gasp aloud. He hunched over the wheel. He could drive no more. As the lights turned green, he somehow managed to steer his way through the traffic and pulled up untidily against the pavement. For a minute or two he sat there doubled up with pain. He had to have air. He jerked open the passenger door, scrambled across the passenger seat and half-fell onto the pavement. Three children running by stopped and stared at him. 'Drunk man,' they shouted. 'Drunk man' and ran off laughing. He took no notice. He took three or four deep breaths before pulling himself upright. He had to get off the street. Somehow he managed to stumble across the pavement, avoiding the passers-by who gazed at him curiously. When he reached a broad, open iron gateway, he went through. Before him he saw a green park bench that beckoned to him like a promise of sanctuary and managed to cross to it and slump down without drawing too much attention to himself. The sun emerged from behind a bank of cloud. He closed his eyes and raised his face to its warmth. It made him feel slightly better. It was only then that he realised where he was: the northern entrance to Parco Sempione. 'Where I proposed to my poor dead darling,' he whispered aloud. He pulled himself upright and gazed about him. He knew what he was looking for. Then he saw it: her oak tree. It was surprisingly close. Gasping, he stumbled up the shallow slope and embraced the oak as if it were a woman: as if she were Frederica. Untypically, he didn't care who saw him. The rough texture of the bark rubbed against his face. Quite suddenly he began to weep, as he had wept during the days following her death. And as he wept, he whispered her name over and over. From his tear-stained mouth tumbled his confession. This time he kept nothing back. Nothing. And when he had finished, his hold on the tree gave and he slid slowly down the trunk until he sprawled spread-eagled amongst its roots. Her roots, he thought.

He stayed there for some time his face turned towards the blessings of the sun. And as he sat, the bitter pain that had gripped him drained away.

When it was quite gone he climbed to his feet. He brushed the dirt and the leaves from his coat and then made his way through the passers-by, who were enjoying the early spring sunshine. He breathed deeply as he walked through the iron gate and into the world once more.

A young woman in a bright red coat approached him, her high heels clicking on the hard pavement. She had her hand tucked into the arm of a tall man in a dark overcoat. Her husband probably, Roberto thought. As they passed he smiled at her. He saw her hesitate for an instant wondering if she knew him or not. Then, to be on the safe side, as it were, she gave a guarded smile.

And Roberto manoeuvring his car through the afternoon traffic, smiled all the way home.

Oh God What Must I do?

I

I have never been a woman for dropping names. Firstly, because I'm inclined to despise that rather shallow purchasing of attention by proxy; and secondly, with the exception of the particular case whose history I am about to relate, I am acquainted with hardly anyone whose name merits the dropping. However, at certain parties, when confronted by the sort of women who collects intellectual celebrities as others collect Dresden Shepherdesses, I have only to mention Allessandra's name and immediately I have their undivided attention. Such an example of the breed I met recently, at a reception that my rather lowly secretarial work at the Embassy sometimes requires my husband and me to attend. Immediately on hearing the celebrated name, the lady in question's hitherto rather bored and condescending air vanished immediately.

Suddenly, I am the most fascinating person in the room.

She proceeds to extol Allessandra's qualities, as the greatest female novelist of our generation and, resting her hand intimately on my arm, enquires, 'You mean *you* actually know La Demercurio?'

It is the condescending emphasis she lends to that little

word *you*, that irritates; the implication being, that somehow I am too dull, too fuddy-duddy, to be worthy of such elevated companions.

'But tell me,' she continues, 'do you know her well?'

'Oh pretty well,' I murmur airily.

'Really! How often do you speak with her?'

'Well, every day I suppose. '

'Every day! Really! How fascinating! So would you describe yourselves as…' she pauses…'intimate friends?'

She gives an oddly salacious emphasis to the word, intimate.

'Intimate?' I consider the question. 'Yes, I think one could say that.'

I know from experience what is coming next: the invitation to the exclusive little dinner party. The smile appears as though switched on by some operative in her brain. 'As it happens,' she says leaning towards me, 'I'm holding a little dinner party next Thursday?'

Oh there's a surprise, I think to myself.

'Nothing very grand. She'd meet some fascinating people.' And she proceeds to list them: their myriad talents, their virtues and their standings in Society. When the list is complete there is a silence. I smile into it. Recognising her omission she adds hurriedly, 'Oh you yourself would be most welcome of course. That goes without saying. And your husband.'

'Well…' I'm good on wells. I keep her waiting. 'I don't know really. You know she's a very private person.'

'Oh I'm sure. Writers often are. But that's the fascinating thing about her. That trick she has, despite her immense fame, of keeping her life so private. No one knows a thing about her. No articles, no interviews. She's a mystery. Apart from that drawing on the fly leaf of her first book no one knows what she looks like. And that was twenty years ago. She never goes round the country signing books in shops as others do. But that only seems to add to her fascination. Don't you agree?'

'Well,' I say,' actually she did do a book signing once.'

'Really?'

'Yes.' I lean towards her and whisper. 'As a matter of fact that was where we first met. Well actually the second. But that's another story. The book-signing was where, I think I can safely say, we sealed our…relationship.'

'Fascinating,' she murmurs.

'Anyway it was a long time ago. She wouldn't dream of doing them now.'

She frowns. 'Why is that do you think?'

'Doesn't need to really. And she hates attention. All those people pestering her; all that pushing and noise. She loathes it all. In her own way she's a very modest person. A bit fuddy-duddy really. Rather like me.'

'Oh what nonsense!'

And the smile switches off and is instantly replaced by a frown. 'But you know I can understand her. I really can. I've written a few things myself. So I can understand how she feels. From what you've said I can sense that we have a good deal in common, she and I. I really do. So you can assure her, that should she decide to come to my little dinner party, should *you* wish to attend, as I genuinely hope you will, she'd have nothing to fear on that score. I'd swear all my guests to absolute secrecy. They're all people in the public eye. They understand these things. You can confidently reassure her on that score. I'm the soul of discretion. We all are. Do please see what you can do?'

'I'll do my best but…' I glance round the room and momentarily catch sight of my husband. He is doing his best to conceal his boredom. He has both hands in the pockets of his rumpled jacket. When he finally spots me, he flicks his eyes with mock desperation in the direction of the door. He wants to go home. I frown and give the slightest of shakes to my head. He shrugs and shuffles off into another room.

The lady's manicured eyebrows are raised.

I smile at her. 'My husband,' I explain.

'Really! And does he know Allesandra as well?'

I notice she is already on first name terms with the famous writer.

'My husband? Oh yes. Better than I do, I should say.'

She laughs lightly. 'Look, about my dinner party. Here's my card. And I'll write the date for you. And promise me you'll do your best to persuade her to come.'

I take the card and note that there are three addresses.

'Ah,' she says taking the card back from me, 'let me underline our town address. That's where we'll be.'

I inspect the card once more. 'Well, I'll do my best. But why don't you ask her yourself?'

'I'm sorry.'

'She's here somewhere. I'm sure I saw her a moment ago going into the other room.'

The lady takes a step backwards. 'You mean she's here? Allesandra is here. Tonight?'

'Yes. Unless she's already gone home. Surprising really. She hates this sort of thing.'

'Oh do you think you could introduce us? Just to speak to her, my dear.' And she flutters her hands and her eyes flick upwards to the ceiling.

'Well, I'll try. But she likes to remain incognito. She's almost a recluse.'

'Oh I understand. I understand.'

'I could tell you how we met if you like,' I say.

She stifles a yawn. I don't think she hears me. She points an elegant finger. 'In the other room you say. Could you tell me how I might recognise her?'

I consider the question. 'She's probably the most unlikely looking person in the room.'

'Perhaps you…'

'No, I have to speak to my friend,' I say, pointing across the throng to an imaginary person.

It's the nearest I come to a brush-off. And I have to confess it gives me a certain guilty pleasure.

She shakes my hand. The smile switches on. 'It's been fascinating,' she said. 'Fascinating.'

And then she is gone, sliding through the crowds in search of her prey.

II

Like many other women, I too had read the glowing reviews of
Allessandra Demercurio's first novel with interest; but it was the
title that intrigued me; and so when I saw that she was doing a
book signing in the city's foremost bookshop, I took a copy
from the pile and joined the queue that led to her table. The
lights were rather dim but I could make out that she was a
smartly dressed woman of thirty or more, rather tall and looking
rather older than her picture in the paper. She smiled on
everybody she met and seemed to be enjoying her moment of
fame and popularity.

As I waited at the end of the long queue that wound round
the shop, I couldn't help recalling another writer I had once
known and sadly lost touch with: my dear friend Franco He too,
a number of years earlier, had enjoyed a brief season in the sun
but now, alas, was almost entirely forgotten. And I prayed that
the same demoralising fate would not be visited on Allessandra.
Success early in a career can become a burden: for poor Franco,
after having so effortlessly scaled the heights of fame while still
a student, the descent into obscurity had been demoralisingly
swift and precipitate. The critics turned against him: *Oh of course
there are good things in that latest novel of his, some very worthy things,
but really it has none of the fire, the discerning originality of his first book.*

And so after a time, despite himself, Franco began to believe
they were right.

His confidence and self-belief   forsook him.   What had
once seemed so easy and natural now became burdensome and

laborious. He would do anything to deflect himself from having to write: put up shelves, vacuum the carpet, do endless crosswords puzzles, watch tiresome television programmes, visit friends - anything that might distract him from the task of writing. He started drinking more than was good for him.

Of course, I knew nothing of this at the time. As far as I was concerned he was beavering away at his latest work, which would serve to re-establish him once more at the top of the literary ladder. And although I was unaware of the reality of his situation, I began to sense that all was not well. He had always been the most gregarious of companions but now we rarely saw him and when we did, he seemed so much thinner. I thought he might be ill. He developed a rash that covered the entire upper part of his body. His beautiful dark hair began to fall out; his so-called friends deserted him. He locked himself away and rarely went out. Initially I respected his need to be alone. Isn't this what all great artists did? And after all, whenever we did chance to meet, he took pains to inform me how well his latest book was going; that he was working on it night and day; it had taken over his life. It was to be his masterpiece.

And I believed him. Why should I not? But then, as the days dragged on into months and the months into years, my concern grew. I though it wasn't healthy for him to be on his own quite so much; cutting himself off in this fashion from all his friends and from me in particular. After all we had been close friends at the University. At one time indeed, we had almost become lovers; but friendship somehow got in the way.

And so, one afternoon, although reluctant to disturb him, I

knocked at his door. There was no answer. And yet I knew for certain that he was at home. I was about to walk away when it occurred to me that he might be ill: lying there in agony, unable to call out or move. I went home and telephoned him several times, leaving messages on his answer phone; messages to which he never responded. I became so concerned that I considered calling the police; or trying to locate his mother who lived in Milan. And then, I thought, I'd give it one last try. I set myself a goal. I would knock at his door for half an hour. If there were no answer by the end of that period, I would call the police. I like rules like that. They make me feel easier. And so, one morning in September, I stood before his door. I checked my watch and knocked. Deep within me I was convinced I was merely going through the motions. But to my surprise, the door opened almost immediately. He peered out like some odd underground creature, blinking into the sunlight. I was shocked at how thin and drawn he looked. He was wearing a stained dressing gown and his feet were bare. He had been an unusually handsome man in his youth with wonderfully symmetrical yet interesting features. Across his lip on the left side ran a small pale scar which far from detracting, served in fact to add to his attractiveness, for it freed him from the burden of perfection. He had always been fastidious about his appearance. But now he was unshaven and I couldn't help remarking the reek of alcohol that surrounded him. Yet he greeted me with something approaching his old warmth.

'Franco,' I said, 'are you all right?'

'Why shouldn't I be?' And he laughed.

I told him I'd called a few times; asked him why he had never answered the door or picked up the phone.

'Oh I'm so busy working. It's at the top of the house you see, my office. There's no phone up there. I don't hear anything. I live my life in a sort of trance.' And he laughed once more.

I asked him if he'd eaten.

'Not much time for that. You know how it is when I'm absorbed in a book. No time for anything.'

I said, 'If you like I'll make you something. I've brought some mince and some peppers and a bottle of wine and some pappadelle.'

He didn't want me to be put to any trouble.

'No trouble,' I assured him. 'I could do with something myself.'

So he let me in and showed me to the kitchen. In the sink, dishes and cutlery were piled up in a bath of greasy, brown water. In one corner flies buzzed about a pile of overflowing black bin bags. In the living room the curtains were drawn. Empty bottles littered the table and were piled up in the paper basket and by the fire. On the television an idiotic quiz game was playing, where scantily clad young women tried to decide which young male contestant should first be pushed into a swimming pool. The sound was turned down. There was an odour of despair about the place.

'Look,' I said, 'how would you like me to make you something to eat now and maybe tidy up a bit?'

'If you like,' he said. He didn't seem at all put out. He gestured at the stairs. 'But I must get on.'

He disappeared up the stairs and soon I heard the distant rattle of his typewriter. I found the sound strangely comforting.

Later we ate, almost in silence. At one point, as he lit a cigarette and drained his third glass of wine, he said, 'I'm not very good company I'm afraid. But you see if you deal in books, that is all you think about morning, noon and night.'

'I understand.'

'I'm glad you understand,' he said with a smile. Pouring himself some more wine, he raised his glass and thanked me. Shortly afterwards he fell asleep on the sofa. I placed a cushion beneath his head and covered him with a blanket before continuing with my work of bringing some sort of order to the place. When I had finished downstairs, I went up to his bedroom at the top of the house, intending to replace the grubby rumpled sheets with clean ones and to vacuum the dusty carpet. But there were no sheets or blankets in the bedroom cupboard. Adjoining the bedroom was a small room. I pushed open the door thinking it might be a store room and realized too late that it was in fact his workroom. I stopped in amazement. Perhaps I should have walked away. After all it was none of my business. But something held me. The curtains were closed and the room was lit by a single bulb. On a table beneath the window was a typewriter, an A4 sheet of paper slotted into place. Other sheets covered the table. They overflowed from it and spilled across the floor. It was impossible to cross it without stepping on them. Once more I was tempted to walk away; to leave things as they were. After all, this was Franco's sanctuary. I knew he would have hated my reading what was, as yet, unfinished. Yet lack of curiosity has never been one of my abiding virtues. I confess it: I am nosy. I tried to convince myself that I was picking up the fallen sheets purely in the interest of tidying up. But that would have been a lie. I desperately wanted to see what had so occupied him for all these long, lonely months. I held the sheet up to the light. The first line read: *Oh God, what must I do?* And so did the second. And the third. And so it continued to the end of the page. I picked up another. It was exactly the same; as was every sheet I looked at. *Oh God, what must I do?* - typed over and over again: thousands and thousands of times. Clutching a pile of these pages in my shaking hand, I crossed to the table and read the sheet still in the typewriter. It was the same. I was finding it difficult to breath. I tore open the curtains, opened the windows and, taking a deep breath, rested my eyes on the red-tiled roofs of the city.

And as I did so, into my mind came a picture of Franco, as he had once been when we were students together in Bologna: a rather thin, winsome creature with an amusing talent for mimicry, who moved with the lightness and elegance of a trained dancer. I remembered too, how he had made me a present of his first novel. It was at a party in the house of a female student I did not myself know. It was she who greeted me warmly at the door and her eyes shone when I told her I was a friend of Franco's and gave her my name. She spoke so warmly of him that it induced in me a slight pang of something approaching jealousy. It was a new sensation for I had always considered him a friend rather than a lover.

The young woman rattled on. She led me into the dusky

interior of the apartment that was lit with guttering candles. 'What a remarkable man he is. Quite exceptional. Talented and yet so modest. The sort of man I have always dreamed of spending the remainder of my life with.' And she gave a self-mocking laugh.

My pangs of jealousy intensified. I studied this pretty, vivacious young woman as best I could in the candle-lit gloom. Could there be something between them? I asked myself.

'Come,' she said, 'I have a present for you.'

'For me?' I was surprised; surprised and somewhat uneasy. Why should this pretty young girl, someone I had only just met, be giving me a present? She took my arm and led me into a large room where couples were dancing, laughing and drinking. Here too the curtains were drawn and the room lit but by two or three candles. There was incense in the air. We sat side by side on a large sofa. From beneath one of the cushions she produced a small parcel, wrapped in red tissue paper.

'But you shouldn't,' I protested.

'Don't be ridiculous. It's not from me. *He* asked me to give it you.'

'He?'

'Franco. He's told me so much about you that I feel I know you. Don't you feel the same?'

I demurred, rather embarrassed and tore the parcel open. Inside was a book with Franco's name on the cover.

The girl said, 'He's written an inscription for you. Read it.'

She lit a cigarette lighter and held it so that I could make out the writing.

I opened the book carefully. On the inside cover between my name and his scrawled flamboyant signature, he had written:
My first book; to my first reader. With love and gratitude.

I was touched. For a moment I thought I would cry. 'I must thank him,' I said. I looked round. 'But where is he?'

'Dah Rah!' the girl exclaimed removing the blonde wig with a theatrical flourish and bursting into laughter.

'You!' I said.

'Of course. I really think I should take up acting. Or perhaps become a female impersonator. I believe it pays rather well.'

'I knew it was you all the time,' I said pushing him away.

'Liar!' Franco put his arm about me. 'I believe you were just a bit jealous.'

'Rubbish,' I said.

I was angry but then my anger dissolved and we kissed each other. Lightly. As friends kiss.

Looking back, it all seemed to have happened in another lifetime. And now, gazing out over the roofs at the broad morning sky it made me weep to think how all that youthful, that boundless energy and ambition had shrunk to the confines of this tiny, dishevelled room; as Franco himself seemed to have shrunk. My tears fell uncontrollably upon those awful sheets with their despairing, endlessly repeated message. So unrestrained were my sobs that it was only when I turned to leave the room that I became aware of him standing there, quite still in the doorway, watching me. For an instant our eyes locked and then a groan of utter despair and abandon escaped from him and he slumped to the floor.

III

After that I lost touch with him for a number of years. But later when we met up once more, he filled in the missing part of his story, informed by his novelist's eye for detail and his amazing memory. Mockingly he referred to is as: *Franco: The Lost Years*

After several months in a psychiatric hospital - in order to further his recovery - he had travelled north to Milan, to live with his widowed mother and younger sister. He was still too weak to think of doing any kind of work. His father had left an annuity to his mother but there was trouble with probate. What was worse, his younger sister, whom he adored, fell ill. It was some kind of complaint that defeated the doctors. She was unable to rise from her bed. The least effort prostrated her. She required constant medical supervision. So, their already meagre resources were stretched even further. Franco's attitude to his writing changed. Now he must write not for the critics, for acclaim but for money. But the fact was – he seemed unable to write at all; neither for love nor money. His talent, or perhaps his will, had deserted him. In desperation he was about to take a job in a hosiery store run by a distant relative, when he remembered an agent, by the name of Falconetti, an admirer, who had been a friend of his father and had often helped him from time to time in the past, with publishers' contracts and other matters. What is more, he was known to be wealthy.

Franco swallowed his pride and went to see him at his office in Via Manzoni. Embarrassedly he explained the desperate nature of his plight.

'Signor Falconetti, I must have money,' he explained. 'I'll do anything. Anything. My sister you see. Please help me. I'll do whatever you say.'

'So you need money?'

Franco stared at the floor. 'Yes.'

Signor Falconetti studied his distraught young friend for some time in silence from behind his desk. Then he rose and from a bookshelf took a slim paperback volume bound in pink and handed it to Franco. Franco studied the cover. It was decorated with a circle of flowers and assorted grasses, in the centre of which a pretty young nurse surrendered herself to the passionate embraces of a handsome young doctor. Franco leafed through a number of pages before suddenly hurling the book to the floor in disgust. 'Why are you showing me this rubbish?'

Signor Falconetti picked up the book. He pointed at the photograph of the authoress on the back cover: a substantial looking lady who smiled contentedly out at the world from beneath a mountain of dyed blonde hair. 'Do you know her?' he asked.

'Of course I don't know her. I have better things to do than to waste my time reading that kind of drivel. '

Signor Falconetti studied him. 'Really?' he said mockingly. 'Tell me Franco, what better things? Like, for example, standing all day behind a shop counter selling stockings while your sister fades and your mother weeps the nights away?'

Franco bridled. 'Signor Falconetti I thought you were a friend?'

'But I am a friend; a friend who tells you the truth even though you may not wish to hear it.' He pointed once more at the photograph on the back of the book. 'Franco, I have to tell you something: I am very fond of this lady whom you evidently despise. Do you see how she smiles?'

'What's it to me whether she smiles or not?'

'Do you know why she smiles?'

'How should I know? What is all this talk of smiles? What has it to do with me? I come to you, practically begging for help. Do you think I enjoy doing that? Do you? And all you can do is talk of fat ladies who grin idiotically and write asinine romantic fiction. If that's all you can do I think I'd better leave.' And Franco suddenly rose to his feet overturning the chair and strode towards the door.

'Franco!' Falconetti said. 'Please sit down.'

Franco hesitated.

'Franco please!'

Franco sighed and relented. He closed the door, righted the chair and sat down. He folded his arms. 'Well?' he said.

The Agent leaned forward, his elbows on his desk. 'Shall I tell you something about smiling?' He tapped the back cover of the book. 'This lady makes over three million euros a year. Three million euros! Every year without fail. That is why she smiles. And as for me, I take ten percent of that. So I smile too. Every day. Look at me. You see how happy she makes me.' And he leaned back in his large leather chair, his hands clasped behind his neck and smiled. 'What do you think of that?'

Franco shrugged. 'There are certain prostitutes who make a

comfortable living in this city selling their wares but I have no wish to be one of them.'

Signor Falconetti sighed staring at the ceiling. 'That's unworthy of you, my dear Franco. And it's unfair to the lady. You asked me for help. I am offering you a way. You have talent. You need money.' He laid the book in Franco's lap. 'So my advice to you is, read this. Study how she does it. And write! You understand me?"

Franco stared at the book on his lap. He could scarcely bare to touch it. 'I can write in my own way,' he said. 'I did it before and I can do it again.'

Signor Falconetti shook his head. 'I don't think so,' he murmured. 'You are mining an exhausted seam my friend. I've seen it before in a number of other writers. It's the truth and the truth hurts, I know. But I want you to do something for me. Go home and think about it. Just think about it that's all. Will you do that?'

Franco hesitated. He slipped the book into his pocket. 'Very well,' he said reluctantly. The agent slapped him on the back and accompanied him to the door, his arm about his shoulders. 'Good boy,' he said. 'When you've decided, call me. We'll work out a contract. The usual ten percent.'

Franco was silent. Falconetti could see he was still unconvinced. He squeezed his shoulder. 'Listen,' he said. 'I'll tell you what I'll do. As soon as you've written the first sentence, I won't even ask to see it, just ring me up and tell me. I'll write you out a cheque for a thousand euros. What could be fairer?'

He held out his hand.

For a second Franco hesitated. Then he thought of his sister lying pale and exhausted in her bed. He took the hand and shook it. 'Very well,' he said, 'but I hate myself.'

The agent smiled. 'Hate yourself as much as you like, my friend. But with three million in your pocket, I can assure you, even hatred tastes sweet.' And he closed the door with a smile that could only be described as enigmatic.

As Franco reached the stairs the door opened once more. Falconetti pointed at him. 'Wait,' he said. 'I've been thinking. Did I say ten percent? Make it fifteen. Ten for the book and five for the advice. The excellent advice. And cheap at the price if you ask me.'

And he smiled once more and closed the door.

IV

For three weeks the pink book lay unopened on the small table beside Franco's bed. He spent time with his ailing sister. He visited lawyers, struggling in a financial world that was alien to him. The bills came in. But there was little money to pay them. At night he drew the bed sheets over his head to muffle the sound of his mother weeping.

After a week Falconetti phoned him. He spoke in his usual style of mocking affection. 'How goes the lover?'

Franco swore. Falconetti laughed. 'A Thousand Euros,' he whispered and put the phone down.

The sun shone through the bedroom window. For a full minute Franco stared at the book. Then he picked it up and took it into the garden. He read it through at one sitting. It took him half an hour. He stared up at the sky, then covered his eyes with his hands. He groaned aloud. 'Oh God, what must I do?'

What he did was to go up to his bedroom and put a sheet of blank A4 paper into his battered old Olivetti. He had a vision of the blonde lady; the incredibly wealthy, blonde lady. She was smiling at him. From somewhere a voice came into his head. He leaned over the typewriter and wrote the first sentence. *Oh God, what must I do?* But he didn't ring Falconetti asking for his advance. Nor did he stop writing. And how he wrote! For the first time in years he wrote with amazing confidence and rapidity, covering page after page with hardly a correction. It was as though the book, as the saying goes, wrote itself. Much later he attempted to explain the phenomenon to me: 'It was as though,' he said, 'I were merely listening. There was a voice in my head: a soft female rather blonde voice. And I merely wrote down what she told me.'

At the end of three weeks the book was complete. He typed the title on the front page: *Oh God, what must I do?* - bundled up the manuscript and posted it to Falconetti.

Two days later the agent rang him back.

'What are you trying to do to me, writing such things? Are you trying to ruin me? I haven't slept all night. I couldn't put it down. What we have here is a copper-bottomed best seller, dear boy or I'll give my body to science.'

There was a pause. Falconetti said, 'Well aren't you thrilled? Is there something the matter?'

Franco hesitated. 'Well there is something.'

'What? What? Tell me.'

'It's difficult.'

'Come in and see me. Tell me about it.'

An hour later Franco sat once more in Falconetti's office.

He began hesitatingly. 'Well, the fact is…I don't know how to say this. But I once had a reputation. As a serious writer.'

'A deserved reputation.'

'Perhaps. And well, you see it's not that I'm not grateful for what you've done. I am, really I am. But I'm also, how can I say, a bit ashamed. You see, I wouldn't like my other readers, my serious readers, to know that…well…that I'd…'

'Sunk so low. Is that what you mean?'

'Not exactly. I mean, I don't want you to think I'm a snob or anything, but I'd rather nobody…that is…I…'

'Rather no one knew?'

Marco picked up the manuscript. 'Actually yes. I'd rather no one knew I wrote this.'

There was a pause. 'Leave it with me,' Falconetti said breezily. 'In fact leave everything to me. I have to think of something.'

Later that afternoon he rang back.

'Franco?'

'Yes.'

'What do you say to Allessandra?'

'Allessandra? I don't understand.'

'As a name.'

'Name?'

'For you. It's a very nice name. I found it in a knitting catalogue. Allessandra the Great, you see the connection. The female conqueror of the world of literature. Now let's think of another.'

'Another?'

'A surname. Let me see,' the agent mused gazing out his office on the second floor. He read the name on a grocer's shop opposite. 'Ah, I've got it. How about Demercurio.'

'What sort of name is that?'

'A very good name I think. After all your dark winter's over and you're going out into the sun once more. The mercury is rising. You know, Balzac took his names off Paris' shops. Why not you? Allessandra Demercurio. It has a certain ring. Like a cash register. Demercurio! It smells of money.'

'Well I…'

'I knew you'd like it. Then, you see, nobody need know it's you. You can write your other books under your own name. Perfect solution all round.'

And so, when the book appeared in print six months later, it was under the name, Allessandra Demercurio.

V

As Falconetti had predicted, the book was a huge success. And not just with the readers of romantic fiction. Franco couldn't help bringing some of his own distinctive qualities to bear. Yes, it was a love story, but it was more than that. It was a great love story. As well as Romance there was Tragedy in there, there was wit, there was irony; and in addition a subtle but beguiling eroticism and passion. And it was beautifully written. In short there was everything that goes to make a story a serious, insightful, yet entertaining piece of fiction. It appealed to practically everybody and flew off the shelves; it flew also to the top of the best seller list and stayed there for months. But its very success brought its own peculiar problems.

One afternoon, some two months after publication, Falconetti asked Franco to come to his office. After they had exchanged greetings and congratulations, Falconetti asked him to sit down.

'Something's come up,' he said studying his fingernails.

'Yes?'

'Well,' he took a deep breath. 'This morning Feltrinelli called me.'

'The book shop chain?'

'Well not the whole chain. The man himself: Feltrinelli in person. Not a man to be trifled with. They're opening a new bookshop in the centre of Milan. Just round the corner actually. He tells me it will be the largest, most modern bookshop, certainly in Italy, if not in Europe. It opens next month. And he wants you to be there.'

'What for?'

'You know, cut a ribbon. Sign books. Smile at your fans. That sort of thing.'

'But I can't do that.'

'Why's that?'

'I'm a man.'

'Yes I'm aware of that. But obviously they don't want *you*. They want Signorina Allessandra.'

'Signorina Allessandra?'

'Yes.'

'But isn't there a bit of a problem here. I mean she doesn't exist.'

'Yes I had thought of that.'

'And any way we've discussed this already. No interviews, no television appearances. And it's worked well. It's part of her charm. Her mystery has, if anything helped to create interest.'

'Yes, well I explained all that to him,' the agent said calmly. 'But he wouldn't buy it. You see he's very influential and used to getting his own way. I shudder to think what the consequences might be if he felt offended. There's a Feltrinelli branch in practically every city in Italy. If we were to turn him down, I wouldn't put it past him not stock your book. Or what is more to the point, any of the books that I handle. It would be the end of you. And what is more important, it would be end for me too.'

Franco stood up. He strode from the window to the door his head in his hands. And then for the lack of anything else to do, strode back again. 'Is it all going to happen again?' he lamented.

'Well,' said Falconetti calmly, 'There is a way.'

'There is?'

'I've been thinking about it.' He rose and walked round Franco studying him carefully.

'What?'

'You're still an exceptionally good looking young man.'

Franco was embarrassed. 'So?'

'So.' Falconetti walked to a rectangular tent on wheels that was standing in the corner of his office. He whipped back one of the curtains. 'Try that for size,' he said, handing Franco a hanger on which hung an organdie dress with ruched sleeves. And then while Franco clutched the dress, dumbfounded, Falconetti pressed the intercom on his desk. Idly inspecting a pair of high heeled sandals sprinkled with diamantes, he said, 'Would you be so good as to inform the make-up girl that we're ready for her now.'

VI

It was the title of the book alerted me. *Oh God, what must I do?* Hadn't I seen it typed on a hundred abandoned sheets six or seven years earlier? But then it could have been a coincidence. Such things happen in life. My curiosity however, got the better of me. In my lunch hour I joined the queue of admirers that snaked across the bookshop to the table where the woman, I presumed was Allesandra, sat smiling and chatting. I studied her. Across my mind flashed the vision of the slimmer much younger *woman* at that party years ago; the woman who had been Franco and had snatched a blonde wig from her head. The queue shuffled forward. As I got closer to the table I could make out the tell-tale scar across 'her' lip and a shock of excitement went through me. I was certain it was him. And yet 'she' was so convincing: the wig was immaculate; the make up impeccable; the voice soft and gently modulated. She wasn't quite as striking as the drawing of her that appeared on the fly leaf of her book - a skilful mixture of a sort of feminised Franco and early Sophia Loren with just a mysterious touch of the Mona Lisa thrown in for good measure - but she was nevertheless convincing and not unhandsome. As I leaned forward curiously, I sensed the aroma of an expensive perfume rising above the neatly coiffed hair. Had it not been for that give-away scar across the lip and the title of the book, the elaborate charade might possibly have taken me in. Certainly nobody else in that long queue in Feltrinelli's suspected a thing. In fact the handsome young man in front of me began to flirt outrageously with her: even inviting her to meet him, after the signing, in the Bar Zero.

'And what shall we do there?' murmured 'Allessandra' with perfect equanimity, glancing up seductively from beneath her false eye lashes.

'Who knows,' said the young man. 'Why don't we let fate take its course?'

'Why not indeed,' said Allessandra in a low seductive voice.

The young man took her hand and bent over and kissed it, before walking away, smiling to himself, the signed book proudly clutched in his hand.

Allessandra wiped her hands delicately with a tiny frilled handkerchief.

'Next,' she said as though she were a rather seductive dentist addressing a room full of patients.

It was my turn.

Without looking up 'she' took the book from me. I must have been the hundredth that afternoon. 'And who is this for?'

'It's for me,' I said.

'Yes,' he said a trifle wearily,' I know that but what shall I write as a dedication?'

'If you could just write, "My first book. To my first reader with love and gratitude". That would be sufficient,' I said.

The pen was suddenly still in his hand. Slowly he raised his head and our eyes met. The eyes are everything. Gradually the familiar face of my old friend emerged through the integument of his expertly applied female disguise. As if by magic, a metamorphosis took place: Franco emerged and Allessandra retreated.

'Of course,' he said.

'I'm so happy to see you looking well,' I said.

And it was true. I was glad. A shaft of exquisite happiness travelled slowly through my whole being. Quite suddenly the shelves, the rows of books and the queue of book lovers that snaked behind me, faded away. I was powerfully aware of his bent head writing my name; the heady perfume, the odour of polish rising from the table and the thought of that hard masculine body beneath all that frothy impedimenta of femininity. The very air was charged with an almost overpowering eroticism. I had to clutch at the table to prevent myself from falling. He wrote out my dedication and blotted it carefully. Then he wrote out his address on a piece of paper and slid it surreptitiously between the leaves of the book. 'My mother and sister would be so pleased to see you,' he said. 'As of course would I.' He leaned forward and whispered. 'We must talk.'

'I'd like that,' I said. 'What shall we talk about?'

'Oh,' he said. 'The usual. Girl talk.'

'Can't wait,' I said.

'Neither can I.'

Then he did the oddest thing. He placed both palms upon the simple, polished table and slowly caressed its smooth, polished surface. 'I will always love this table,' he said. 'I may very well buy it.' With his thumb and forefinger he softly gripped the tongue of a belt that hung down from my dress. 'You understand?'

'Yes,' I said, 'I understand.'

The woman behind me in the queue was growing restive. She had a home to go to; a husband and children to feed.

He wasn't in the least put out. His eyes were mine.

He said, 'Is there anything else you want?'

'No,' I said. 'That is yes. As a matter of fact there is something.'

'Anything. Anything at all. What is it?'

'Well,' I said, 'I wonder if you could possibly give me the name of your hairdresser?'

VII

'I've had enough of this,' my husband said. 'Let's go home.'

I took his arm and leaned against him. Making for the door,

I saw the lady I had spoken to earlier, pushing her way through the crowds in our direction. She put her hand on my arm.

'Alas I haven't been able to locate our Allesandra,' she said pouting almost sulkily. 'But then I have no idea what she really looks like.'

I gazed round the room. 'She must have gone home' I said. 'I told you she hates this kind of occasion. Doesn't she darling?'

'What's that?' my husband said.

'This lady was dying to meet Allesandra,' I said.

'Ah Allesandra,' he repeated nodding.

'I was explaining that she hates this sort of thing.'

My husband nodded. 'Loathes it,' he said.

I smiled at the lady. 'But let me present my husband to you instead. That will make up for your disappointment.'

She hardly evinced a smile. She extended her hand briefly and shook his. As she turned away she said, 'You will remember about my invitation now won't you?'

'I'll do my best,' I said.

VIII

In the taxi home, Franco put his arm about me. 'Hello wife,' he said.

'Hello husband.'

'Thank God that's over,' he said. He smelled faintly of whisky and tobacco. 'Did you enjoy it?'

'Sort of,' I said. 'Although I don't really like parties.'

'Nor me.'

'All those strangers.' I leaned my head on his shoulder. 'This is the part I like best.'

'Who was that rather superior looking lady with the jewels you introduced me to?'

'Oh just somebody I got talking to.'

'She could hardly wait to get away.'

'She found me rather unexciting too.'

'Imperceptive of her.'

'That's what I thought. She thought we were a real couple of fuddy-duddies.'

'Nothing wrong fuddy-duddies.'

'No.'

'Though let it be said that we're sort of post-modernist fuddy-duddies.'

I turned to him. I felt the buttons of his shirt on the side of my face. 'Wish I'd thought of saying that.'

He pressed his lips to my hair. 'So what did you talk about all evening?'

'You mainly.'

'Ah yes. The story. Did she enjoy it?'

'Up to a point. But she got bored with me and went off looking for Allesandra. She was desperate to meet her.'

'They all are.'

He leaned forward and rapped on the window. 'Third on the left,' he said to the taxi driver. 'Just past that lamppost.' He removed his arm from about my shoulder. The taxi slowed.

'I quite enjoyed frustrating her actually. It's like being in a play.'

'D'you know, I think there's something of the sadist in you sometimes.'

'Post-modernist fuddy-duddy sadist.'

'Something like that.'

He closed the taxi door with a clunk.

'I rather like it actually,' he said and he kissed the top of my head softly.

IX

In the bedroom, as if to a preordained pattern, he set out our table and chair and placed a number of books on it. He sat down and ran his hands sensuously across it. Then he slowly lowered his head and pressed his lips softly to its polished surface. 'I love you, table,' he said. He got up and opened a large wardrobe. He ran his hand across the line of dresses. 'What would you like for tonight?' he said.

I wasn't really listening. I looked across the city roofs. A sliver of moon that I could obliterate with the tip of my little finger hung above a bank of dark blue clouds. 'I love this time of night,' I said.

I went to him. He began to remove his jacket. He nodded at the wardrobe. 'Well?'

I laid my head against his chest and put my arms tightly about him. 'Oh I don't know,' I said. 'I think I'd just like you to hold me.'

'Hold you?' he said.

'Yes. Just hold me,' I said.

The Camel

When she read in the local paper of her brother's shameful fall from grace, Simonetta could scarce believe her eyes. *Our Roberto!* she thought. *No, there must be a mistake. It can't be possible.* Yet there it was in black and white on the third page. The photograph, although blurred, was undoubtedly him: the anxious, fixed half-smile pinned to the round face; the thinning hair. There were pictures too of the wrecked hotel room: the curtains torn down, windows broken, the television set lying wrecked on the pavement four storeys below, the charred remains of the bed and furniture. Beneath it was a photo' of the waiter, with his bruised sorrowful face and bandaged head; and alongside, his account of the events, as told to *our reporter:*

It was a Thursday evening just after eleven. I was in the kitchen having a smoke waiting for the night-relief-porter to take over. The bell rang. A gentleman in room 304, I now know to be Signor Melotti, asked for ham rolls and a glass of warm milk to be taken up to his room. When I knocked on the door and explained that I had taken the liberty of substituting tuna, as we were out of ham, he seemed to go insane with rage. He screamed with anger and began to beat me about the head and body until I passed out. I have had two weeks in hospital. I can't understand it.

He seemed a decent enough man; a quiet sort. I'd never seen the man before in my life. I have been a waiter here for thirty years. Nothing like this has ever happened to me before. I don't know when I will be returning to work. I can't sleep at night. The whole incident has severely shaken my faith in humanity.

It didn't stop with the assault on the waiter and the damage to the room: there were further charges pending, for facial injuries sustained by one of the four arresting policemen and for damage to the squad car.

Even after three readings Simonetta still found it difficult to believe the story. It was so completely out of character. Roberto was the least violent and most undemonstrative man she had ever met. Even under extreme provocation she had never known him resort to violence. Like the good Catholic he was, he was always ready with the turned cheek and the soft answer; even under the most extreme provocation. On a number of occasions indeed, both Simonetta and her mother had earnestly wished that he had stuck up for himself more readily. There had been that incident at the School, when the overbearing and universally disliked Signor Facetti, had mocked and pushed him before the rest of the school staff and a group of children, after Roberto had been made Head of the Maths Department over Signor Facetti's head. His mother had been outraged when she heard of it. But Roberto had explained it all away in his habitually mild manner: 'Suppose I had hit him back. Or shouted. What good would that have done? After all he was a senior candidate. Who's to say I wouldn't have felt the same had I been in his shoes. He's not such a bad fellow you know. And anyway I'm not perfect by any means. You have to remember there are always two sides to every question. You have to be philosophical about these things.'

'Madonna!' his exasperated mother had cried, throwing her hands in the air, 'We have a Socrates in the family. A Socrates!'

'Better a Socrates than a Mussolini,' Roberto had replied softly.

'Ah if only your poor father were alive, God rest his soul,' muttered his mother, crossing herself and squeezing his round, red cheeks between finger and thumb with such immoderate affection, that his lips had pouted like those of a bewildered cod fish. 'Roberto you are too good for this world. Too good! Listen to your mamma now. Don't be a saint all the time. You hear me? Sometimes a little of the devil is not so bad you know.'

And she would have marched down and settled matters there and then with the loathsome Signor Facetti, had not Simonetta forcibly restrained her. It was following this incident that his mother persuaded him to enrol in assertiveness classes at the local night school; but after a couple of visits he had cancelled his subscription saying the atmosphere did not suit him and joined a wild flower and rambling club instead.

His mother, in whose vocabulary the word diffidence had no place, and who, when provoked, had the tongue of a fish wife, shrugged her ample shoulders despairingly. 'He was born without a temper,' she muttered resignedly, thereby conveniently exonerating herself from all responsibility. Simonetta, who had studied psychology, was not so sure; she suspected that Roberto's amiable passivity was a reaction to his mother's famously touchy character.

Signora Melotti saw slights everywhere; even where they did not exist. Her famed touchiness sprang in part, from the bitter rivalry that had always existed between herself and her older sister, Antoinetta. Such competitiveness is common enough between siblings but generally speaking the protagonists tend to mellow with the years. With Roberto's mother, Barbara, there was no mellowing. On the contrary, her skin, if anything, appeared to grow thinner as she grew older; her always strident competitiveness hardening into a coruscating and habitual resentment. Her touchiness became as much part of her nature as the colour of her hair.

It had begun with the death of her father on the eve of Barbara's twentieth birthday. She had been his favourite daughter. Following his exit from the world, hers seemed to darken. She was constrained to stand by, fuming and tight-lipped, as her elder sister, as to the manner born, assumed her deceased father's position as head of the family. All the decisions were hers, while poor Barbara, by contrast, felt powerless, undervalued and neglected. It was at this time that an inner cry that was always and for ever: *Me! Me! What about me?* began to take possession of her. Resentment gnawed remorselessly at her soul. She felt like a bit-part actress whose role was, and would ever be, to stand unacknowledged in the wings, while her sister, effortlessly gathered to herself the plaudits of the adoring audience.

Of course there had been the odd occasion, when she had enjoyed her longed-for moment in the limelight. In her middle thirties, for example, and resigned to a life of spinsterhood, she had been somewhat taken aback when, one frosty January morning, as she was bending over a pile of newspapers in the newsagents where she was employed as a manager, her employer, Signor Melotti had enthusiastically flung himself upon her. As they threshed about on the newspaper-strewn floor, he passionately implored her to marry him. Signor Melotti, fifteen years her senior, and the owner of two newsagents in the town as well as a profitable kiosk near the station, was perhaps not the man of her dreams - but he was flesh and blood. He was *there*. And he had asked her. There was no one else in the offing. Perhaps it was surprise at the timing and enthusiasm of the offer, as much as anything else, which induced her to accept him. For a few brief weeks, flaunting her diamond engagement ring, she revelled in the attention she received. But her time in the sun, sadly, was all too brief. It was, of course, her perennial nemesis, Antoinetta, who brought it all to a premature close by casually letting slip at Barbara's engagement party that she too was to marry. To Barbara's chagrin, Antoinetta's future husband - a handsome, wealthy and well-connected patents' lawyer from Florence, scored significantly higher on the desirability scale than the rather humdrum and elderly Signor Melotti. Barbara felt herself being shuffled out of the light and into the darkness once more. It was a place with which she was growing all too familiar. 'If the truth be known,' she would confide to her children and to anyone else who would listen, 'she did it on purpose; deliberately to spite me. Why did she have to announce it at my engagement party? Why? I'll tell you why. She couldn't bear for me to be the centre of attention for once in my life, that's why.'

Then, when she produced a male child a year later, she had once more, to her obvious delight, basked in the enthusiastic familial attention that she craved. But once more glory was snatched from her when her sister's husband chose the eve of Roberto's birth on which to succumb to a rare and exotic blood complaint. Although even Barbara could not bring herself to believe that he had expressly elected to pass away on that particular day merely out of spite, she still felt that the angel of fate had once more used her ill: and it was an angel who, she firmly believed, was in some mysterious fashion, deeply in cahoots with her sister. 'And where was *she* while I was going through the agony of childbirth?' she would ask Roberto and Simonetta who had heard the sad tale a thousand times before. 'I'll tell you where. In that villa of hers playing the brave widow for all she was worth; dressed head to toe in those elegant black weeds by Versace. Oh Bravo! Bravo!' And she clapped her hands sardonically. 'And where was I while all this wonderful performance was going on? Lying alone in the state hospital that's where. And who came to see me? Oh your father deigned to come once! But my mother? My mother came! Oh yes. But how long did she stay?' - Signora Melotti's discourse at the peak of embitterment frequently took a rhetorical turn that was positively Ciceronian – 'How long? Ten minutes that's how long. And what did she talk about? Not about me. Oh no. Not to ask about my new beautiful baby boy. My Roberto! Oh no. None of that. All she spoke about was of her beautiful Antoinetta. Of her terrible loss! How bravely she was facing up to bereavement; how tragically pale and beautiful she looked. She couldn't wait to get out of that miserable hospital and to shoot back to the real show.' She snorted derisively. 'The miracle of childbirth! Well let me tell you something: this miracle came a poor second to Antoinetta and her rich husband in his oak coffin with the brass handles. Not that I'm bitter of course. It's just that sometimes I think life is just so unfair.'

Her misfortune, as she saw it, did not stop there.

When, some months later Antoinetta, herself produced a fatherless boy-child of her own, the field of competition shifted to occupy new ground: La Guerra dei due figli; the War of the Two Sons. Who was taller? Better looking? The more intelligent? Had the more beautiful girl friend? The better job? The stronger character? Produced better exam results? Had the greater charm?

The grounds for conflict and resentment were endless.

And somehow Antoinetta, by insouciantly appearing not to compete at all, always emerged the victor. Thus the resentment deepened until Signora Melotti's bitterness, which had up till then focused exclusively on her elder sister, began to spread indiscriminately, taking in Anoinetta's son, the son's wife, the grandchildren - until by increments, the entire world bore the brunt of her resentment. For her children it became an increasingly onerous burden. Simonetta could see how this burgeoning bitterness was gnawing at her mother's soul, until it showed signs of consuming her entirely; it became a form of madness. As for Roberto, though they never spoken of it, Simonetta was convinced that his refusal to take offence; his extreme philosophical detachment, had its origin in his fear of becoming a carbon copy of his mother. This is not to say that there wasn't a deep affection between mother and son, for there was; they doted on one another. Which was why, Simonetta instinctively understood that not one breath of Roberto's crime must reach her mother's ears. It would break her heart. She was convinced of it. It must be kept from her at all costs. A decisive and intelligent woman, she knew immediately what to do. She cancelled the newspapers until further notice and spent the remainder of the morning on the telephone, swearing everyone that she knew to absolute secrecy. Most difficult of all, of course, was the conversation with Aunt Antoinetta. Before dialling her number, Simonetta worked out carefully what her strategy should be. In the end she decided that the best policy was probably to be utterly blunt. In an attempt, however, to more effectively padlock her aunt's tongue, she did add a small lie: informing her that her mother had been feeling unwell for some time and was in no fit state to hear bad news of any kind.

Aunt Antoinetta was all understanding: 'Poor Barbara! Oh how dreadful,' she murmured in her soft disarming fashion. 'No of course. Not a word. I understand. My poor sister. Roberto of course has always been a problem for her, we all know that. But this. So out of character. It makes me realise how fortunate I have been with my own dear boy.' Then she changed tack. 'Tell me Simonetta dear, how did poor Roberto get on with his application for the inspectorate by the way? Ah no this scandal wouldn't have helped. Of course, not a word. You can rely on me absolutely.'

Simonetta was carefully cutting the offending article from the paper with a pair of dress-making scissors, when she heard her mother enter the room. She attempted to screw the paper into a ball but in doing so only succeeded in drawing her mother's attention to it.

'Something interesting in the paper?' her mother asked.

'No. Not really.'

Simonetta wasn't good at lying. She improvised recklessly. 'Just thought I'd cut this recipe out. Looked quite interesting.' She smiled, what she hoped was a guileless and enthusiastic smile. And her mother, who could spot discomfiture at fifty paces, homed in unerringly on the untruth.

'If it's so interesting why are you throwing it away?'

It was a good question.

'Ah well I *thought* it was interesting,' Simonetta said feeling the water deepening about her. 'You know, when I first read it. And well then, you know, I decided it wasn't...so interesting, that is.'

'Well it might interest me.'

Simonetta looked hard at her mother's large red hand, palm-up, that reached for the paper.

'Ah well you see...' she began, and then having no idea what there was that her mother should see, she shrugged her shoulders and lapsed into silence. Fortunately, at that moment, the ringing of the phone saved her. Simonetta heaved a sigh of relief and was about to leave the room to dump the offending article, when the word 'Antoinetta' on her mother's lips, stopped her short. She turned slowly thinking to herself: *She wouldn't would she? Not even Antoinetta. Not after what she had said.*

Her mother cupped the mouthpiece. 'It's Antoinetta,' she mouthed. Simonetta sat down on the sofa.

'Antoinetta! To what do we owe this honour?'

'It's just that I was concerned my dear,' Antoinetta said.

'Concerned?'

'Well about you really, dear. When I heard you were poorly.'

'Poorly? Me? First I've heard of it. What's supposed to be wrong with me?'

'Oh, she didn't specify.'

'She?'

'Yes Simonetta rang me and…'

'Simonetta?' Signora Melotti turned towards her daughter, who sat hunched on the sofa, her head in her hands.

Antoinetta clicked her tongue. 'Oh dear perhaps I shouldn't have said. But I just couldn't bear it darling. The last thing you want when there's trouble in the family is to feel under the weather.'

'Trouble in the family?

'Oh dear, perhaps I shouldn't have said. It's just that...'

'Trouble? What trouble?'

'Darling I've said enough already I…'

'WHAT TROUBLE?'

There was a pause. Antoinetta sighed. 'Simonetta told me not to say anything about Roberto so really I'd better go before I say too much.'

'Roberto! What about him?'

Simonetta gave a cry. She couldn't bear it. She rose and went into the kitchen where she stood leaning on the sink, staring at her reflection in the little mirror. She could still hear the conversation. It was largely one-sided; Simonetta's mother, being for the most part, silent.

When it was over Signora Melotti slowly replaced the phone. She stood staring down at it for some time. Then she walked across the room and stood, grey-faced in the doorway, staring at Simonetta. Simonetta couldn't bring herself to look at her.

'Mamma I'm so sorry,' she said, her hands kneading.

Her mother held out her hand. 'Give it to me.'

Simonetta shook her head. 'Oh mamma you don't want to…'

'Give!'

Reluctantly Simonetta handed the article to her mother. Signora Melotti sat down on the faded green kitchen chair and smoothed the crumpled paper on her knees. She read it slowly a number of times. Now and then she shook her head. A gulping sob came from her. She looked up helplessly at her daughter and finally murmured, 'My poor Roberto. They are wrong. All of them. He would never do that. Something must have happened.' She let the paper slip from her hand. During the long silence that followed, Simonetta's mother stared down but she no longer saw anything. Then she said softly, 'This is how they will think of him from now. To the end of his life. This will be Roberto's story. All the good in him will be forgotten. When they speak of him, this is what they will remember. All of them.'

And Simonetta knew that by 'all' - her mother meant Aunt Antoinetta. She gave a little animal cry of sympathy and crossed to her. She put her young arms about her. She whispered in her mother's ear. 'He was so good. He never thought badly of anyone. To do that! I don't understand.'

Signora Melotti shook her head in agreement but she wasn't really listening. She was thinking of *Before* and *After;* of how, if she been at his side when he had most needed her, she might have prevented the former from toppling over into the latter; of how her strong mother's arms could have drawn him back from that dark *After* that lay in wait for him in that lonely Rome hotel room.

She could have asked him. Why? Darling Roberto there must have been a reason. Some mistake. Tell your mother. Tell me.

*

Roberto is sitting on the edge of the bed. It is six o' clock in the evening. He removes his jacket and hurls it to the floor with a cry of vexation. He has just returned from the Central Offices of Education. He knows the interview has not gone well; he understands why they turned him down. He knows, in addition, that he has made something of a fool of himself. Not for the first time. He remembers it all; every word that passed between himself and the people who studied him so gravely, seated behind the long table in the high-panelled room. He goes over it in his mind for the twentieth time. He cannot help himself. It is an age-old habit. And as he remembers, the old familiar pain in his stomach begins to gnaw at him. Was it really necessary for them to do that: to insult him like that? For that is what they did. The Director of Education had removed his spectacles and looking at him, as though he were some sort of inadequate schoolboy, had said: 'Apart from the question of ability, Signor Melotti, we have to ask ourselves, if you really have the drive, the sort of energy that a job in the Inspectorate requires.'

And Roberto had shuffled when he should have been still; had been evasive and hesitant when he should have been forthright and calmly articulate. It had been a sorry performance. He knew it. None better. He gave an audible cry of regret to the empty room, recalling how, as he had closed the door, he had overheard the grey-haired man with the moustache whisper quite audibly to the Director: 'Disappointing. Not really the sort of material we're looking for.'

'Material?' he said aloud to the empty hotel room. 'I am not material. I am a human being.'

He didn't need their pity. Wasn't it enough for them to turn him down without adding patronising insults? He took a couple of indigestion tablets from his pocket and swallowed them. He lay on the bed. The pain in his lower stomach, thank God, began to ease. He saw himself walking: striding across to the grey-haired man. Saw himself leaning on the desk, quivering with pent-up rage saying, 'And who are you to say I am disappointing? How dare you? I have extensive experience. I have written papers for respected journals. I have taught for ten years. I have been an advisor for three. When did you last stand in front of a class of unruly children? No, don't answer. I'll tell you. Never! And you! You dare to sit there and judge me!'

The sound of his own shouting surprises him. His face is swollen and red with anger and his heart thumps rapidly. He lays his head down slowly on the pillow. Once more the interview plays in his head. This time though he changes his answers. He is bold, knowledgeable and forthright. He falls into a troubled sleep. When he awakes it is almost eleven o'clock and the room is dark. At first he cannot remember where he is. Then the memory of the failed interview seeps back into his consciousness. Tomorrow he must catch the train, back to his small town and explain his failure to everybody. He knows what he will say:

As they explained the parameters of the job responsibility to me I realised it just wasn't for me. I told them so too. No good beating about the bush. I think they would have offered it to me but I told them it wasn't for me. You should have seen their faces.

The old familiar pain in his lower stomach is back. It travels up over his shoulder and into his gums. Now his teeth ache agonisingly. He knows he should eat but he isn't really hungry. It is too late. The doctor has told him several times not to eat after nine o'clock. He folds both hands behind his head and stares at the ceiling. His mind begins to pick its way, like a haggard bird through the myriad slights he has suffered throughout his life: a tall thin-legged, ragged-feathered, discontented, screeching bird. It picks at the scattered jibes and insults that have blighted his life; plucks them up in her long beak and then flings them savagely away. And each peck is a pain to him.

He has always done this.

Signor Facetti who had mocked him before the whole staff. And he had said nothing. Peck! The headmaster who had questioned his wisdom as an advisor and later phoned his superior to complain. Peck! The ugly, loose-mouthed youths on the train to Bari who had mocked his attempts to talk to the pretty young woman who sat opposite him. They had patted the top of his head patronisingly; called him 'baldy' and one of them - perhaps no more than fourteen - had struck him so hard in the stomach that he had fallen groaning in a crumpled heap on the floor. Peck!

Back and back through the entire history of his life the dark bird stalks. Pecking. Always pecking.

Now he is nine. He is in love with a pretty fair-haired girl in his class: Elisabetta. Even now he can conjure her image in his mind; see her even now as clear as a photograph in black and white. He knows that even now he is, in a way, still in love with her. Perhaps he always will be. His love for her is like an ache beneath his heart and he carries it with him as he walks home after school to where his mother is waiting. He tells his friend who shares his desk at school, of his love. His friend tells him he should write his Elisabetta a letter: a letter in which he explains that he loves her. He understands that this is what he has to do. He writes it out during the next lesson in his best handwriting, keeping all the lines as straight as he can. When he has finished, he folds the letter and writes her name on the front: Elisabetta. As his pen traces her lovely name he groans with his love for her. He watches as the letter is transported from hand to hand across the classroom. Now she has it. Her hand is clasping the letter he has written. He watches her as she unfolds it. He follows her lovely, dark eyes as they scan *his* letter. He knows what she is reading. She has finished. She whispers something to the girl who sits at her side. Then she glances across to where he is sitting. She smiles at him. And he, heady with adoration, smiles back. Later in the playground, he stands alone and watches as she walks towards him. He can see his letter in her hand. His letter. She stops opposite him. She is very close. He looks into her eyes and smiles. She does not smile. She holds his letter up before his face and tears it into tiny strips. Then she throws them in his face. She has put her finger and thumb elegantly to her nose. She wrinkles it as though he smells, then walks away laughing.

Peck, peck, peck!

He gives a cry of anguish and rolls over convulsively onto his side. The pain in his stomach and teeth rages now. He has a name for this pain. He calls it Elisabetta.

So severe is the pain that he thinks he may die. No matter what the doctor says he must have something to eat. He rolls from side to side groaning on the bed, clutching his stomach. He picks up the phone at the bedside and rings the main desk. Apologising for the lateness of the hour, he asks the waiter for a ham sandwich and a glass of warm milk. He rises from his bed. He bends double. He splashes cool water upon his face. When he hears the knock on the door, he crosses the floor and opens it. The waiter stands there with a tray. The waiter is a small, middle-aged man. Beneath his eyes are dark shadows. He speaks through his nose as if suffering the remains of a cold. His black jacket with the shiny lapels is spotted with stains.

'Signor Melotti,' he says apologetically. 'Here's the milk you ordered. I hope you don't mind. We seem to be out of ham, so I've made the sandwiches with tuna instead...'

Fault

Whit the loudspeaker announced that the express would be delayed for twenty minutes, Marion stepped back from the edge of the platform. She sat on a bench and watched the monitor. Somewhere between her heart and her solar plexus she felt the sudden ache for a cigarette. Seven years ago she had given up smoking: for her health's sake. But now what difference did it make? She took the escalator up to the main platform and bought a packet of twenty and was walking away before she realised she had no matches. Only smokers carry matches.

The girl at the kiosk glanced up at her curiously. 'Are you feeling alright?' she said as she handed her her change.

Was there something about her? Marion wondered. Did it show? Almost automatically she replied, 'Fine' to the question. It was what she always said. But she wasn't fine. She hadn't been fine for eleven years. She didn't know what 'fine' meant anymore. She walked across the concourse. She looked back to see if the assistant was looking at her. But already she was busy with another customer. *She'll read about it in the morning,* she thought. Perhaps there'll be a photograph. And she'll tell somebody.

'That's the woman who bought cigarettes off me yesterday. She forgot her matches. You know, I thought there was something funny about her. You can tell, don't you think. I think you can anyway.'

And then she would begin talking about something else. *As for me*, Marion thought, *I shall be beyond memory*.

It was what she most wished for.

She stepped on to the escalator and descended once more, watching the faces that rose towards her: one stranger after another: upright and stiff gazing straight before them. On the platform she discovered that the express was still delayed. The green message on the monitor informed her that a stopping train would be along before it.

I am waiting for the train, she thought. My train. The train that won't stop for me.

She searched for the cigarettes in her coat pocket and her fingers closed over the boy's glove. It was always there. She took it out now and laid it on her lap teasing the fingers out gently. A small green glove with a striped lilac and cream horizontal pattern. She had knitted them for him herself for the boy's fourth birthday. It was still curled to the shape of the small left hand that had gripped hers as he had skipped beside her on that freezing January morning.

'I thought I'd take him for a little walk in the park,' she had told Mr Evershed, the boy's father. He had one foot on the library ladder. The other hung free in the air, pointing like a ballet dancer's, as he stretched across to replace a book in the shelves.

'Excellent notion,' he had said smiling down at her over his half moon spectacles.

She had turned to go but he had called to her. He came down the steps and patted the boy on the head. It was a clumsy gesture. The boy's cap fell to the floor and his father laughed and bent to pick it up for him. He was a good man; a kind man - but not really completely at ease with children; even his own.

'Freezing outside. You wrap up warm.' He had crouched down and pulled Alan's gabardine tighter and tried to button it about his throat. The buttons defied him. In the end she did it for him.

'You be a good boy for Marion now won't you?'

The boy raised his gloved hand. 'Going to see Colin,' he said.

'Colin?'

'It's one of the ducks. He gives them all names,' she said.

Mr Evershed nodded. 'God gave names to all the animals,' he said.

'There were ducklings last spring. Just been born. And he pointed at one and asked me, "What's he called?"'

'As if they were born with a name.'

'Yes. I'd have said, "What are we going to call him". I just thought it was funny.'

The boy spun round almost losing his balance. He stopped, his arms spread. 'Ducks and books. Ducks and books.' He lifted a magazine and picked up a book that was underneath. He held it in both hands sniffing at the spine. 'Lots of books. Lots of books. Millions and millions and millions.'

Mr Evershed had smiled up at her. 'Yes there are a lot of books aren't there?' He said to his son, 'Do you think you'll read them one day?'

'No,' the boy said. 'Definitely not. Definitely, definitely not.' And he shook his head frowning. He took Marion's hand. He said, 'My favourite duck is called. He's called. He's called…'

'What's he called?'

The boy frowned again, his gloved finger to his lip. 'Alan,' he said. 'He's called Alan.'

'Like you,' his father said.

'Yes. And his father is called Doctor Quack.'

The boy made quacking noises and ran to the window and looked out. They had both smiled but when she glanced up at him she saw he was avoiding her gaze. Still not looking at her, he said with his slight stutter. 'I wanted to say…' but then he stopped. He picked up the leather bound book the boy had found. 'Been looking for this everywhere,' he said. He leafed through the pages. He said, 'I wanted to say: how good you are with the boy.'

And she had shrugged and started to say something but he had interrupted her.

'No. It's true. He's so much happier. I was worried you see. After my wife… you know. Well I just wanted to say how genuinely grateful I am.'

'Oh I enjoy it,' she said.

'Yes I can see that. And what I wanted to say… It must be dull for you here sometimes. I understand that. But I really don't want you to go. You know if you get another offer I…'

He left the sentence unfinished. Then he said, 'It worries me sometimes. He needs the stability. You know if it's the money. You know I've been thinking…'

'No, no,' she said, 'I love it here. Really. It's no trouble. And he's a good boy really. An interesting boy. He just needed to be…' she was about to say 'loved' but then she thought it might sound like criticism. 'He needs attention.' she said.

'Yes of course. But you do more than that. Much more.'

His eyes were on her now. He was in his mid forties: twenty years older than her. She wondered if he was falling in love with her and how she would feel about it if he were. They stood there looking at one another. The sunlight fell in patterns on the oak boarding and the red carpet. The boy had his arms outstretched and was running between the tables being an aeroplane now. He made engine noises with his mouth. She wondered why she had shied from the true word. Now she said it.

'Love,' she said softly.

'I'm sorry?'

'Is what he needs. Love.'

'Ah yes. Yes of course.' He took off his glasses and polished them with his handkerchief. 'I do love him you know. Sometimes perhaps I don't show it. Perhaps I don't know how to. But I do love him. More than my life actually.' It was so typical of him to add the 'actually'. He nodded his head briskly. 'Yes I do,' he said emphatically as if she might doubt him.

The boy came back to them. 'Swing Park,' he said. It was his name for it. His left glove had fallen. She crouched before him and tugged it on over his small hand. She looked up at his father. 'We'd better be off,' she said.

'Yes of course.'

She took the boy's hand in hers. As she was closing the door, Mr Evershed said. 'Perhaps you'd like to have dinner with me tonight?' Before she could answer he said,' Of course I'm sure you have other things to do. Perhaps, you know some other…'

'I'd like to,' she said. 'Thank you.'

And he had nodded and smiled. She closed the door and she and the boy left the house hand in hand.

It was only a short walk to the park along the clean pavement lined with pillared houses, past the German delicatessen and the Museum of Tropical Medicine to the Park. All the way the boy talked of the ducks. For a short time the previous year the pond had frozen. He had laughed as the ducks had floated in to land, only to slide comically across the ice on their tails, their leathery, webbed feet grappling with the air. What was funny was that their eyes, their expressions didn't change. The boy had laughed with his whole body. He kept asking her now as he skipped beside her, 'Will the ducks do slide today, Marion?' She said she thought they very well might and made up a rather silly song about sliding ducks which he joined in with, singing at the top of his voice, his head thrown back, frowning with the effort to hit the high notes. 'Again. Song again,' he implored. And so they sang it again several times until they reached the main road before the park. She gripped his hand tightly as they stood at the zebra crossing waiting for their crossing light to turn to green. She went through the drill with him.

'No singing now,' she instructed and held his hand tighter still and they repeated together the little rhyme they always chanted when crossing the road. But when he saw the duck, stranded halfway across the road on the small bollarded island, he stopped and pointed. It was a miracle that it had managed to reach it without mishap. The boy called to it, telling it to wait but the duck flapped its wings furiously and began to half fly, half waddle directly into the roaring traffic. Every day and during long sleepless nights in the years that followed, she saw herself grasping the boy by the shoulders; pulling him back. It tormented her. She saw herself doing it: the duck flying free and both of them laughing; she with her arm about him and he leaning hard against her body, shaking with laughter. But she hadn't done it. She hadn't. His impetuosity had been too quick for her. Though she clung hard to his hand and called his name, he had slipped from her, leaving the little empty glove in her hand. He had plunged screaming into the murderous flow of cars, oblivious of everything but the shattered body of the duck, spinning and bouncing amongst the wheels. And when she had herself tried to catch at him it was all too late.

*

In the hospital where she lay with a broken femur and two fractures to her skull, the nurses and the doctor kept from her the fact of the boy's death. They had had to prise the small woollen glove from her clenched hand. Her memory of the incident was vague but she remembered the duck, frantic on his island and the sound of the speeding car as it struck the boy, hurling him over the windscreen. And so they lied to her, evading her questions. 'The boy is as well as can be expected,' they told her. And when the surgeon was out of earshot, he had told the nurse and the student doctors, 'Time enough to tell her the truth when she's out of danger.'

It was the boy's father who told her. She saw him standing in the doorway of the ward in a black overcoat, a red scarf about his neck while the other visitors pushed past him. Then he had walked slowly down the ward and stood looking down at her as she lay propped up on her pillows. His eyes were red and his whole face was lined and grey. It was difficult for her to turn her head. She felt the tears pouring from her eyes and down her face. 'I'm sorry,' she sobbed over and over. He continued to stare down at her not saying anything. She wiped the tears from her. 'How is he? Have you seen him? Is he going to be alright?'

But he wouldn't speak. He began to breathe heavily and his head shook.

'What is it?' she whispered. 'What?'

His mouth opened and closed but there were no words. Then he said, 'He's dead you know. Dead. My son is dead.'

A groan came from her. 'No, no, no.' She banged her fist hard on the bed.

'Dead. Dead. Dead.' He kept repeating the awful word over and over. She put out her hand to him but then his gentle, sad face seemed to suddenly inflate and change colour - from grey to a suffusing red. His fists beat at her. Beat at her breast and her face. He was screaming now. 'And it was you. You did it. It was you. It was you. Your fault. You did it.' And he fell upon her raining blows down on her. 'I'll never forgive you. Never. Never.' And he punctuated each repetition with a savage blow.

It took four nurses to drag him away from her. As they pulled him through the swing doors at the end of the ward he turned round one last time and pointed at her. 'Never!' he roared.

How she wished she could have died then. She longed for the doctor to sit down beside her bed and take her hand; to shake his head sadly and tell her there was no hope.

She would have thanked him.

But almost against her will she made a full recovery.

She only saw the father once more and that was in the courtroom. She could hardly bring herself to look at him and he for his part kept his face studiously averted. He seemed old and bowed. She spent most of the proceedings with her hands clasped tight to her ears so that she wouldn't have to hear the boy's name.

After, she went to stay with her mother and father and found he had sent all her clothes and belongings there. She couldn't bear to touch them. She piled everything that was to do with that house and that time in the garden and set fire to them. She stayed in their small house with the long garden for over a year, rarely venturing out. Sometimes she would go out into the back garden and sit in the doorway of the greenhouse, staring at nothing. One day she saw her father filling a watering can from the large rusted tank that leaned against the back of the house. She saw him almost fall and clutch at the tank rim. The can fell from his hand and spilled water across his shoes. His cap dropped to the ground. He crumpled. She called out his name and ran to him. She thought it was a heart attack. She called out to him. But when she reached his side she found that he was sobbing like a child. When she asked him, he told her it was for her that he was crying.

Perhaps it was this that encouraged her to emerge into the world once more. She tried working in a children's home but whenever a single child was put in her charge, she saw and anticipated dangers everywhere. She was knotted with fear. One day, one of the supervisors found her in the day room, surrounded by a small group of bewildered children who were gazing up at her as she sat with her head in her hands, weeping uncontrollably. Very kindly it was put to her that it might be better if she did something else. She moved to a large anonymous city and took a job in a car broker's office, performing simple, repetitive secretarial tasks. The doctor thought things were improving. But then the sight of a child, in a street or crossing the road, would fill her once more with the familiar, all embracing sense of dread. There was danger everywhere. One day, seeing a small boy on a bus sitting beside his mother, a sense of the danger he faced, his utter vulnerability, seized her. She stood up suddenly and walked to where he was sitting. She had crouched beside him and clutching his hands in hers, begged him to be careful. She implored the mother, when she took him home, to take a route that avoided crossing any main roads. She lectured her vehemently on what she must do.

Through the long days and nights she re-ran the events of that awful day over and over in her mind. And always in these waking dreams she saw herself pulling the boy back from his fate; saw him turning up towards her, his face smiling. It continued in this fashion for seven years until one morning she awoke from a fitful sleep and heard a voice which was her own saying 'This life I am leading is a living death. A living death.' And then the thought struck her. Why not a real death?

Why not indeed?

And as the thought came in, an overpowering sense of relief took possession of her. She ached for nothingness. To be something that had no memory. As she looked up the times of the trains, she found herself singing to herself.

It was a tuneless nonsensical song about ducks.

*

It wasn't until the train began to pull out of the station that Mr Evershed, glancing up from his paper, noticed the small figure seated alone on the bench, smoking. Although it had been over seven years since he had last seen her, there was no doubt in his mind that it was she. He was so happy to see her. So happy that chance had provided him with this opportunity. He banged at the window and shouted and waved at her. But she didn't look up. Nor would the carriage window open. He ran down the aisle to the door and lowered the window. 'Marion!' he shouted. And when she seemed not to hear, he shouted louder. 'Marion!' He leaned far out of the window frame, waving both his arms. 'Marion it's me.'

And finally when she looked up, she too knew who it was right away. He saw the dawning realisation on her face. The train was past her now gathering speed. He beckoned with both arms. 'Marion I want to tell you something.'

And she began to walk then to run along the platform alongside the moving train. A porter shouted a warning but she took no notice. The throb of the engine was drowning his voice.

'Marion!'

She was running headlong but the train too was accelerating. The porter was running now. He shouted at Mr Evershed to get inside the carriage. But he only leaned out further. The end of the platform drew closer. She was almost there. But then she stumbled.

'Marion,' he screamed. She looked up her arms outstretched. 'I wanted to tell you,' he shouted. 'It wasn't your fault.' He roared it with all his strength above the scream of the wind and the pounding of the diesel. 'It wasn't your fault.'

And he kept shouting, even though he feared she might be out of earshot. 'It wasn't your fault. It wasn't your fault.' He saw her climbing slowly to her feet. He waved. When he saw her hand raised he knew that she had understood. It was only then that he finally closed the window and returned to his seat.

The porter helped Marion to her feet. Her hands and knees were grazed and her stockings laddered. 'Woman your age. Ought to have more sense,' he said. 'Could have killed yourself there.'

'It was someone I knew a long time ago,' she said as she brushed herself down. He was trying to tell me something.'

'Oh yes. Important was it?'

Marion shook her head. 'I don't know,' she said. 'I couldn't hear.'

The porter escorted her back to the bench and then entered a door marked *Enquiries*.

The platform was deserted.

When the express was announced Marion stood up slowly and walked towards the edge of the platform.

Gilded Butterflies

I t was but the slightest of oversights. At the time he had thought nothing of it; in fact he was able to joke about it in the bar afterwards with the rest of the cast. Later when he phoned his young wife, Sarah, from his hotel room, he decided not to mention it; not out of embarrassment but rather because he'd decided to save the story for Sunday lunchtime: Eva, his daughter from his first marriage would be there along with, among others, Richard Sachs, his agent, and the Arts Editor of the Sunday Telegraph who was planning to do an interview with him. Too good a story to waste on just one person, he thought. So he told Sarah the show had gone pretty well. 'Rather boring if anything. Thank God there's only a week left of the run.'

'And then we're off to Lucca the week after next. Oh Hugo I'm so looking forward to it! Aren't you? I love Italy and we both need a break.'

'Yes. Oh yes, enormously,' he said with simulated enthusiasm. He tended to see holidays merely as lost job opportunities. Visualising the coming Sunday's lunch he saw himself at his dinner table, a glass of Chardonnay in his hand, surrounded by the rapt and admiring faces of his listeners as he picked his way dexterously towards the punch line of this latest anecdote.

'Will you be coming straight home after the Saturday show?' Sarah asked.

'No, Sweetie. I've decided to stay over Saturday night. I'll be down Sunday morning. In plenty of time for lunch, don't worry.'

'Oh yes of course.'

She tried to disguise her disappointment; as she did all her disappointments. She loved waiting up for him on Saturday night: just the two of them sharing a small supper and a glass of red wine in their new kitchen, late at night before they went to bed; gossiping of the London Theatre life and the friends they shared. And Hugo would tell her with the utmost sincerity how he sometimes longed for the simple life; he'd nuzzle her ear, call her his Cordelia and whisper how they would: *tell old tales, and laugh at gilded butterflies, and hear poor rogues talk of court news; and we'll talk with them too - Who loses, and who wins, who's in, who's out; and take upon us the mystery of things As if we were God's spies.*

And she, on the other hand, would think that she wouldn't half-mind being a gilded butterfly at the Court for a bit; or indeed any theatre; even the Provinces. But she never said anything to Hugo, as she knew any sign of disappointment on her part distressed him. She loved being at home in Brighton with little Sean of course - but after five days with just a baby, she often craved adult company. She sometimes had the feeling that she was living her life by proxy.

It crossed her mind, that after the weekend, she could drive back with Hugo and stay over at his hotel; she might even be able to fit in a gossipy lunch at the Ivy with Claudia who was having such a success with her new TV series.

'Hugo, we could drive back together Monday afternoon,' she suggested, her expectancy of a refusal lending an upward inflection to the statement. Just in time, she stopped herself from adding - *if you like*? In order to deflect the most obvious grounds for his refusal she added, 'Delia said she wouldn't mind looking after Sean for one night.'

'Mmh,' Hugo murmured. He was inspecting his reflection in the hotel mirror: wondering should he wear the grey suit with the tie or something more casual for his coming TV interview; possibly the open-necked Italian shirt and the taupe sports jacket. He might even wear jeans. Why not? After all I'm only fifty, he thought to himself. Well fifty two. But the waist's still only 34. It'll show that I'm still...He wasn't quite sure what it showed but he was certain it showed something.

'So what d'you think?' Sarah asked.

'Sorry?'

'Monday? Got some shopping to do anyhow.' She managed to make it sound as though the shopping was her primary objective.

'Ah yes,' he said. 'When were you thinking?'

'Monday darling.' And then with an unconvincing attempt at mild irritability. 'I just said.'

'Oh yes, Monday. I'm sorry, Sweetie, I'm tired.'

'As I said, we could drive up to town together Monday morning. I could stay over if you like. I mean, you know, if you want me to? It's up to you entirely.'

'Monday? Well….'

It occurred to him that the story of the missing pistols would make a suitable closing anecdote for his TV interview. It was genuinely funny and at the same time suitably self-deprecating. He began to rehearse a few phrases in his head.

You see, he would say with a shrug, *even the best of us can make mistakes.* On reflection better to leave out the *even the best of us* part: smacked of arrogance. Something like… *Even those of us who rightly or wrongly are supposed to be enormously experienced can do the most stupid things-.* No - *Stupid things* was weak - *gaffs* would be better…*can be guilty of the most idiotic gaffs.*

Yes much better.

The coming Sunday lunch, he thought, would allow him a useful opportunity to refine the anecdote. He might even chance standing up and walking about, at the point when he discovered he'd left the pistols on the props table: right arm akimbo. Yes that would work well. Sitting on the hotel bed, he rehearsed the movement in little: crooking his right arm and pulling an appropriate expression.

'Hugo?' Sarah said. 'Are you there?'

'Yes. I was just thinking, Sarah love. You know Monday. It's a lovely idea, darling. Naturally I'd love you to be here. Unfortunately there's my TV interview after the show Monday. Wouldn't want you hanging about, darling. You know what a bore it can be.'

In fact Sarah could think of nothing she'd rather do than to hang about. She loved TV studios; or at least the memory of them: the lights, the cameras, the nervous yet exhilarating expectancy; even the smell. It was there she had first met Hugo. She had played a waitress in a rather silly comedy in which Hugo was the grumpily amusing husband. Afterwards she had asked him for advice about her career. He had been suitably attentive: no sense of the great actor in his manner or of the gulf in experience and achievement between them. He had laid a sympathetic hand on her forearm. 'You've got talent,' he had said nodding gravely, his eyes on hers. And she had believed him. 'Don't you worry, it'll come right. I'll have a word with Richard, my agent. I'll see what I can do to help.'

That night she had slept with him in his London apartment. Since their marriage and the arrival of little Sean, she rarely spoke of *her* ambitions.

'Yes *I* hate TV studios,' she said. It was what he wanted to hear.

'Don't be too disappointed. You'll be able to watch it live. Why don't you record it and then we can watch it together later? Not sure exactly when it goes out. Elevenish? Something like that.'

In fact he knew to the nearest second when it began.

He said goodbye, telling Sarah and Sean that he loved them, before resting back on his pillows sipping his chocolate drink and eating a ham sandwich. He thought of taking a bath before turning in for the night but instead he put on his jacket and went down to the hotel bar, where he told the story of the missing pistols to the Spanish barmaid and two Cypriot waiters. The little walk went well. They'd laughed at that. He had pretended not to notice the other guests covertly observing and whispering to one another.

Before going back to his room he autographed two bar menus for the waiters.

*

On the Monday night, Sarah dutifully watched the programme on the TV in her bedroom, with little Sean at her breast. Through the bow windows she could see the looping string of street-lights reflected in the grey shifting mass of the sea. Although she had already heard Hugo's anecdote at lunchtime on the previous Sunday, she still laughed out loud. He had added further grace notes and curlicues, she noted. She admired the practised hesitancy which lent an improvisatory air to the tale: as though it were something that had only that moment popped into his head.

She held up little Sean in both hands. 'Look there's your daddy,' she said. 'Your daddy's a famous actor.'

Hugo was standing up now as he had rehearsed. The camera followed him as he walked about the studio. The audience laughed. He was into his stride.

'Well, there I was,' he said, strolling languidly across the studio floor. 'There I was, the complete aristocrat: dolled up to the nines in my top hat, tail coat, white kid gloves, silver-topped cane; the full Monty. Under my arm, this highly polished mahogany box containing a set of duelling pistols: absolutely vital in the coming scene as I had to despatch a careless intruder. And like a complete idiot I thought, It's going well tonight; the words *before, pride* and *fall* come to mind. It was time to place the box on the table. But Oh oh! No box. Nothing but an empty armful, as Mr. Hancock might have said. Silly me. I'd forgotten to pick the box off the props table. So I walk about the stage muttering to myself, as one does. And then it came to me. I'm an aristocrat, I thought. What's the point of being a toff if you don't have servants to fetch and carry? So I shouted out in my most imperious tones. "Adam! My duelling pistols!" Unfortunately it so happened that the actor playing Adam, Jeremy Horton bless him, absolutely brilliant actor, was in the toilet doing, well, what one *does* in the toilet. Well, as you can imagine, it's a bit of a shock to hear your name shouted over the tannoy when you're occupied with' - he hesitated – 'your er own affairs. I don't know what the toilet to stage Olympic sprint record is, but poor Jeremy shattered it. And that included pulling up his pants and picking up the box. Arrived on stage at a full gallop. His tongue was out to here and he was panting like a race horse. Unfortunately he'd forgotten the first and most basic rule of the acting profession. Always check your flies. Well I took the pistols from him and he stood there awaiting further orders, mouth and flies agape. God forgive me I couldn't resist it. I raised my cane and pointed at the offending buttons and said with all the aristocratic gravity I could muster. 'Do button your fly my dear chap.' Of course we all corpsed.' He looked into camera three. 'Jeffrey dear boy, wherever you are, forgive me.'

Sarah sniffed Sean's backside. 'Who's a smelly boy?' she said. She was out of the room, changing Sean's nappy and didn't see Hugo sitting down once more to a rush of applause and laughter from the studio audience. He waited until the applause peaked and began to die, before saying, 'Well mistakes have their part to play. Where would we all be without our mistakes? It's the only way to learn. The vital thing of course, is to make sure you never make the same mistake again.'

But on the Friday evening performance, much to his bewilderment, that is exactly what he did. That night, after the show he decided not to have a drink with the cast but to go straight back to his hotel. When Sarah phoned him he made no mention of what had happened. Secretly he was rather ashamed of himself. And worried. He felt immensely tired. But when he turned out the light, sleep would not come. The scene played itself out over and over again in his head. He saw himself standing in the wings, reminding himself not to forget the box: but then unaccountably he found himself on stage without it. It was after three o'clock before he finally fell into a fitful slumber. And with sleep the old, familiar nightmare crept in. He stood at the side of the stage, the audience already filling the auditorium. The director, his old friend Tim Evershed, asked him to take the lead in a play he knew nothing about; that he had never even read. The director and all the actors brushed aside his protests. *You're Hugo Melville, remember. You can do anything. Don't worry. You'll be fine.* A terrible fear gripped him but to his surprise, he somehow managed to get through, making the thing up as he went along. At one point he turned and searched the audience. Sarah was there. She smiled and stood up holding little Sean in her hands. The whole play had come to a standstill. Then with a cry she flung the baby looping over the heads of the audience knocking him to the ground. The baby began to wail like a police siren. From beneath her dress Sarah produced the two duelling pistols. She pointed them at him and the barrels exploded with light.

When he awoke the phone was ringing and his pyjamas were drenched with sweat. It was after eleven. He picked up the phone, still fogged with sleep.

'Yes?'

'What about Malvolio?'

'Sorry who's this? '

'Rich'

'Rich?

'Who else?

'Rich it's half past two in the morning.'

'I know. So what d'you say?'

'Sorry?'

'Malvolio. What d'you say?'

'Sorry I'm not with you.'

'We talked about it last Friday?'

'Did we?'

'Did we! Come on Hugo! Look, things have moved on. It's the National. Twelfth Night. Was such a sell out last year they've decided on a revival. Same production. Same set. Pretty much same cast. Except Desmond definitely can't do it. The prostrate thing looks more serious than they thought. Yes I'm sorry too but anyway… Tim Evershed has just rung me. He wants a name. A name who can act. In short he wants you. O.K.? No listen. It's a month. On top of that there's talk of an American film deal with music and singing. Sondheim's involved. I'll firm them up on that. If no film, it's no go our end. Right? They start rehearsing next week. I know it's one show after another but, hey you know, that's show business. What d'you want? Now look, he needs to know *toute suite*. If not before. What am I to tell him? Are you in or out? I'm your agent – I say in. So speak to me.'

'Well…'

'I hate "Well" Hugo. Say something that's got a Yes in it please.

'It's not easy Richard.'

'Hugo I'm being terribly patient here. Explain to me about not easy.'

'I've arranged this holiday.'

'Cancel it. You got cancellation insurance?'

'I think so but…'

'I'll get Joy to do it for you. Who's the company? What's the number?'

'It's not just that Richard.'

'What else is there? It's prestige. It's enormous exposure. It's Hollywood doing its culture bit. Not to speak of money. And you want to sit on a beach somewhere looking at the sea? Come on!'

'It's just that Sarah's been looking forward to it. You know she's stuck in Brighton with the baby and…'

'I know. It's terrible for her. I love that girl. You want *I* should tell her?'

'No it's not that Rich. I just hate to disappoint her.'

'I'm good on disappointment. Try me. I'll call her now. Then we can call Tim straight after.'

'No. Look. Just give me an hour or two. Let me talk to her.'

'An hour max. He's waiting on the other phone now. Other fish in the sea you know. If you go with it, Tim says he'll come to the last show tomorrow to glad hand you.'

'Rich…'

'I'll tell him you'll phone me within the hour.'

'Richard I don't know I…Richard?'

But Richard had rung off.

Hugo put his phone down and lay back on the pillow staring at the ceiling. He hated having to make choices. Like most talented actors he was a man guided more by instinct than by reason. But this, he decided, was a dilemma that could only be resolved by logic. He took a piece of hotel notepaper and a pencil from the bedside drawer and drew a line down the centre. At the top of the first column he wrote in large capitals the words *Hugo/Malvolio* and at the head of the other *Holiday/Sarah*. He chewed the end of the pencil and stared blankly in front of him before giving a deep sigh and adding the words - *and Hugo* to the *Holiday/Sarah* column.

Half an hour later when he totted up the totals he found the pros in the *Hugo/Malvolio* column outnumbered the other by eight to five. No arguing with logic, he thought. For a further ten minutes he walked up and down the hotel bedroom in his dressing gown composing the speech he would make to Sarah. Then he sat down and wrote it out in printed capitals on the note paper.

When he told her he was sorry for calling her in the middle of the night; that it was important, she was immediately awake. He cleared his throat and began to read but she began to talk with such excitable volubility that he could find no chink into which he might inject his speech.

'Oh Hugo darling,' she said excitedly, 'the tickets arrived this morning. Oh and the other good news is, there's a language school next to the apartment and they have a crèche for their students. The lady in charge is half English and she'd be happy to take Sean for a few hours each day. They could also do some baby sitting. Have to pay of course but it's amazingly reasonable. Oh and the other thing is, they say we can have the ground floor apartment, somebody cancelled, so no lugging the pram up piles of stairs. And did I tell you there's a little garden out the back which nobody else can use. And, Oh Hugo, best of all there are orange trees, can you believe. I've never been in a garden with orange trees. Isn't it wonderful, Hugo? Hugo?'

And into the breathless silence she eventually left, Hugo began to read with instinctive naturalness the words on the paper.

'Sarah darling,' he said. 'Look, something's come up.' He paused.

'Yes?'

He could hear the anxiety in her voice.

'Yes. Well, you see Rich has just called me.'

'Rich?'

'Agent Richard. I don't know if I mentioned it to you but

Tim wants me to take over Desmond's Malvolio.'

'No. Actually you didn't mention it.' There was a frost on her tongue.

'Well Richard really wants me to do it. There's a film tied up in it too. You know how persuasive Richard can be and so…'

'You've decided to do it.'

'Well…' he became confused. Her questions were throwing him off his script.

She said, 'You have. I know. You've decided to do it. Oh Hugo.'

In the silence he could hear that she was crying softly. 'I knew it wasn't going to happen. It was just too good. I knew it. I knew it. Why does it always have to happen to me?'

'Sarah darling.'

She said with exaggerated lightness, 'Forget about it. You don't have to worry. I'll phone up and cancel.'

'Sarah,' he said.

'No please don't talk to me anymore.'

'Sarah listen to me.'

'No I don't want to listen to you. Not now. I'll get over it, don't worry.'

'Sarah please!' He was shouting now. He screwed the script up and threw it into the waste-paper-basket. 'I just wanted to tell you that I've turned it down.'

'Turned it down?'

'The Malvolio thing. I decided to say no. I'm about to phone Richard now.'

'But I thought…Why didn't you say?'

'Didn't give me a chance.'

'So we're going. We're really going. The three of us?'

'Of course.'

'And you're sure you don't mind giving up this film and everything?'

'Never crossed my mind. To be honest I'm ever so slightly hurt that you'd think I'd let you down over something like this.'

'Oh darling. I'm so sorry. And I thought…Oh I love you. I do. I really do.'

'And I love you too.'

After a further rather prolonged exchange of endearments, he waited for her to say her final goodbye and ring off, before he replaced his phone. Then he took a deep breath, picked up the phone once more and dialled Richard's number.

*

At the Saturday night performance, the final one of the run, he didn't have to think about the pistols. The prop lady Beattie handed them to him with a smile. 'Just in case you forget,' she said.

'No chance of that.'

He thought how stupid his anxieties had been. He relaxed once more into the part. Perhaps that was the problem. He was too relaxed. In the final scene with David Harsnet, who played his son, - a rather precocious, graceless and unlikeable boy, he suddenly and unaccountably dried. It had never happened to him before. He was at a loss how to deal with the situation. He knew he was supposed to walk down towards David who was sitting at a table and say something. But what that something might be he had not the slightest idea. He backtracked mentally: repeating the previous half page or so of the script they had just covered but a terrible blankness yawned when he reached the same point. His whole body seemed to be burning. He wondered if he was ill. Perhaps he was having a heart attack. The thought crossed his mind that he was on a stage and that out there in the darkness was an audience who had come to see him: hundreds of anonymous strangers who had chosen this particular night, of all the nights of their lives, to travel from their various homes to this particular theatre in cars and buses and trains to watch and listen to him for a few hours. And what he did here was to pretend to be somebody else, who moved and lamented and laughed his way through a life that was entirely fictional. And at the end they applauded. That was the nature of the contract. But of them and their several lives he knew nothing and in all likelihood their paths would never cross again. He was suddenly struck by the absurdity of the whole enterprise. It wasn't in any sense a normal way to behave. He experienced an almost irresistible desire to cross that unseen, purely notional barrier that existed between himself and them; to talk to them directly as himself; to explain to them what was happening: that a break had occurred somewhere in the super subtle complex of nerve endings that linked his tongue to his memory. It was only habit that saved him; some odd atavistic adherence to an unwritten protocol that kept him from breaking through that ageless unseen divide between himself and his audience. Them and him. Him and them - that was the story. And where were those words? Did they reside somewhere in him or were they flying about under the sky like errant birds bound for regions he could never reach. These thoughts took mere milliseconds. And as he was thinking, he turned his back on the audience: moving upstage once more as if bound on some carefully rehearsed journey. He muttered some nonsense in an attempt to demonstrate to the audience that he was involved in some desperate inner struggle with his conscience that justified this silence: a struggle utterly germane to the action of the drama. At the stage wall he turned and saw a mild alarm in the eyes of the boy. It was his first part. During the early days of the run Hugo had practically carried him. Now he saw in those young eyes, the dawning realisation that he, Hugo was lost. He wondered why he had not had a prompt. He walked back towards the boy and rested his hands on the small rustic table. But nothing at all came into his head. Nothing. He stared hard at the wood of the table. The grain of it was unnaturally well defined. The scattered objects seemed enlarged and hard and yet strangely unreal. Look, he thought, there is a hammer. How like a hammer it looks; and that cigar on the edge of the plate. It had the look of an iconic cigar: as though it defined the universal qualities of cigarness. Everything he saw, hammered at his eyes and brain with a revelationary impact. For a second time, he wondered what was keeping the prompt. Didn't he realise what was happening? The vacuum seemed to have lasted for hours but it can all only have been seconds. He tilted his head away from the audience and whispered hoarsely to the boy out of the corner of his mouth. 'Help me. What do I say?' And the boy stared back and shook his head. And he hated him for it. Then someone said in a voice that rang across the auditorium: 'What are you saying?' And he realised it was his own voice. It was a reflex: it was as though his throat and tongue shaped the words which were beyond the recall of his brain. He beat at the table with his fists and said the line again only louder. 'What are you saying?' Whether it was the right line or not he had no idea. But it must have been, because the boy replied. For the remainder of the scene until the end of the play he abandoned himself to another persona: a mere hollow representation of himself: whose mouth opened and closed without any volition on his part or on the part of his consciousness - and somehow said the right things. He walked and spoke the remainder of the scene as though on automatic pilot, trusting that this meta-self knew better than he what he was about.

As the curtain came down he suddenly felt more ill than he had ever felt in his life. Somehow he managed to take his curtain; even smiled. The applause was thunderous. *Didn't they realise what had happened?* he wondered. He forced himself to walk steadily back down the long corridor and up the stairs to his dressing room. He half expected the technicians and other actors that he passed, to mention the disaster that had just happened to him but they all greeted him cheerily. *They're trying to protect my feelings,* he thought to himself. It was idiotic. It was as though he were walking through a building where a bomb had just exploded and yet the occupants were all going about their business as if it were a perfectly normal day. *Why don't they tell me what they're really thinking?* he thought. *That I lost it. Anything's better than this cheery hypocrisy.*

It was crazy.

Once across the threshold of his dressing room he staggered, groaning to the wash room and threw up with such violence that it brought him to his knees. He must have fainted because when he came to, he was lying, his arms about the bowl, his head resting on the toilet seat.

There were footsteps in the dressing room; a tentative knocking at the wash room door.

'Hugo?' He recognised Tim Evershed's voice. He flushed the toilet and raised himself.

'Just a minute.' He ran the cold tap and splashed water on his face.

'You all right?'

'Fine. I'm fine,' he called simulating a brightness he didn't feel. When he emerged, dabbing his face with a make-up-stained towel, Tim was standing with his back to the solid wooden clothes rack that ran down the centre of the dressing room, his arms folded. He inspected Hugo's damp face anxiously. 'Jesus, you look terrible.'

'You wait 'till I get my make-up off.'

He sat at the dressing room table and smeared his face with cream. He could see Tim's handsome young face in reflection, studying him. He was hoping against hope that Tim hadn't been in the audience. He said, 'I'm sorry about the Malvolio thing. I'd love to work with you more than anybody. You know that.

Always loved working with you. Don't know if Richard explained but we've got this holiday all arranged. And you know Sarah...well, both of us could do with a break. You know I'd love to do it and well I suppose it's just that she comes first.'

Tim sat down beside him. He began to play with one of the make-up sticks. His head was down. 'I didn't come about that. You said no. You made your choice - which you have every right to do, naturally. And I wasn't going to come tonight but I'm glad now that I did.'

Hugo scrubbed at his face with a tissue. 'Oh Jesus, you didn't see it tonight?'

'Yes I did.'

'I don't know what to say Tim. I don't know what happened out there.'

'I think it's better.'

Hugo turned his head from his reflection and stared at him disbelievingly. 'Better?'

'Oh absolutely. I've seen it before of course. Couple of times actually. The character somehow, he's just much more interesting. I don't know. Less sure of himself. So the balance of sympathy has tilted. It's much more dense, more finely textured in terms of characterisation. Beautiful moments. And you know what I loved best?'

'Don't tell me.'

'I loved, you know, that moment when you come down to your son towards the end. That pause. That walk.' He shook his head. 'That absolutely devastating hesitation. And then turning away and mumbling to him as though the words are being forced out and then to shout that ordinary, utterly commonplace line.'

'What are you saying?'

'What?'

'No that's the line. *What are you saying?*

'Devastating. Absolutely devastating. And to say it twice. My God where did that come from? I just thought the whole thing was…well it was amazingly courageous. And courage is… ' he formed a small jerking pyramid of his thumb and four fingers, searching for the words…'the absolutely indispensable gift of a real actor. That and imagination of course. And that terrible blankness after. As if you were sleepwalking through your life. That it was over. That everything was over. I thought, you know, it was tremendous. It's as if you've found a new dimension. Shifted up a whole emotional gear.'

Tears were streaming down Hugo's cheeks. But he was sobbing not from the weight of the praise but from relief. He hadn't noticed; Tim, whom the Guardian had named in their review of the year, as the most perceptive young director of his generation, hadn't noticed. The chances were that neither had anybody else. He had got away with it. *Getting away with it* was what Hugo felt, in the nether region of his actor's soul, was what he had been doing all his life. And tied to this belief was its corollary - that one day he would be found out. It was something he had never admitted to anybody. It was something he scarcely admitted even to himself.

He wiped the tears away and Tim hugged him. 'It's taken it out of you I can see,' he said. He turned him about and held him by both shoulders. His face was no more than three inches away and his bright blue eyes burned into Hugo's. 'That's why you have to be my Malvolio,' he said.

'But did Richard tell you. Sarah and I...'

'I know. I know all about your holiday. But there's plenty of time for holidays. This is a once in a lifetime chance.'

'Tim I'd love to but...'

Tim held up his hand silencing him. 'Listen. Let me tell you something. To be perfectly honest, when I heard from Richard about your position, I made enquiries about somebody else. I've even spoken to him. It was practically settled. Nothing signed of course.'

Hugo was overwhelmed with curiosity to know who this rival might be.

'Naturally I can't tell you who it was.'

'No of course. I understand,' Hugo said.

'But look. Here's what I feel. No bullshit. If *you* won't do it, and I hope against Hell that you will, - I'm not going to do it at all.'

'Tim!'

'No listen! Listen to me. I want to tell you something and it's important, right. Here's where I am. I wouldn't do it because if I did it and you weren't Malvolio then I'd always know, through my whole life, I'd know...' and he spelled it out slowly and clearly, 'it–could–have–been–better. You understand Hugo? And that's something I'm not prepared to live with. I'm sorry but it's true.' He took a deep breath and stepped back. 'So ok it's up to you really. I don't want to put pressure on you. I know

Sarah. And I love her deeply. You have to remember I knew her before you did. We were at RADA together. Talented lady. But that's it. That's what I feel ok? What do you say? A simple yes or no will do it.'

Hugo took a deep breath. He stood up and walked from one end of the dressing room and back again. Sarah, he was thinking. Oh Sarah. Then he stood before Tim again and looked at him for some time without speaking. Then he nodded his head slowly three times.

'Do I take it that's a yes?' Tim asked.

'Yes,' Hugo said. 'It's a Yes.'

Tim threw both his arms about him and kissed him. 'Thank God,' he cried. 'Thank God. You won't regret it. You will not regret it.'

There was a tap on the door and David Harsnet entered followed by his mother. When she saw Hugo and Tim clenched in an apparently passionate embrace she covered the boy's eyes with her hands. 'Oh dear me I'm sorry.' She turned to leave.

Hugo released himself from Tim's passionate embrace. 'No come in, Mrs Harsnet. Come in.' He put his hand on the young boy's shoulder and ushered him towards Tim. 'This is David, one of the boys who plays my son.' he said.

Tim and the boy shook hands formally.

'And I'm his mother,' the woman said still rather flustered. 'I'm so sorry to burst in on you like that.' She turned to Hugo. 'That's the last night. So I just wanted to say thank you for looking after David during the play. I'm sure it's been a huge privilege for him. And I know he's learned so much. Haven't you David?'

The boy shrugged his shoulders. He was squeezing one of Hugo's tubes of make-up that lay on the dressing room table. A red shiny worm of carmine issued from the tube and sat fat and inert on the table top. The boy dipped his index finger in it and smeared it across the table. He mumbled something that Hugo couldn't catch.

Hugo smiled. He'd never cared much for the boy. Now he saw him as dangerous. As someone who knew his secret. He changed the subject. 'Tim's directing *Twelfth Night* at the National. He's just asked me to play Malvolio. And I said, yes. So we're both a bit excited. That's why we were, you know...' He made an embracing gesture in the air.

'Snogging,' the boy said. His right hand was stained red with the make-up.

'David leave that alone!' his mother said, snatching the tube from him.

Tim said to her, 'I was just saying to Hugo how terrific that last scene was between the two of them tonight. Absolutely electrifying.'

'Oh did you think so? It was just so different tonight. You see I come for all David's performances. And I go through his lines with him at home so I practically know it by heart. '

'Really? How interesting,' Hugo said. He was aware of the boy watching him.

'I was just saying, the courage of those huge, extended pauses.' Tim said. 'Amazing. Quite amazing, don't you think?'

'Well to be honest, at first I thought something had gone wrong.' Mrs Harsnet said. She was wiping the boy's red-stained hand with a tissue. She glanced up at Hugo. 'I was wondering - did you and David work that out beforehand. Or…?'

'Course not,' the boy said. 'He comes down to me, right, and he says…'

'No!' Hugo said cutting across him with sudden vehemence. The boy was watching him with a frank, unflinching gaze. He knows, Hugo thought to himself. The little bastard knows. He smiled at the mother. 'No. Sometimes, you know, those things come to you on stage. You just have to follow your instincts.'

'Yeah but…,' the boy sidled towards his mother; leaned against her. All the time his eyes were on Hugo. 'Yeah but, like when I'm sitting at the table, right, he comes down to me and he says…'

'I'm afraid we have to go now,' Hugo cut in swiftly. 'People to see. Things to do. Last night and everything. You understand.'

'Oh yes of course,' Mrs Harsnet said. 'I'm sorry. We have to be running along too. Well goodbye and thank you once more. Come along David.'

Hugo shook hands with her, smiling. 'It's been a pleasure meeting you.' He tousled the boy's hair as he ushered them from the room. 'And who knows, perhaps we'll work together again one day.' But as they disappeared down the corridor he said to no one in particular, 'In your dreams you toxic little bastard.'

Then he began to think of Sarah.

*

It took him three days to tell her. A number of times he got close but then retreated, as if from the edge of a cliff. And then one afternoon as they walked together along the seafront, with Sean asleep in his pram, the cellophane cover dotted with rain, he decided it was now or never. The next day he would be attending the first read-through. Seven days later they were scheduled to fly to Italy. It had to be now. He formulated a stratagem. It unrolled in his head like a scene in a film.

Grey sea crashing onto the beach. Close up Hugo. He glances at Sarah. She is smiling.

Pretending his mobile has rung, he takes it out, shielding it from the wind. Tight Close Up. Hugo. He is anxious, concerned.

We only hear his side of the conversation.

Hugo: *Yes... This is Hugo...Oh Hi...What?...Oh God...No...Yes I can hear you...That's terrible...I can't believe...No she's here now...I don't know how I'm going to tell her...Yes...Yes...Well thanks for telling me...And listen - don't do anything stupid...Yes...Goodbye.*

Close up Sarah. She has been watching him. Silence

Sarah: *(Anxiously) Hugo what is it?*
Cut to Hugo. He closes the mobile. Pockets it. He cannot speak. Then:

Hugo: *Sarah, I've got the most terrible news.*
Sarah: *What?*
Hugo: *I don't know how to tell you.*
Sarah: *Is it Daddy? It's his heart isn't it?*

Hugo: No.

Sarah: It's not Eva? Oh my God there's been a car accident. (She begins to weep) Poor Eva.

Hugo: No, not Eva.

He holds her by the shoulders. Forcing her to look at him.

Hugo: Sarah, I don't know how to tell you this. It's about Tim.

Sarah: Tim? Tim's died?

Hugo: No. That was him calling. It's just that he's lost all his money in some terrible venture capital scam. He's absolutely broke. He's at the end of his tether. He's talking of suicide. The only way he can recover is if he makes this film in Hollywood. Trouble is they won't do it unless they have me along.

Sarah: (With immense relief) Oh darling is that all. I thought it was something terrible. Then of course you must do it.

Hugo: But I told him I couldn't. There's the holiday. I know what it means to you. I couldn't let you down. I told him, No.

Sarah: Oh Hugo darling never mind about the holiday. Tim's welfare is much more important than any silly holiday. We can go on holiday anytime. Hugo we have our whole lives ahead of us.

Hugo: Darling!

They embrace. The sea rolls. Slow fade to Blackout.

But when in reality he took out his mobile, Sarah had walked on out of ear shot, unconcerned. He ran panting to catch her up and when she asked him smiling who had called, his resolve melted.

'Wrong number,' he told her.

*

The next day, after telling her he had business with Richard, he attended a morning read-through. It was over by 12.30. He shared a lunch with Tim and an official from the film company - but all the time he was thinking of what he must do. He hardly touched his food. Tim asked him if anything was the matter but he told him he was fine.

On the train home, he knew that between three and four she always took the baby for a walk along the beach. The house would be empty. She wouldn't be expecting him home till after four. He decided he would write a note explaining everything and leave it on the mantelpiece. Then he would go and sit in a pub somewhere and, after a decent interval, when he knew she would be back and had read the note, he would call her. But when at three-thirty the train pulled into Brighton Station, he knew he couldn't go through with it. He went into a phone booth and dialled his home number. As he suspected there was no one in the house. He heard his own voice telling him that neither of them was at home; that he should leave his name and number and speak clearly after the tone. And then, taking a deep breath, he told her the whole story and how desperately sorry he was.

When he put down the phone, he was shaking. He walked into the station buffet and ordered a double whiskey. Then he had another. And then another. When he was sure that she must have returned and heard the message, he walked out into the street. It was raining. He ordered a taxi. But just as he was approaching his house, to his dismay, he saw her bending over, folding the pram. A feeling of shameful nausea and desperate pity gripped him as he watched her struggling up the steps through the rain, with Sean under one arm, dragging the pram behind her. He knew he should have leapt from the taxi and helped her but instead he sank down in his seat and told the taxi driver to drive on. He wasn't sure where to go. Eventually, outside the Regent Hotel he told the driver to stop. He thought of going in and ordering another whiskey; perhaps ringing Sarah once more before she had time to listen to his message but instead he crossed the road and sat huddled in a small shelter staring out at the sea. After an hour, shivering with the cold and the rain, he got up and walked slowly home.

He hung up his coat in the hallway and walked from one room to the other. He didn't call out her name but whispered it with an odd desperation. Sarah, Sarah, Sarah. He could hear her up stairs. In the living room he switched on the answer phone. His message had been deleted. When he turned she was standing in the doorway, looking at him. He sobbed aloud and held out his arms for her but she didn't move.

'No,' she said.

'Darling I'm so sorry.'

She turned her head away. She said, 'Why till now? You must have known days ago. Maybe weeks. And to tell me like this. Like this. I'm your wife. Your wife, Hugo. We're supposed to be able to talk about things like this. That's what people do if they love each other. We're supposed to be able to tell each other the truth. But now, I don't really know. I don't know anything anymore.'

'Sarah!'

'No! Don't come near me. How could you do this? When you knew I'd be out. It's so...It's so fucking pathetic. It never occurred to me that you were that before. And I don't know if I can love somebody who's pathetic. I really don't.'

He could think of nothing to say. For what seemed an eternity they stood at opposite ends of the dark blue carpet; the empty space a palpable barrier. Then finally she said. 'I'm going up now. I don't really want to see you. You sleep where you want as long as it's not near me. Tomorrow I may feel differently. Or perhaps the next day or the next. I don't know how long it will take for me get used to the idea of having someone pathetic for a husband. I suppose you can get used to anything. Meanwhile I'll talk to the travel company tomorrow.'

He took a step forward. 'Darling let me do that.'

'No. You've got your rehearsal to go to. You think about yourself. You're good at that. And don't call me *darling*. Not for a bit anyway.'

And he watched her cross the hallway and mount the stairs. Not looking back.

*

To try and make it up with her, he drove to and from the theatre each day. He hated the driving but he felt the need to make himself suffer. To let her see that he was suffering and that it was for her sake. But they lived apart, like strangers. And the rehearsals didn't go well. The unreality he had felt on that last night at the Royal Court came back. The remainder of the cast were talented and ambitious but for the most part younger than him. He was the one they looked up to; the experienced one. He had never been nervous or unsure in rehearsals before - but now he dreaded the moment when the call went out for him. He spent most of his time going over and over his lines in dark neglected corners of the theatre.

One afternoon the girl who was playing Olivia came across him. He was sitting with an old blanket about his shoulders going over his lines. She was wearing pink leggings and drinking a coffee. She said, 'My tutor at the Central School kept telling us, that the people who are good are the one's who are always dissatisfied. They know how hard they have to work in order to be good. I never understood what he meant until now.' She was a pretty girl with auburn hair and an attractive excitable frankness about her. Perhaps a year ago he would have taken her on one side; bought her a drink at the bar; flirted with her. But now he just smiled wryly and went back to his text.

At home in a neglected part of the house he recorded the parts of the other actors on a tape and then walked about speaking his own lines into the pauses. It worked well until he began to think that he would be doing this for real the next day, with the eyes of the admiring young cast upon him and immediately the words became fugitive, alien things.

Driving in his car to and from the theatre he would play the tape in the car and roar out his part. And the other drivers who pulled up alongside him at traffic lights would look at him askance as he bellowed, 'I'll be revenged on the whole pack of you. Cross stage to down stage left. Turn. Gesture. Exit Left.'

Five days before the opening night, during the prison scene, the lines went from him completely. He scarcely knew who he was or where. He began to cry and his body shook. He turned the terror into a joke and asked for a prompt; was given it and managed somehow to finish the scene with no further mishaps. Nobody else thought anything of it, after all prompts were often given during rehearsals. It was normal. But for Hugo, who prided himself on an almost uncannily instant and infallible memory and had never missed a word in the theatre since he had played Portia thirty nine years earlier at school, it was devastating. A stark terror invaded his soul and would not lift. From that day on, he carried his lines scrawled on a piece of paper into the darkness of the stage jail; reading them by the light of a small torch. But it wasn't just the lapses of memory that worried him. He found himself confused by the meanings of the simplest lines and the almost limitless possibilities they offered. Anything seemed possible; the old, easy, unerring certainty seemed gone for ever. Walking on from the wings to his mistress's call he knew that he was supposed to say 'Here madam at your service.' He knew it. And yet, myriad syntactical alternatives presented themselves to him. Why not - 'Madame here at your service'? Or 'At your service here Madame'?

Anything was possible. The freedom was bewildering.

Where previously, he had seen any part he played, as a

straight highly coloured thread sewn boldly into the fabric of the drama - now, it was a wild muddy and multi-coloured, directionless scribble. He longed to share his terror with someone. But how could he? It just wasn't in his nature to do something like that. They all depended on him. At one point he did confide to Tim that if he wasn't satisfied with his performance he could get someone else to play the part. But Tim had laughed uproariously thinking it was a joke. Sarah was the only one. But they were still not speaking. Sometimes he would hear her moving about in the upstairs section of the large house that she had elected to make her own: hear her feet on the stairs or in the hallway or on the floor above his head. Sometimes, inevitably, their paths crossed but though he would hesitate as she crossed the hallway in the hope that she might stop and speak to him or broach some form of a truce, she always brushed past him without a word; as though he weren't there. And as he worked alone with his tape recorder, the lines became more and more fugitive. He knew he was working too hard - or rather, trying too hard - but he didn't know what else he could do. And everyday, instead of improving, things were getting worse. What he had been relatively certain of early on, even on the first run-through, was now becoming more and more uncertain. He wondered if he was going mad; or possibly having some form of a breakdown. Somewhere in his consciousness, he had the feeling that he was being punished for something.

There had to be a get-out. But what? The preview was but two days away. He couldn't possibly ask to be released on such short notice. And then, lying in bed that night, it came to him. He would engineer a car accident. Not something violent enough to kill or maim him for life of course. But a gentle shunt; occasioning a minor, relatively painless injury. But one that would offer him a justifiable pretext for withdrawing from the play; his pride intact. Suddenly he felt better; happier than he had been for weeks. He knew exactly the spot where the 'accident' could take place. It was a notorious black spot. There had been an accident there only the previous week. The road turned suddenly right after a hump-backed bridge. There was a warning sign but it was hidden in the thickness of a hedge. To the left was a wooden fence through which he could gently crash, before sliding down a small slope into a cushioning field of barley. He needn't be hurt at all; or only slightly. He could easily simulate a concussion. After all you're an actor, he said to himself.

And so the next morning, as he approached the bridge, he steeled himself. But as he did so an awful premonition gripped him. He saw the broken fence and the car on its side in the field. Ambulance men were stumbling up the slope, bearing a stretcher covered with a red blanket. One of them turned his head away sadly. Hugo shook the vision away. He knew he had to do it. It was too late to back out now. Fifty metres from the bridge he slowed somewhat. No need to be reckless. All he needed was sufficient speed to break through the fence. Twenty five miles an hour should do it. His mouth was cloyingly dry. He tried to swallow but there was not a trace of saliva in his mouth. Now he was on the slope of the bridge. He glanced down at the speedometer. Too fast. Too fast. But it was too late to brake now. He glanced in the mirror. Nothing. That was good. All that was required was a swift pull on the steering wheel. His knuckles were white. Now! Now! Now! He screamed aloud. He jerked the wheel savagely. The car slewed left mounting the raised grass verge with a sudden thump that almost knocked the wheel out of his hands. He saw the fence loom. A glimpse of a grey sky. Wood tore screechingly at the near-side door and it swung open with a bang. He closed his eyes and instinctively and uselessly stamped on the brake. The wheel leapt in his hands and the car stopped with a force that thumped his head hard against the wheel before flinging him back. And then everything was still. The silence was a vacuum. Slowly he opened his eyes. He was still alive. And apart from a slight pain in the region of his right temple and a stiffness in his neck, he didn't seem to be hurt. The car was on the side of the road, the near-side tyres on the grass verge, the others on the tarmac. The engine had stalled. For a moment he sat there; wondering what he should do. A car passed slowly going in the opposite direction. A man and a woman peered at him curiously. He raised his right hand to signal that he was not in need of help. They drove on. He must phone somebody. He couldn't sit here all day. He took out his mobile and with a shaking hand called up the A.A. A woman's voice said, 'Hello.' A voice that he knew to be Sarah's. In his confusion he'd called the wrong number.

Sarah said, 'Hello. Who's this please?'

He said, 'Sarah?'

'Yes?'

'It's me.'

'Hugo?'

'Yes.'

It was the first time they had spoken in days. His mouth was so dry he could hardly form the words. Eventually he managed to whisper, 'Sarah help me. I'm frightened. I'm terribly frightened.'

'Hugo my darling where are you?'

The old tenderness and concern was back in her voice. A wonderful peace flooded through him and he sat back and closed his eyes. He did not see the Jaguar saloon that took the bridge so fast that it had no chance of stopping before it buried itself into the back of his car with a sickening, tearing of metal.

*

What he saw when he next opened his eyes, was a nurse at the foot of his hospital bed making notes on a clip board. When she had finished she hooked the clip board back onto the bed, glanced at her watch, shook down the mercury in the thermometer and turning, became aware of Hugo's eyes watching her.

'Ah there you are Mr. Melville. Nice to have you back,' she said.

He had been semi-conscious for almost three hours. There was a severe whip lash injury, three broken ribs, some damage to his pelvis and to his right leg. Mr Mehta, who was in charge of his case, was most worried about the possibility of diffuse axonal trauma with its attendant, what he in doctor-speak called, 'permanent deficit of brain function'. However, since Hugo had come-to for a brief period in the ambulance shortly after the accident, the doctor informed Sarah that there was every reason to be optimistic on that score. The state of his right leg also gave grounds for concern. Indeed during the first week of his stay, Mr. Mehta informed him matter of factly, indeed almost jovially, that they might have to remove the leg permanently. Hugo replied that if he had any choice in the matter he would prefer the non-permanent option. Dr Mehta was later moved to assure Sarah that Hugo's mental powers, based on the evidence of his verbal dexterity, appeared to be unimpaired. As it happened, he was eventually to regain full function in the damaged leg, although he would limp for the remainder of his life. Of the accident he could remember nothing; nor indeed anything of the week preceding it. Mr. Mehta's term for this condition was - retrograde amnesia. He felt there was no real reason for concern. He was optimistic. He said, 'Mr Melville will recover full function although it could take as long as three years.' The last memory Hugo could dredge up of his pre-accident life was of being on a beach in the rain with Sarah and Sean. He thought Tim might have been there too. There was something vaguely uneasy about the memory and it occurred to him that it might have been part of a film he had been shooting.

When Sarah was allowed to visit him for the first time that evening, he had recovered to the extent that the actor in him couldn't forebear playing the part of a severe amnesiac. As she sat down and asked with tender concern how he was, he had slowly turned his head, his eyes blank, his jaw sagging idiotically. 'Mum,' he mumbled.

'It's Sarah, darling.'

'Sarah,' he had mumbled thickly. 'Not Mummy.'

But when he saw her genuine anxiety, he had clutched at her hand and laughed. And she had clicked her tongue and slapped his hand and cried and laughed and then cried again.

'Sorry I just couldn't resist,' he told her

During the second week, Tim came with some other members of the cast. He told him that he had bad news: that the play was doing very well without him. They had found an actor who had recently played the part in Birmingham and he had slotted in well. He wasn't Hugo of course but then as Tim said, 'One can't have everything.'

After three weeks, he was home. In a strange way he began to enjoy the rather dull day-to-day lives they led together: the necessarily slow family walks along the beach with Sean, he in a wheel chair; sitting down to watch television together in the evening; the shared meals and of course the growing familiarity and burgeoning relationship with his son. The one blot on the horizon was a financial one. While their lawyer assured them they were more than likely to win the action against the speeding driver of the Jaguar, as it was *he* who had run into the back of *him* – the action showed every sign of being prolonged. In the mean time, there was the pressing question of the mortgage on their large house to be paid; not to speak of the other domestic bills. In the mean time they made daily inroads into Hugo's savings.

'It looks as though we may have to sell the house,' Hugo said one evening. With sad hearts, since they loved the house, they visited the Estate Agent and put it on the market.

But then one evening after supper the phone rang.

'Hi Hugo. Rich here. How you feeling? Good. Good. Look. There's a part going. New play, young writer but I've got a feeling it may do something. Got a nose for these things. Good character part. Not huge. But significant. Whoever plays it will get noticed. There'd be an audition of course.'

'Sounds good,' Hugo said. 'Tell me more. When's the audition. Is the character in a wheelchair?'

'Wheelchair?'

'Didn't you know? I'm still in a wheelchair But I could be walking in about three weeks. I'll have a limp of course. Not too bad. I can pretty well disguise it. Tell me when do I need to be there?'

'Oh I'm sorry, Hugo. I wasn't thinking of you.'

'What d'you mean?'

'It's a woman.'

'Woman?'

'Just about Sarah's age. It's tailor made for her.'

'For Sarah?'

'Yes. Well, you told me the money was getting tight: you not working and everything. So I thought why not? Hugo? Hugo are you there?'

After a pause Hugo said, 'I'll go and get her for you.'

And it all happened exactly as Richard had predicted. Sarah, with the help of some coaching from Hugo, travelled up to London for the audition on the following Wednesday. She took Tim's advice and dressed and made herself up as the character and much to her excitement and not a little anxiety, she got the part.

The opening was to be in Guildford so they rehearsed there for a week. She drove herself up there each day. Occasionally she stayed overnight with her friend Claudia. But usually she drove home, where, each night, she rehearsed with Hugo. Really she wanted him there for the first night but he decided to stay in Brighton and look after Sean. As he explained, 'If you are worrying about Sean and the baby-sitter it could affect your performance.'

And she had finally agreed.

On the preview night there were one or two hitches but in Sarah's estimation it all went off satisfactorily. Which, as Hugo said, is what you want on a preview night. By the time the press night came round, the play had settled down. The following day the reviews were glowing, with Sarah in particular picked out for her honesty and what the *Evening Standard* the next day called…'her translucent yet joyful gravity of purpose.'

'I've always been good at translucent but joyful gravity of purpose,' Sarah informed him when he rang her after the show that night. 'It's my thing really.'

'How's Sean?' she asked.

'Oh he's fine,' Hugo said and held him to the mouthpiece so he could send his gurgles down the line.

'I'm glad he liked it,' Sarah said. Her voice dropped. 'Oh darling are you lonely? What are you going to do now?'

'Well, I'm going to read Sean the *Guardian* review. Then we'll probably watch *Horizon* together. He'll be asleep by the time you come home.'

He could hear the noise of a party in the background. 'Sounds like revelry by night.'

'Oh well you know how it is. Don't breathe it too loudly but we may have a hit on our hands.'

'What do you mean *may*? You enjoy yourself, darling. You can tell me all about it when we have supper tonight.'

'Oh that's what I wanted to ask you. Would you mind awfully if I stayed over tonight? I've already had a glass or two. Don't really want to drive home. And this party looks as if it's going to go on some time. Would you mind terribly if I stayed at Claudia's tonight? You won't be too lonely will you?'

After a moment's reflection to compose himself, he said, 'No of course not darling. You enjoy yourself. You never know how long it's going to last.'

'Oh darling you are a sweetheart. Don't forget to take your pills. And I'll be back tomorrow night to tell you all about it.'

'Gilded butterflies,' he said.

'What? What was that?'

'Nothing. Nothing.'

'I can't hear. Such a racket here. Look got to go. Love you. Give Sean a big kiss from me.'

And she was gone.

After changing Sean's nappy, Hugo fed him and tried to settle him down for the night but he too seemed infected by excitement and stayed stubbornly awake. So finally Hugo carried him up the stairs and settled him beside him in the large double bed. The sheets smelled of Sarah. He made himself a cup of sweet chocolate and cradling Sean in his arms, they both of them settled down to watch a recording of his Parkinson interview. But before the end they had both of them fallen asleep.

Sixteen

Not long after my sixteenth birthday, while waiting to go to Sixth Form College, I worked for a time at the Local Infirmary. My work consisted of little more than portering: I carried used sacks of dressings to the incinerator, pushed patients in wheel chairs to the television room or onto balconies, went to the station to collect consignments of blood, cleaned the ward floors with large electrical polishers and made endless pots of tea. I had led a fairly sheltered life up to that point and some of the things I experienced rather shocked me: like seeing the tiny aborted foetus of a baby boy suspended in a bottle of preservative on a shelf in one of the ward offices. And then, also on my first day in the job, I noticed one of the other porters standing before the incinerator with a bucket in his hand. As he flung the contents into the furnace, I saw an amputated leg arching through the air and into the fire.

Later in that same week George, the Head Porter, asked me to accompany two rather genteel old ladies down to the mortuary. He gave me a key with a number on it. 'I wouldn't ask but there's nobody else about,' he whispered in my ear. 'Will you be all right with this d'you think?'

I told him, 'Yes'. What else could I say?

The mortuary was lined with large metal drawers each with its own name and number printed on cards - for all the world like giant filing cabinets. I found the name and number in question and drew back the drawer. In it lay the corpse of a dead woman. Tied to her big toe was a label with her name and number so there could be no mistake. I had never seen a dead person before. The two old ladies gazed down at the body of their sister. 'Yes there she is poor dear,' one of them said softly. They gazed on her for a few minutes. I wondered what I should do if they became hysterical or even fainted. I needn't have worried. They were both calm and collected; indeed almost matter of fact:

'That will do,' one of them said.

They both kissed her 'Goodbye'. I pushed the drawer back into place and locked it. Then I escorted them out of the hospital and showed them to their bus stop. They thanked me for my trouble and smiled politely.

The strange thing is that I never had nightmares. Perhaps it was because I was so young and just took everything in my stride. Sometimes when the work was light I would chat to some of the patients. There's a wonderful democracy about a hospital ward; the barriers of class and wealth are lowered: rich and poor, the educated and the illiterate, dressed alike in pyjamas and dressing gowns, all mix together more or less as equals. And I became an accepted part of that democracy.

My sojourn in the hospital started to break down another barrier. At the age of sixteen you divide the world into two distinct camps: the young and the not young; and ne'er the twain shall meet. But on those several wards, I found that men who were roughly the same age as my father or my headmaster, those I had hitherto regarded almost as aliens, began to treat me as some kind of equal. In the Infirmary there were neither young nor old - there were just people. Or rather there was a more elemental tripartite hierarchy: the healthy, the sick and the mortally sick. Of course they pulled my leg and gave me nicknames but it was done in a spirit of fun. Boredom probably had a lot to do with it. I was their link with the outside world of normality, where people were healthy and caught buses and went to work. And yet it was strange to find men in their forties, or even older, talking to sixteen-year-old me quite openly, of their troubles and their fears, their health, their wives, their children and their finances.

It was strangely flattering.

Of course there were some that you got closer to than others: such a one was Mr Raymond Edgeworth. He had been rushed in one afternoon after having suffered a near fatal heart attack. Three times during that first day, an emergency call went out and three or four young doctors and nurses ran in dragging equipment behind them and pulled the screens noisily about him. You could hear their shouts and the thump of the defibrillator. It didn't look very promising. Old Mr Jefferies waved me over. He was a pessimist by nature, even when healthy. He shook his head dolefully. 'Looks like that one's on his way out.' He nodded towards the screen. 'Don't think our friend there will see the sun come up if you ask me.'

But when I came to clean and polish the ward floor the next morning, the screens were still there. Staff Nurse Rogers drew back the screens and said I could wipe round and under the bed with a damp mop as long as I was quiet about it. Even with the near dead, the floor had to be cleaned. He lay there with his head thrown back on the pillow, his face pale and drawn. I thought he must be asleep so I worked as carefully and quietly as I could. Then I noticed that his eyes were open and he was following me with a distant yet interested expression. He even managed a wan smile.

'Feeling better?' I asked him.

He nodded feebly and said something I couldn't catch. I leaned closer. 'Let's say,' he whispered, 'if I was the slightest bit worse I'd be dead.'

Over the following days I noticed that he had any number of visitors: some of them rather attractive, smartly-dressed women. By the fourth day the screens were gone and he was sitting up in bed. Staff Nurse Rogers had given him a shave and a bed bath and combed his hair. I had a feeling he enjoyed that. He was a handsome man just past forty with longish, shiny auburn hair and eyes that twinkled with an air of amused detachment. And yet, occasionally it was possible to discern a deep sadness in him. For some reason he seemed to take a liking to me. And I liked him in return. Perhaps it was because he had a son the same age as me. He had a way of joking dryly with the nurses that outraged and at the same time amused them. But with me he was often serious. He listened carefully to what I had to say and occasionally would even ask my advice but always in an oblique sort of way that was oddly captivating. This was immensely flattering to a callow and rather over-protected sixteen-year-old. When the nurse had finished tidying his bed, or checking his temperature, he would glance about the ward before discretely beckoning me over. He would lean towards me as if to share a secret. 'Tell you what citizen,' he whispered, 'that Nurse Rogers is definitely a dangerous piece of goods.'

'Dangerous?'

'Body on her, she shouldn't be allowed out without a licence. It's the uniform, my friend. That bosom. All that crisp whiteness. That purity. And then those black stockings. They should make a law against it or Sister Palpitation will get me by the heart strings. What body music we could have made together her and me when I was in my prime. Now it'd kill me.' He punched me gently on the shoulder. 'But what a way to go my friend. What a way to go.'

And I, who up to this point in my life had scarcely even held hands with a girl never mind kissed one, would give a wry and complicit smile that acknowledged we were both men of the world and understood all there was to know of women and their complex yet seductive natures.

He'd often say, wrinkling his nose, 'Come and talk to me for a bit, citizen. Tell me what it's like to be young. I can hardly remember.' He'd glance covertly about the room before asking me to refill his already half-full water jug. 'That way if anybody makes a fuss, I can say you were just filling it up for me.' And he would wink at me knowingly.

When I got back he would give a surreptitious glance about the ward, as if he had some outrageous piece of information to impart, then incline his head towards me confidentially and speak in an undertone.

'Talking of the fair sex. Know who that lovely piece of prime womanhood was who came to visit me yesterday?'

'What, Nurse Rogers?'

'No not Nurse Rogers. Although I do not deny for one minute that little Nurse Rogers, as you rightly point out, is a tasty item. I don't deny it.' He beckoned me closer after another swift glance up and down the ward. I leaned forward the better to hear. 'No. Came in yesterday. Full motley. High heels. Christian Dior suit. The lot. You must have seen her.'

'No.'

'You didn't? Oh you missed a treat. The ward was redolent with the scent of Chanel No 5 for two hours after. Raised the olfactory tone a few notches I can tell you. My wife.'

'Your wife?'

'Love of my life! But oh Jesus I thought I was a goner there for a minute. Quack told me in no uncertain terms. No excitement. Absolutely verboten. Slightest whiff of excitement and the old ticker would go on the blink for good. No reprieve this time. Well, there I was talking to my wife. She was sitting where you are now. Me - extremity of calm. Keeping the ticker strictly under control. Doing what the Quack told me. Then I happened to glance in that little mirror there.' He pointed to a small mirror on his bedside table. 'What do I see?

I shook my head.

'Only my girl friend.'

'Girl friend?'

'Louisa.' He clicked his tongue in irritation. 'I'd told her not to come. Why don't women listen? Women eh! Women!'

And I complicitly shook my head, as if the warding off of legions of elegantly dressed, predatory women was a problem I had to deal with on a daily basis.

'Bloody Louisa! Beautiful example of prime womanhood. Beautiful! She was talking to one of the nurses. I was sure my wife would look up and see her any minute. The ticker starts going into clapper mode. My whole body was rocking with it. Boom boom! I thought, Oh my God here we go again. This is the end Raymond my son. I put my hand up behind me and waved at her to clear off out of it. Thank God she saw me. It was a close thing. No excitement he says. God help us!'

I must admit I was quite shocked that he, a married man, should also have a girl friend. I'd read about such things in novels but in those days, fiction and real life were two entirely different things. This was the first occasion on which I'd spoken to a man who admitted it. Who actually lived that life. He waved me to come closer. He shook his head dolefully. 'All over now, that life. All over'

'It is?'

'Oh absolutely. Climbing through windows; doing a runner from irate husbands and daddies; thrashing away in the arms of Venus the live-long night. Thing of the past, my friend. Don't believe I'll get the old leg over again this side of paradise. Sad isn't it. And I loved my life. Loved it.'

I could see he was in a mood to talk and I was happy to listen.

He'd always been good with his hands and even when he was still in junior school, he learned to tinker with his father's car and repair it when it went wrong. Later, his father built him a small garage at the end of the garden when he was still in his teens. He began to repair neighbours' cars. Word of mouth spread his reputation for honesty and efficiency and he soon had enough in the bank to put down a deposit on a small, local garage. His reputation grew and the business expanded. By the time he was thirty he had three garages including a large complex in the centre of town with a concession from Mercedes Benz.

'And then,' he went on, 'a couple of weeks before my fortieth birthday I was out with some pals fishing for salmon. Loved it. I loved it. All that life. I was blessed. We fished into the evening and then we'd go back to the Inn and eat and drink. You never saw the like. Lords of conspicuous consumption wasn't in it my friend. And then while we were eating and drinking and laughing the thought came to me. *I've got to get up tomorrow at six o'clock and work like stink till seven or eight. If I go on like this much longer I'm going to kill myself. It's inevitable.* I've seen it happen too often to other men. Work eighteen hours a day - houses, money in the bank, villas abroad. The lot. But what's the good of all that if you're an invalid or worse still, defunct. Zilch. I could see it happening. One day I'd be into a decent-sized salmon and bang, my heart'd go mad with excitement. The old watch would run out of time. Stop for ever. What's the point of that? So I decided then and there to get out of it and enjoy the rest of my life. Left my manager to run the business. Gave him half of the income and just lead the life of Reilly.

Should have changed my name to Reilly. I was that pleased with
myself. I knew I'd done the right thing. I was a lucky man. And
the point was I *knew* I was lucky. I never stopped reminding
myself: *Raymond*, I'd say, *you are one lucky guy. Fortune has blessed
you.* But I tell you something, my friend: in order to be a lucky
man you have to be lucky all your life. To be unlucky - you only
have to be unlucky once. And one afternoon bad luck clobbered
me in the heart. And it was funny really because it happened
just as I'd predicted. You know, I think sometime you need to
be careful what you dream because there's a good chance your
dreams'll come true; the good and the bad. But especially the
bad. So there I was one warm, dusky evening into this enormous
salmon. And you know - Do you fish? You don't - well let me
tell you, you're missing something special. There is nothing to
equal that electric feeling when a huge fish makes a grab at your
line. Nothing. Thrill? What! It's electric. E-L-E-C-T-R-I-C! In
fact it was all too much. I got this unbelievable pain in my chest
and the next thing I knew my pals were pulling me out of the
water. If they hadn't heard the splash I'd have drowned to
death, never mind cardiac arrest. So you see we buggered it all
up me and that salmon. I don't blame him though. I often
wondered what happened to him. He's probably swimming
about somewhere poor sod with fifteen metres of line and
fishing rod hanging out of his jaw. You know, up to that point, I
was set for another - I dunno, thirty years of the life hedonistic:
wine, women, song and salmon. And what happened?' He
tapped his heart. 'This happened that's what. This rotten blasted
heart put the kybosh on everything. Next thing I know I wake

up in here with three big nurses jumping up and down on my chest. Was a time I would have enjoyed that. Not any more though. Not any more, citizen.'

He shook his head relapsing into a melancholy silence. After a few moments his eyes slowly closed and he fell asleep.

I crept away.

For some time I didn't see him or talk with him. I was sent to help out exclusively on another ward for a few days. Then I had a couple of days off and the weekend came. So, it was about six days later before I saw him again. His bed had been moved about five spaces down from the door. This was a good sign: the patients most at risk are always in beds nearest the door so the nurses can get at them fast. I gave him a wave but he didn't see me at first. He had his nose in a book. He was a voracious reader. Good books too. Not the usual rubbish. When he saw me, he took off his glasses and waved them at me. I went over. He gave his customary, conspiratorial glance up and down the ward. 'Come here citizen. Been wanting to tell you something. I want to get something off my chest.'

He motioned me to sit down. There were no jokes this time. He was staring straight ahead in front of him. It was late November. Only four o'clock but the darkness was coming down.

'You know I told you about me and the salmon?'

I nodded. 'The story of how it buggered up your life.'

'Got it in one.'

Still he wouldn't look at me. He was obviously having difficulty saying what he wanted to say. His lips moved but no words came out. He closed his eyes and then opened them again. I didn't say anything; just waited. When he at last spoke, it was with unusual force.

'Lies!' he said.

'What lies?'

'What I told you. All of it lies. Well yes, there was a salmon. And yes I did think this might be just the moment when I might have a heart attack. But it didn't happen then. No, there was something else.'

For the first time he turned and looked at me full in the face. His eyes were immensely sad. 'It was much worse. It was a terrible thing. Terrible. And I don't want to lie to you. I like you. You've been a good friend to me.'

I was embarrassed. I tried to deprecate this sudden outburst of praise and familiarity. But he wouldn't let me. He put up his hand.

'No, a good friend. And I don't know what's going to happen with this.' He tapped his heart. 'I could go tomorrow. And I wouldn't like to go out on a lie. Not to you. I've told a lot of lies in my time, most of them not serious. Show me a man who says he's never told a lie and I'll show you a liar. But this was a big one. The worst of it was, I lied to myself. So I want to tell you the truth of it. If you want to hear that is?'

'Of course,' I said.

He showed me the cover of the book he was reading. *Myths and Legends of the Rhineland.* 'Was reading one of these stories. Something hit me. There *I* was. It was *me* he was writing about. I tell you, my friend, it gives you a bit of a turn when you read the truth about yourself in black and white.' He turned the pages. 'Where is it? Here it is: *A Ride Across Lake Constanz*. You ever come across this story?'

I shook my head. 'Never,' I said.

'Nor me till today. It's a sort of legend. Well, what happened was this: there were these men in a coach. You know it was, like, the nineteenth century. And they wanted to get to this town. They were in a hurry. They thought they were going to be late. But this town they're going to, it's on the other side of the lake. It's winter and the lake's covered in ice. The road goes round it but because they're in a hurry they decide to drive the carriage across the lake. Over the ice. And they do it. It's fine. They arrive safe and sound on the other side. Then, they're in the Inn eating, and the host, the landlord says, "How long did it take you to go round the lake gentlemen?" And one of them, the sort of leader, says, "Oh we didn't go round. We drove across on the ice."

'And the landlord looks at them in amazement. "You came across on the ice?"

'"Yes of course," the man says. "Why d'you ask?"

'"Why? Because you're lucky to be alive."

'"Lucky why?"

'"Because the ice is only thin. It may look thick but it's not. We never get thick ice here. There are salts in the water. Everyone here knows that. Nobody risks going on it. Only last month three children went sliding on it."

'The man goes: "What happened to them?"

'"They drowned. Fell through the ice and drowned. So if

small children can break the ice what chance is there for a coach and horses? It's a miracle you got through."

'The man stared at him. He couldn't speak. The horror of what might have happened struck him. In his mind's eye, he saw the coach and the horses, himself and his companions capsizing and floundering in the icy water before sinking to their deaths. The vision was so real to him that it overwhelmed him. He gave a sudden, terrible groan and fell to the floor. Stone dead.'

He paused looking at me steadfastly. There was an awful expression in his eyes. One I'd never seen before.

I shook my head. 'He died. But why? I don't understand.'

'He died of recollected fear.' He closed the book with a snap. 'Recollected fear.' He looked at me hard. 'You don't believe it do you?'

'I don't know,' I said.

'Well I believe it. Because it almost happened to me. Let me tell you. Listen.' He beckoned me even closer. 'I've never told this to anybody. It's a terrible thing I did. I have to tell somebody.'

Just then the Ward Sister called my name. She had a job for me before I went home. Just before I left he clutched my sleeve. 'Come back tonight. I'll tell you the rest of it. Please! It's important.'

After I'd finished work that night I hung my dust coat up in the little room the porters used and went back to the ward. He was sitting up waiting for me, drinking a cup of tea.

'I've been thinking about you,' he said. 'Did you notice Old Jeffries has gone?' He nodded to the empty bed by the door. 'Couldn't stand those tubes down his nose. Pulled them out.

Now he's in heaven. Or Nowhere. I'd put my money on Nowhere.'

'You said you'd been thinking about me.'

'That's right. That's right. I wanted to give you some advice. You're just starting off in life. Don't mind telling you, I envy you. I do, I envy you. Listen. I just wanted to say when you're your age… How old are you?'

'Sixteen.'

'Sixteen. Yes well, when you're sixteen, you think it's going to last for ever. But let me tell you something from one who knows. It doesn't. I've learned one big lesson in my forty years. Know what it is? Nothing lasts. Nothing lasts. Not even Nothing. Think about it. It's a big thought is that. So my advice to you is: enjoy it while you can, because you're a long time dead. And this…where we are now…' and he pointed round the quiet ward: at the lines of patients; some hunched in sleep, others lying on the tops of their beds reading books or newspapers or listening to radios on their headphones… 'this my friend is the Waiting Room.'

He laughed a sudden explosive laugh that degenerated into a fit of coughing. When he'd recovered himself, he rested his hand affectionately on my shoulder. 'I bet you're glad you came aren't you? All this cheerful news.'

He wiped his mouth with a paper handkerchief.

I said, 'Was that what you wanted to tell me?'

He shook his head. 'No. No, not that. Something else.' He pointed at the water jug on his table. 'Pass me a drink of water would you?' He drank deeply then settled back. 'I want to tell you. This isn't easy. This is not easy. I wanted to tell you, I did a terrible thing once. I didn't think it was so terrible at the time. Didn't think much of it at all. But I do now. And it's caught up with me. They say your sins catch up with you, don't they? In my case I think they're right.

'It was about five years ago: actually five years ago this week. I was going out with this girl. I was married too. But, you know, that never stopped me. That's me. That's what I am. She wasn't the first by a long shot. She was a really nice girl. Came from a good family. Her father was a vicar, can you believe. Quite a big noise in the Church. God knows how she came to get mixed up with me. That was her one big mistake in life. I was in love with her. I really was. Going to get a divorce. The wife knew nothing of course. Hadn't got round to telling her. But I was intent on marrying the girl. Well, let's say I made myself believe I was going to marry her. Probably I was lying to myself as well as to her but there you are. Anyway the inevitable happened. She got pregnant. I didn't know what to do. There was my wife. I had two kids. There was the business. What were they going to make of it all? Then there was her side. She was religious. She thought the world of her mother and father. She couldn't bear to think what it would do to them. She was going mad with worry. She was so ashamed. She started talking about killing herself. In the end I told her: there was another way. Another way. She knew what I meant. She didn't want to do it. She thought it was like murder. It was like killing one of God's creatures, something that was part of herself. A sin. It went against everything she believed in. But I talked her into it. And it was difficult. Her father was well known in the town. He was involved in organising hospital visits. Not just in our town but across the country. If she'd gone into hospital, someone would be bound to see her. It would all come out. There'd be hell to pay. But I had a customer who was a doctor. I'd done him a few favours. His son had been in trouble with the law and I'd given him a job. I'd wanted to help him. There was nothing in it for me. I'm not a bad man you know. Not a bad man. So he agreed to do it. But where? That was the problem. Couldn't use his surgery; too much of a risk. Then I thought about my great aunt. She had always favoured me. She had a nice house up Alderley. Fairly isolated. We used to go there often when we were kids.' He smiled as he reminisced.

'She had this huge plum tree in the garden. Once a year she had this ceremony where all the family went and picked the plums. Made jam and things. She liked me. Don't ask me why but she did. I was her favourite nephew. Well, about this time she was going away on holiday with a friend. I called round to see her. She was pleased to see me. I made up this story. I told her, I was worried about her going away. There'd been a lot of burglaries in the district: people who'd gone away having their houses turned over. I told her, I didn't mind looking after the place while she was away. Keep an eye on things. She was very grateful. Let me have the key. I told her to let the neighbours know what was happening: that if they saw the lights on or whatever, they weren't to worry. It would be me just checking up. I said I might even stay there a couple of nights. I covered myself.

'So it was all set. I bought red sheets and blankets. Red sheets wouldn't show the blood; a rubber underlay. I thought of everything. We did it at night. I say 'we' but while it was going on I stayed downstairs. I just sat in the kitchen staring out at this beautiful plum tree. But I could hear her crying and screaming sometimes. I turned the radio up full blast. I didn't want to hear.

'Then it was over. It was in a plastic bag. The doctor he handed it to me. "There's your son," he said. I went out and buried it in the garden. I went out that night. And it was me doing that. Digging this little hole. It didn't need but a little hole. But I dug it deep. It was the digging that made me realise what a terrible thing I'd done. My son, I thought. That's my son in there. Under the ground. He wouldn't have seen anything. He wouldn't have known he'd been in the world. Not seen the moon or the clouds. Not seen his mum's face looking down at him. My face. Not even that.

'I went up to see her. There was a pile of sheets thrown in a corner of the bedroom. They were red but I could still see the blood on them. The girl and me, we didn't say nothing. We just stared across the room at one another. She just kept shaking her head. Very slowly shaking her head from side to side. That's all. It was like too big for words. Too big, you know.

'It didn't last. How could it after something like that. We didn't see each other again. I think she went a bit crazy. She was in hospital for a time. I don't know where she is now.'

He took a deep breath and asked for more water. He turned to me. 'You alright with this?' he said quietly.

I nodded.

'You want me to go on? You see there's only three of us know about it. Me, the doctor and her: the mother.' As he pronounced the word 'mother' - he choked. The water spilled from the glass. He wiped himself down and then looked at me. 'Now there's you. There's four of us. You do what you want with it. I just wanted to tell someone. To tell you. You want I should go on?'

'Go on,' I said.

He drew another deep breath. 'O.K. So, about three weeks ago I was back there, you know in the area. It was about a week before I came in here. I was going to see a customer. Potential sale. There was a motor he was interested in. I still did the odd job like that. And I realised I was near my great aunt's house. She'd been dead about two years. There was a young woman in the front garden of her house. I said hello. Her husband came out. They were very friendly. We talked about this and that. I told them my great aunt had lived in the house; how we all used to come for what we called our Plum Day. The husband said, "Well we've made a few alterations. Would you like to have a look round?"

'I wasn't sure you know. It had terrible memories for me that place. But they were very keen and it seemed rude to say no. Well I had a guided tour. I didn't like everything they'd done but I made the right noises. What was awful, was standing in the bedroom where it had happened. My heart started going. I thought I was going to faint. Thinking about it my heart must have been in a dicky condition for some years but I knew nothing about it. It just needed something big to trigger it; to push me over the edge. I thought I hid it pretty well but the woman must have noticed. She made me sit down and brought me a glass of water. I said no. I had to get out of that room. It was like being in a room where a murder had been committed. And it was me who'd done it. She took me out into the garden. "I bet you'd like to see the famous plum tree. It's still there you know."

'It was strange to be back. Something kept drawing me to the spot where five years ago I'd buried him. But the grass had grown over. There was nothing to show. Nothing you know. I'd dug the hole really deep because I'd thought, whoever bought the house after, might change the garden. Dig it up. But it was still lawn with this old plum tree growing out of it. Then her husband called her into the house. There was a telephone call for her. I just wandered about on my own for a bit. I was still feeling a bit groggy. It was strange because I hadn't thought about it much at all, about what we'd done. It wasn't on my conscience. That baby had just been something inconvenient. It had to go. That's how I thought about it. But now...

'So, I just walked about taking deep breaths trying to steady myself. I heard singing coming from the bottom of the garden. I saw their little boy in this bit of a greenhouse that leaned against the wall. My aunt had been a great gardener. When I was a kid I used to like going in the greenhouse because it was always warm, even in winter. You could hide there and I liked the smell of tomatoes. He was pottering, their lad, just like I used to do: pouring water onto the plants from a watering can. It was a struggle for him to reach, him being so small. But it didn't seem to bother him. He just carried on singing to himself. And you know I was thinking - I ought to change. I'd never been much for kids: not even my own. Too busy thinking about myself I guess. So I gave him a shout and a wave. Something I wouldn't normally do. I usually keep kids at a distance. And this little kid, he just looked up but he didn't say anything. I thought, that's kids for you. Just then anyway, his mum came out. I said I had to go. I had a customer waiting. I thanked them. I was thinking, What a nice family. They had no need to show me round. And I told them that. I told them I was glad such a nice family was living in my great aunt's old house. They liked that. I could see them smiling. The husband said, "She must have been a great old lady. You can tell that by the way she kept the garden." He said. "Sometimes I can feel she's still around."

'I got in the car. I was feeling a lot better. Back to my normal self. The wife said, "This house. It's haunted you know." She was smiling as she said it.

'Well I never believed that stuff.

'She said, "You don't believe me do you? But I've seen it. It doesn't worry us though." She looked like a happy kind of lady; good wife; good mother to her little boy. Straightforward. Uncomplicated. I felt almost envious. I started the engine. As I was turning the car round I passed them. I opened the window and gave them a wave. "Thanks for everything." And then as a kind of jokey afterthought, I called out. "And when you see my great aunt, say hello from me would you?"

'I never saw them again. But the whole thing left a good feeling. But then…'

He stopped in mid-sentence. He was taking rapid, shallow breaths and his eyes were closed.

I gave him a glass of water but he just held it without drinking. I said, 'You alright Mr Eldridge?'

He nodded. He was concentrating on his breathing. 'Just give me five minutes.'

He took the water and sipped at it. 'Five minutes!' he said. 'One'll do.' He tried to smile then exhaled slowly. He looked at me. 'Where was I?'

'You were saying it left you with a good feeling.'

'Right. Right,' he said. He drew in a long breath through his nostrils then breathed out. 'Then a couple of days later,' he said, 'I went to see my sister. She wanted some advice over a mortgage she was getting involved in. I was always close to my sister. I told her the story. How this nice family had invited me into our great aunt's house. Of course I didn't tell her about the baby. The one I'd buried. My sister said she knew them: the wife anyway. She'd met her somewhere. Turns out they were quite friendly. And then we started to reminisce, you know. How we used to all go there when we were kids: to my great aunt's Plum Day. All that. How we'd all make jam and she'd preserve it. We'd both loved those days. And then I told her how they'd said it was haunted. And my sister says, "Yes she told me about that too."

'I told her I didn't believe in all that stuff. I said I'd made a joke about it. I'd told them that when they saw my auntie wandering about next time they were to say hello from me. I was laughing.

'My sister was looking at me. She wasn't laughing. And you know what she said. Oh God! Oh God! You know what she told me? She said, "No," she said…she said…

He clutched at my sleeve. He was stuttering then he started to cough. His head fell back on his pillow. He waved his hand feebly. 'Better get the…'

I ran down and got the nurse and told her what was happening. I stood by the door watching her. A doctor rushed passed me. They pulled the screens round his bed.

I never saw him again.

When I went back the next day the bed was empty. Nurse Rogers was laying new sheets on the bed. I asked her what had happened.

She said, 'Mr Etheridge died at four o'clock this morning.'

I had to turn away. I suppose there's never a good time to die. But four o'clock in the morning must be one of the worst. And I kept on thinking: he'd never finished that story. He had wanted to tell it. It was important for him. But now I'd never know. The rest of that day I went about my work in a kind of a daze. I'd liked Mr Etheridge. He wasn't perfect, but I liked him. He was the first adult I'd got to really know; as a kind of equal. He was a friend. I asked Nurse Rogers to tell me when the funeral was. I'd never been to a funeral in my life before. I didn't like the idea. But somehow I wanted to be there. Maybe it was part of my growing up.

*

More people than I had expected were crowded into the little chapel. A lot of people must have liked him. I could understand that. He was somebody you wanted to be around. Even when he was dead. Naturally I didn't know anybody who was there. I hung about on the edges of the crowd trying not to be noticed. Glancing round the burial plot, I noticed a number of the mourners were smartly dressed women.

After, as I was walking away, one of them caught up with me.

She said, 'It's Jamie isn't it? Am I right?'

'Yeah,' I said.

'Ray told me about you. Oh I'm sorry. I'm Esther. I'm his sister. I wanted to ask you something? Have you got a moment?'

We sat down on a green bench. She stared down at her shoes; shifting them from one side to the other in a sort of dance. She said, 'I can't believe he's gone. Oh I know what he was like. He thought he hid everything from everybody: from his wife. From everyone. But she knew. She knew. We all did. He was a rascal. But we all loved him.' She glanced at me and half-smiled. 'I don't know why I'm telling you all this. You must think I'm stupid.'

I didn't know what to say. I felt a bit embarrassed. 'I don't think you're stupid,' I said.

'Bless your cotton socks,' she said giving a half-smile. 'The thing is you see, you were the last person to speak to him. I was there of course but it was all too late then. But I'm sort of happy that the last words he spoke were to you. To a friend. You know what I mean. Not to a doctor or a stranger. I wanted to thank you for that. So thank you.'

She leant across and kissed me on the cheek. I didn't know

whether she expected me to say something. I was relieved when she went on talking. She said, 'There's something else.'

'Yeah?'

'Yes. I know it's silly but I'd like to know…that's why I wanted to talk to you apart from thanking you... I'd like to know what was the last thing he said before he … you know. What you were talking about. I know it sounds silly but I'd really like to know.'

She looked at me intently.

And I thought back to that evening. I remembered sitting beside his bed; handing him the glass of water. I said, 'He was telling me how he went back to see his great aunt's house.'

'Ah yes, *we* talked about that too. How funny. Was it about it being haunted?'

'Yes. He made a joke about it.'

'He would do. Even if he was dying he'd somehow turn it into a joke. I loved him for that. You know he was the sort of man, no matter what he did, you couldn't help liking him.' She brushed her skirt softly with the back of her hand. 'I'd like to think of him going out on a joke.' She put her hand on my arm. 'What did he say? D'you remember?'

'I think so,' I said. I thought about it. Then it came back to me. 'He'd been invited in by the people who lived in the house.'

'Auntie's house?'

'Yes.'

'He told *me* about that too.'

'They showed him round. He went into the garden to see this tree. This plum tree.'

'He told you about that did he? We all loved that tree.'

'Then, after, he was driving away and he said to them about the ghost, he said…'

'Go on,' she said.

I paused. I wanted to get his words exactly right. I knew that was important to her. 'He said - he said to these people as he was driving away. He said, "If you see my great aunt say hello from me." It was a joke.'

'Is that all?'

'I think so.'

'He didn't tell you the rest?'

'Rest?'

I thought about the baby. I didn't think it was up to me to tell her about that. I told her. I said, 'No. That's where it ended. He was going to tell me more but then he began to cough. He wasn't well. I had to call the nurse. I never saw him again.'

'He didn't tell you what *I* said to him after that?'

'No.'

She was staring out above the dark trees.

'That's what was so funny,' she said. 'He came to see me just after that. Told me the same story he told you. About the ghost and everything. But he'd got it all wrong, you know. All wrong. I tried to tell him. But he wouldn't listen. He was having such a laugh. He was telling me he wouldn't have been scared. He'd like to see her. He said, "How could I be scared of her? Of Auntie. I'd love to meet her. I'd say, *Hello Auntie*. I'd ask her how she was. I'd say *—How was the jam this year. I'd warn her. I'd say, - Look here Auntie - it's alright you going round trying to scare the likes of me but don't you go scaring their little boy."*

'That's when I stopped him. I said to him, "What little boy?"

'And Ray said, "Their little boy. He was playing in the garden."

'I said, "What boy Ray? They haven't got a little boy."

' "What?" he said.

' "A little boy. They haven't got one."

'And as I said it, he looked at me so hard. As if I was someone he hated. And his face was grey. It was terrible. Never seen anything like it. He said, "What you talking about? What you mean, they haven't got a little boy?"

'I said, "Exactly what I say. They haven't got a little boy. The wife, I know her quite well. She told me. They can't have children. That's what I was trying to tell you. When they were talking about the ghost. It isn't Auntie that's the ghost. It's this little boy."

' "Boy?" he said. He gave me an awful look.

' "Yes," I told him. "He appeared about five years ago. Auntie used to see him. It was after she came back from this holiday. She warned them. She told this woman, the wife, when they bought the house. Then the wife, she started seeing him as well. She got used to seeing him now and then. Always in the garden near that tree, singing to himself. Didn't scare her, she said. She got used to it." And as I was telling him this, his whole face creased up. It crumpled. I thought he was going to laugh at first. But then his face sort of stuck like that. Rigid. He stretched out both hands and got hold of my shoulders. Really hard by the shoulders. And I said, "Ray what's the matter? What did I say? What's wrong?" But he just looked into my eyes with a terrible expression. Terrible. Then he gave a groan and slid to the floor. It was awful. And I rang for the ambulance. That was his first heart attack. It nearly killed him. And I wondered if it was something I'd said. I mean a minute before he's been joking about this ghost of my auntie. I mean what was the difference between Auntie and a little boy; silly ghost stories. That's all. I couldn't understand. Couldn't understand it at all.' She turned away for a moment. Then she turned back to me. 'I just thought he might have said something to you. Because what ever it was it helped kill him in the end. I thought he might have said something you know, that would explain it. I'd really like to know.'

I couldn't look at her. I didn't say anything. I was thinking about the red sheets on the bed. The boy in the greenhouse, singing to himself. And I understood it all. I couldn't look at her. She said, 'Well was there? I'd love to know. It's preyed on me. That it might have been me. That *I* might have said something.'

And still I couldn't speak. The mourners had all left by now. I could see the black car waiting for her in the roadway. The chauffeur was standing on the pavement in his black uniform. He took off his cap and glanced at his watch.

I shook my head. 'No,' I told her. 'He didn't say anything else.'

I was sixteen. I lived at home with my mum. I'd only just finished school. But I was learning. And what I learned that day was - that there are some things that are best left unsaid. Even if they happen to be the Truth. Especially if they happen to be the Truth.

She offered me a lift in the car but I decided to make my own way home. Before she drove off she leaned out of the car window. 'Nearly forgot,' she said. She handed me a plastic bag. 'Ray wanted you to have this,' she said. 'He's written your name in the front.'

I watched her car until it had disappeared from view. After, I stayed there for some time just looking at the place where the car had been. Then I walked out and caught the bus home. On the bus I looked in the bag. It was a book: *Myths and Legends of the Rhineland*. There was folded paper marking one of the pages. I opened it. The title said: *A Ride Across Lake Constanz*. I unfolded the paper. I thought he might have written something. But there was nothing.

When I got home my mum was coming in from the back garden. Her face was shining and red from the sun. Some words Mr Edgeworth had once said to me came into my head.

Nothing lasts. Nothing lasts. Even Nothing.

I looked at my mum. It was the first time I'd looked at her like that. As if she weren't my mum. As if she was another person. Her hair was tangled and she was smiling.

'Just in time for your tea,' she said. She held up her apron. It was full of potatoes. 'Look,' she said, 'our own new potatoes. You like new potatoes.'

'New potatoes, I said. 'Good. That's good.'

Cleaning Lady

R eturning from his holiday, he learned from the lady who served behind the counter in the Health food shop, that Dorothea had had a fall.

She was nervous of callers since Stefan had died but she had let him have a key. She trusted him absolutely. Once a week he'd got into the habit of dropping in on her.

'It's only me Dorothea,' he called up the stairs.

Her frail voice told him to come up.

He mounted the dark, narrow stairs and stood for a moment to get his breath back, taking in the small upstairs living room.

She sat draped in a blue blanket before the electric fire. The side of her face was swollen and blue and one of her eyes was almost closed.

She looked up at him smiling. 'Home is the sailor.'

'But not from the sea.'

'Always out and about,' she said. 'I'm green with envy.'

'Black and blue, I'd say.' He sat opposite her, leaning forward. 'My goodness what's happened to you?'.

'I had a fall. So silly of me. I was outside the bank and tripped on the pavement. An awfully kind lady helped me. I was quite the centre of attention. I was in hospital for three days. I shouldn't really go out on my own but you can't just stay in the house.'

'You see what happens when I'm away for a couple of weeks!' He smiled to make sure she got the irony.

He noticed the birthday cards on the small table at her side.

'You've had a birthday.'

'Wednesday.'

'And I missed it. I'm so sorry.'

'Oh it doesn't matter at all. Who wants to remember being seventy eight?'

She reached clumsily for one of the cards and handed it to him. Some of the others tumbled to the floor. He bent to pick them up. He noticed the trembling had worsened even in the two short weeks he'd been away.

'Margaret gave me this,' she said. 'Look inside.'

He unfolded the card. Inside was a black and white photograph of a handsome young woman.

'Is it Margaret?' he asked.

'Margaret! No it's me.'

'You!' He stared from Dorothea to the photograph and then back again. Gradually he was able to discern something of the lovely younger woman's features emerging out of Dorothea's bruised, aged face. She had been beautiful. Truly beautiful. And now...

Dorothea began to tell him of her long friendship with Margaret; how they had met at a Primary school in Norfolk. She told him of her childhood; her father's archaeological discoveries. He half listened, while the other half of his mind mused freely.

Could be me in nine years, he thought to himself. *Stuck at home with Parkinson's or some other ailment; being visited by stout, unattractive women from Meals on Wheels, shouting at me as though I were simple.*

Although after the bitter conclusion to his second marriage he had sworn never to marry again, the silence of his empty house was beginning to oppress him. The realisation grew in him that he needed a woman in his house. Good looking of course and younger than he; someone capable; a doctor or possibly a nurse. That would be useful. But at sixty nine, the chances grew remoter with every passing day. He still fancied himself as a ladies' man; still attractive and younger looking than his years. But with the passing years, the effort of projecting a younger man's demeanour required more and more concentration and effort. Whenever he saw an attractive woman, of no matter what age, approaching him on the pavement, he habitually straightened his back, lightened his stride and induced an alert curiosity to his manner. Sometimes he even broke into a trot to demonstrate his relative youthfulness, though the ladies in question rarely seemed to notice.

'You looked like a film star,' he said handing back the photograph.

She fluttered a self-deprecating hand.

He thought, fifty years ago we might have met by chance and become lovers. A gap of ten years was nothing when you were under thirty. Or even forty. After all Andrea, his second wife had been twenty five and he nearly forty when they married.

He resurfaced for an instant. Dorothea was telling him of a French lady who had escaped from Russia at the time of the revolution and whom her father had engaged out of charity, to teach Dorothea French. He nodded with a faint smile and then began ticking off the women in his life. As always when he reached the figure forty he became confused: wondering if he had counted some of them twice; who he had omitted. He abandoned the exercise. For the last eight years there had been nobody. He hated to admit it but it was probably his age. In Bodenhams changing room a month earlier, he had glanced up to see an elderly stranger struggling into a pair of trousers and been dismayed to discover it was his own reflection in the mirror.

He took to his bed for three days and began dyeing his moustache.

'God, seventy next birthday!'

He was surprised to hear his voice ringing round the room.

Dorothea interrupted her discourse to glance up at him in some surprise. 'You don't look it,' she said.

It was what he wanted to hear.

Three weeks earlier, wanting to know what to do with his money, he had enquired in a bank in Shrewsbury of a new high interest savings account. The lady on the other side of the desk was stout and in her fifties. Not his type at all. Too young anyhow. Wasn't she? But despite this he couldn't help showing, what he considered to be his best profile; moving and gesturing with an alertness that he imagined emphasised his youthfulness.

'How long would I have to leave the money in?' he enquired.

'Well,' the woman said, peering over her spectacles at the monitor, 'it's a bond you see. You'd be wise to leave it untouched for five years.'

'Five years!' he said. 'No good to me then.'

'Why's that?'

'I'm nearly seventy,' he said.

She sat back in her chair, raising her eyebrows. 'You're not!'

A current of pleasure and satisfaction ran through him which he was at some pains to conceal. And then to his own chagrin, he found himself leaning forward and saying, 'How old d'you think I look?' And immediately regretted it. He smiled to show that the matter was of little consequence to him; that it was a joke. Nevertheless he left a pause for her answer.

'Oh I don't know,' she said frowning. 'Sixty. Maybe less.'

Sixty! Maybe less! He mused as he closed the glass doors and issued into the street. Sixty! So, perhaps he should be looking for a woman of that age; or maybe younger. He drew back his shoulders and smiled out at the world; *fifty, fifty, fifty,* he sang. Covertly he glanced at the women who passed him; widening his net now to include those who might be in their fifties. Yes, he needed a woman in the house. And quickly. Soon it would be too late. A woman of, say fifty five? Would that be asking too much? *I think not,* he thought. *I think not indeed.* A woman who had retained her looks and her figure of course; someone capable; a doctor perhaps or possibly a nurse. One never knew what lay round the corner.

'A cleaning lady,' Dorothea said, taking the photo' from his hand.

He awoke from his reverie. 'Mmh?'

'It was Margaret put me on to her. Because I'm an old woman and have this silly Parkinson's, the council pays for her.

She's going to get me a fridge and a washing machine and I won't have to pay a penny. She's wonderful. Such a nice person.'

'A cleaning lady,' he said stifling a yawn. 'That's interesting.'

*

He awoke the next night after only an hour or so of sleep. His chest whistled and wheezed alarmingly when he breathed. He slept sitting up for the remainder of the night and in the morning he felt a little better. Nevertheless he decided to go to the doctor.

'I'm going to give you an inhaler,' the young doctor said. 'Use it night and morning. And I'll put you down for a flu jab. I wouldn't worry too much about it. Do you keep your house warm? That's very important you know. Cold is the killer when you get to your age.'

My age! What do you mean, my age? He bridled. *Talking to me as though I were one of those wretched pensioners huddled in the waiting room.*

But he took the prescription and said nothing.

Approaching his front door, he spotted a woman in a smart brown overcoat, struggling to fit the key into Dorothea's door. He wondered if she was the cleaning lady of whom Dorothea had spoken. But she looked too elegant and well dressed; though he had to admit to himself, his knowledge of modern cleaning ladies was rather limited. Her hair was honey-coloured and shiny and secured with a slide. What was she? Fifty? Maybe even a little younger. He hovered behind a parked van, observing, as she finally won the battle with Dorothea's obdurate lock and stepped through the door and closed it. Nice legs too, he thought. Not too thin. He abhorred thin legs; especially in the thigh area. He had never been out with a woman with thin thighs. Never. *And I'm not going to start now*, he thought with some determination. His mind wandered cheerfully through a sensuous forest of shapely female legs he had enjoyed in the past.

*

When he next saw Dorothea, later that week, he worked his way round to finding out about the lady visitor.

'Your front door's getting very sticky,' he said casually.

'It's always been difficult,' she said. 'Quite maddening,' She pronounced it in the manner of those English screen actresses of the forties; as though the "a" were an "e". 'My Stefan said he'd fix it but he never got round to it. He wasn't the most practical of men.'

He had met Dorothea's husband only two or three times, before he had suddenly died. Dorothea had come knocking at his door at midnight. 'I think Stefan's died,' she said and stood with both hands to her mouth in the middle of the room. It was he who arranged for an ambulance to call and helped her with the funeral arrangements. It had made something of a bond between them.

'Like me,' he said.

'Like me what?'

'Not very practical. All the best men are impractical. Never trust a practical man.'

'I'm sure you're right,' she said agreeably. 'But I miss him. It's awful to be lonely.'

He nodded. 'I mention the door because...well it doesn't matter for me because I've got the knack. It's just that I saw somebody on Thursday, a lady I think it was, and I couldn't help noticing she was having an awful struggle with the door.'

'Thursday?' she said. 'Oh that would be Diana.'

He deliberately misunderstood her. 'Ah Diana. She's your niece isn't she?'

She drew her head back. 'No, not my niece. Diana's my new cleaning lady.'

He waited for her to continue but she sat there in silence.

'Mrs Mopps didn't look as smart as that in my day,' he prompted, laughing.

'She is smart. You're right. I like her so much. It's not just that she's so capable and thorough but she talks to me. And she's so intelligent. She was quite a pianist when she was younger.'

The word younger induced an involuntary frisson in him.

'Younger? Well she doesn't look very old now.'

'That's what surprised me. She looks so young. But she told me she has two children over thirty.'

'Perhaps she married when she was very young.'

'Oh no, she told me. She was thirty.'

He performed the necessary calculations in his head, smiling and nodding the while. He wondered how to get round to the existence or non-existence of a husband.

'I think I saw her,' he said glancing out of the window, 'with her husband in the High Street the other day. Of course it might have been someone else. I don't have much of a memory for faces.'

'Oh no. Her husband died about three years ago.'

'Ah ha!' he said brightly; then swiftly collected himself and composed his face to sudden gravity. 'Oh dear,' he said. 'I'm so sorry.'

'Yes. She told me all about it. I was telling her about Stefan. And how helpful you'd been. And one thing led to another. She was quite tearful.'

He felt a pang of jealousy at this. Three years and still weeping for someone else!

Dorothea said, 'It seems incredible to me but she must be nearly sixty.'

'Sixty? Really?'

'I'm sure. How old did you think she was?'

The question jarred him with its directness. 'How old? I don't know. I hardly noticed her. It was just the lock I was worrying about.'

'Oh yes. That door. Quite maddening.' There was that "e" again.

'I'll see what I can do,' he said, rising to his feet. 'I'll try to get it done before she comes next time. Wednesday did you say?'

'Thursday. Thursday at eleven.'

'Not that it matters,' he said. 'I'll try and fix it before then.'

'Oh you are kind,' she said.

'What are neighbours for,' he said smiling.

She stood up as he left. It surprised him.

'Look at me,' she said spreading her arms and smiling. 'I'm feeling so much better today. It's these new pills the doctor prescribed. The trouble is, sometimes I forget to take them.' She put her hand on his arm. 'You don't realise how good just feeling almost normal is if you've been ill. Just to be normal is wonderful.' She held on to him and he felt her shaking through his body. She tapped his arm. 'Tomorrow I've a good mind to come and visit *you*.'

'The door's always open,' he said, though he knew she would never make it.

As he made his way carefully down the narrow, dark stairway, he repeated the word 'sixty' to himself over and over. Sixty, sixty, sixty.

December was coming on and there was frost in the air. Remembering the doctor's instructions he turned up the central heating. *Cheeky young pup.*

He made himself a cup of hot coffee.

He sat down and created in his mind the image of the lady cleaner with the soft shiny hair and the good legs. She wasn't a doctor of course. Or even a nurse. But she was evidently someone who could order his house. And then perhaps she had done some medical training. She looked the type: one of those women who attended classes on what to do if someone had a stroke or choked on a piece of meat. At the very least she'd keep the house up to scratch. The image of his mother drifted into his mind. He hadn't thought about her for years. But now she was there. He recalled how every Thursday she cleaned the brasses; laying them on newspapers on the dining room table;

pulling on stained gloves and rubbing them vigorously with Brasso until they gleamed. The memory of its smell pervaded his memory and for a moment a wave of sadness swept over him. He saw Diana, the cleaning lady with the good legs, performing the same task. Perhaps humming softly to herself as she worked. The sun beamed through the window.

He day-dreamed:

I'll wash those curtains next, she remarked and brought him the paper to where he sat sipping his coffee.

No, not the paper, he told her and pulled her over on top of him and she complied laughing.

The appealing vision faded and he couldn't get it back. He tapped the edge of his saucer with the spoon. Thursday, he said to the rhythm. Thursday at eleven. And then by way of variation. Sixty, sixty, sixty.

He fell asleep.

He dreamed of mending a large door that refused to open. Suddenly it wrenched free and fell on him. 'Oh my poor darling.' Diana, the cleaning lady, was dressed in a crisp nurse's uniform. She crouched like an Olympic weight lifter and with a grunt raised the door from his prostrate body. Her strength amazed him. Then she cradled him on her lap crooning softly. In his dream he looked up at her.

Legs, he whispered in her ear. You have lovely strong legs.

*

At five to eleven the following Thursday, he applied himself to mending the lock on Dorothea's front door. An icy wind blew up the narrow street between the rows of terraced houses. His eyes watered and he found it difficult to see what he was doing. The lock proved obstinate to remove and his cold hands fumbled at the work. He glanced at his watch. 11.15. He looked up and down the road. There was no sign of her. His nose ran with the cold. He stamped his feet. He decided to abandon the task. He returned the tools to his house and decided to walk up and down the street as though he were going somewhere. When she appeared he would look surprised and they would fall into a conversation about Dorothea. He would suggest she borrow his vacuum cleaner. Dorothea had remarked that hers was inefficient. He'd suggest she came round and pick it up whenever she needed it.

What a kind man you are, he heard her saying. She was smiling up at him.

He walked to the end of the street then paused, looking back. The cold was entering his bones. He pulled his collar up and stood in a doorway. A young girl with a bad complexion, delivering the free newspaper, looked at him suspiciously.

He retraced his steps and waited at the other corner. The exhaust fumes of the passing cars and buses hung white in the air. He walked back down the street again; to keep warm as much as anything. Then returned once more; five times. Still there was no sign of her. He swung his arms and blew into his cupped hands. Then he rubbed his eyes with his handkerchief.

Looking up, he finally discerned her blurred figure at the far end of the street. He returned his handkerchief to his pocket and set off in her direction, head down as though bent on some important errand. At the last moment he looked up, feigning surprise, managing to smile broadly despite the shivers that shook him. The bespectacled woman had a gaunt, raw looking face and was much taller than him.

'Sorry,' he said and moved aside to let her pass.

He looked at his watch once more. It was nearly twelve. He walked back to his house muttering angrily to himself. Who did she think she was? Keeping him waiting in the cold like this. And after he'd offered to lend her his vacuum cleaner. No vacuum cleaner for you my girl. And then more loudly than he intended. 'No vacuum cleaner at all.'

He looked about him. The street was empty.

Oh God, I'm talking to myself! he thought.

His house was warm and welcoming. He removed his overcoat and sat at the desk that looked out on the street, spreading the paper before him. *Well, she'd missed her chance. Oh yes, she'd missed it all right. And there were no second chances in this game, my girl. No never.*

It was then he heard Dorothea's door slam shut. He listened. He heard what he supposed were Diana's footsteps mounting the stairs. Voices. Then the faint purring of the vacuum cleaner. He waited. He was good at waiting. Hadn't he been waiting eight years? What was half an hour? He wondered how to manage the 'surprise' encounter. He could hardly rush out when he heard the door open; bump into her, face to face outside his own doorway. That wouldn't work; clumsy. Far too clumsy. She'd see through it in an instant.

At that moment he heard the Dorothea's door shut and saw the Cleaning Lady's handsome profile pass his window. Beautiful hair, he thought; beautiful, youthful hair. He opened his front door carefully and peeped out. She was turning the corner to the right; climbing up the street towards the shops and the town. There was no time for the overcoat. She'd be lost in the crowd in a moment. He ran towards the corner, turning up the collar of his jacket. He turned the corner and then withdrew instantly. She was staring into the Estate Agent's window; her face turned in his direction. She hadn't seen him. Or had she? He thought not. How shaming, he thought, if she caught sight of him stalking her furtively.

It made no sort of sense to come upon her from behind. That wasn't the strategy. He risked another peek. She was still at the window but now her back was towards him, talking to the lady vicar with the grey hair. What he had to do was meet her face to face. Then the surprised look. Then the conversation. So he had to overtake her; then approach her walking down the hill, as though on his way home. She was walking away now. In a tip-toed run, he crossed the street and ducking low behind the parked cars, ran up to the top of the High Street. Once he'd gained the higher ground he crossed to her side of the road. Looking back, he caught sight of her among the other pedestrians. She was about eighty metres from him, walking in a leisurely fashion in his direction, staring into the shop windows as she went. He put his head down, as though engrossed in thought, and moved rapidly in her direction. When he glanced up she was nowhere to be seen. He looked about him in case she had passed him unnoticed. *Can't have disappeared into thin air,* he thought with some irritation.

He continued down the street looking into each shop window as he went. And then he saw her emerging from the flower shop with a shop assistant in a blue house-coat. He made an immediate about turn without breaking his stride and walked back up the hill away from her. Oh God, he hoped she hadn't spotted him. He stopped in the doorway of the men's tailoring shop and glanced back down the street. She was still talking on the pavement, amongst pots of Christmas flowers. Then they both entered. He would wait. He had waited long enough already. He wasn't going to give up now. He would wait until she emerged carrying her bouquet of flowers and then walk down to meet her. The flowers would provide a convenient pretext for conversation. He began inventing one in his mind but his brain seemed numbed by the cold. He felt weak with it and his teeth chattered. He should have gone back for his overcoat. He blew on his hands once more and waited, stamping his feet. Then at last she emerged, the heads of the flowers poking colourfully from the hessian bag she carried. Casually, he began to stroll in her direction. But then, to his dismay, instead of walking up towards him she turned and walked down the street. Away from him. What was she up to now? He increased his pace. But she had crossed the road walking rapidly. On the opposite side of the road, she climbed into a small red Fiat and pulled away while he was still twenty metres away.

He stood watching, as the car turned the corner and disappeared from sight.

'Bloody Hells bastard bells and Fanny Martin,' he said aloud.

Then he began to cough. The coughing wouldn't stop. In the end he had to lean against the wall of the Bank, a handkerchief to his face.

'Are you all right?' asked the woman from the flower shop, touching his arm.

He pulled his arm away. He wanted to say. *—What d'you think? Of course I'm not all right. That's why I'm leaning on the wall coughing my guts up.*

But he could say nothing because of the coughing that wracked him.

At last he managed to stumble home. He turned up the central heating and ran himself a hot bath. He sat in the bath sipping at a tumbler of whisky, looking down at his old man's body. When he tried to get out, he found himself unable to raise his leg over the rim of the bath. He sat staring at the Nirvana of his longed-for bed, that seemed to beckon to him through the open door as the bath water emptied itself around him. At last he somehow managed to lever himself from the bath. The effort brought on another fit of debilitating coughing. He knelt down. It took him a full half an hour to crawl across the upstairs hallway to his bedroom and finally up into his bed. He pulled the coverlet up to his chin. And lay staring at the ceiling. Through his mind ran the vision of the women who had loved him. It was like a beguiling queue passing before his bleary eyes. And as they passed, they turned and shook their heads and smiled sadly before moving on. As always, as the fortieth women passed he began to lose count. He closed his eyes and tried to work out what it could all mean. What did anything actually mean? He had a feeling he was quite close to the answer but always, at the last moment, the great truth swooped out of his reach. Like a kite caught in a sudden gust of wind. Like that other question that always perplexed him: imagining nothingness.

He decided to postpone the pursuit until tomorrow. Now he was too tired. He closed his eyes slowly and something that wasn't sleep overtook him.

When Dorothea knocked at his door the next afternoon, there was no answer.

She tried again several times. Then she lifted the letter box and shouted his name.

He's probably out, she thought. Always out and about.

With the help of her stick and her hand on the wall, she returned to her house and shut the door.

Underpass

When Mr. Urban's car failed to start that Friday evening, his first thought was to ring for a taxi. But when he discovered that his mobile had discharged itself, he decided to walk to the Ringway and catch a bus home. He removed his briefcase and the flowers he had bought for his wife's birthday from the back seat, locked his car and walked out of the office car park towards the large traffic island. He experienced a pleasurable tremor of anticipation at the thought of travelling on a bus once more. How long ago was it since he had last travelled on a bus? He must have been a schoolboy. He had no idea what it might cost now. A pound? Perhaps two - or even more. Did they still have conductors? he wondered. He increased his pace, humming softly to himself. The exercise would probably do him good. There were railings to his right and a scrub of dishevelled lawn that ran down to high-rise blocks of flats. Each had a name: *Trident, Portland, Venice*. At the bus stop he glanced up at the time-table but the glass had been smashed. He had no idea which bus ran near his home. He would have to ask the bus driver. Beside the stop, was a machine instructing him how to buy a ticket. He took out his reading spectacles and as instructed, placed a pound coin in the slot and pressed the green button. It jammed. With some irritation he punched the machine with his gloved fist but it stubbornly refused to produce a ticket or to return his coin. When he dug into his trouser pocket he discovered a handful of small change but no pound coins. He looked in his wallet to discover the smallest note he had was £20. He prepared a tart answer for the anticipated objections of the conductor. The traffic poured by. Of course, he would never have dreamed of raising his thumb to beg for a lift, as he had often seen others do: students or unkempt tramp-like individuals, or middle-aged men clutching red number plates. However he faced the oncoming traffic with a half–smile hoping that someone he knew might recognize him and offer him a lift. Most of the cars contained only one driver and each stared fixedly ahead, pointedly ignoring him. Now he was a walker not a driver, how swiftly his sympathies switched. When he got his car back, he promised himself, he would look out for people like him, standing at bus stops. But he understood himself well enough to know that it was probably an empty vow. He turned up the collar of his overcoat and glanced at his watch. Nine-thirty. The night was turning cold. He began to look out for a taxi but the few that passed were all occupied.

An icy drizzle began to fall. He stamped up and down to keep his feet warm. At last he saw the welcome lights of a bus looming out of the mist and rain. He picked up his briefcase and stepped out onto the edge of the pavement holding the flowers out. Madge would laugh at that when he got home. He'd embroider the tale a little. 'Should have seen the driver's face when he saw me with my flowers...' He had time to see the numerous empty seats before the bus swept past without reducing speed. He gazed after it, cursing the driver. A biting wind had sprung up, whipping through the canyons between the tall buildings. Mr. Urban began to walk up and down again. Ten paces this way, ten paces back. Another bus swept by, ignoring him with an effrontery that was almost personal. The cold was entering his bones. He'd not long thrown off that nasty bout of bronchitis. Madge would be beginning to worry soon. He should phone her. He reached into his pocket and then remembered it was useless. He made a pact with himself. If the bus didn't come in ten minutes, he'd go and look for a phone booth. The paper that wrapped the flowers was drenched. A fire engine roared by, its bell clanging vigorously. He leant his back against the bus stop. A straggling gang of youths lurched by shouting and pushing one another. Why did they try so hard to look ugly? One of them stopped and shouted something at him. He looked fixedly in the other direction. One urinated onto the grass, making no attempt to turn away from the passing traffic. The others laughed. Ignore them and they'll go away, Mr Urban thought. After a short while they did, one of them banging at the railing with his stick. Ten thirty. He'd been waiting for over an hour. Two buses. What did he pay his rates for? Or was it private now? He couldn't remember. There was just too much news to keep up with. His head couldn't hold it all.

A pack of stray dogs scampered across the road and onto the huge traffic island, barking and chasing one another. The ten minutes had passed. He should phone Madge. Wasn't there a phone booth on the other side of the Ringway? He decided to find out. When he reached the subway he broke into a run, a determined expression on his face, as if he had a train or a bus to catch. Emerging on the other side, he was relieved to discover that he had been right about the phone-booth. As he approached, he noticed that it was occupied by a man in a torn overcoat who was leaning heavily on the glass wall. The receiver was still in its cradle. Mr Urban tapped on the door. The man did not look up. Then his body heaved convulsively. He was vomiting. Mr Urban shivered and hurried on. He seemed to remember that there was another phone on the northern extremity of the Ringway. There was no subway this end. He would have to walk all the way round.

Half way round he darted and shuffled across the dual carriageway, avoiding the racing traffic as best he could. It took him nearly ten minutes to reach the second booth. Madge could get a taxi from home and pick him up at a pre-arranged spot. That would be best. He placed the flowers and his brief case onto the floor of the booth before digging into his trouser pocket for some coins. The pages of the phone book were scattered on the floor and the booth smelled of stale tobacco and urine. It was one of those new-fangled phones. You put in your money before you phoned. Then followed the instructions. But he found difficulty reading the instructions in the gloom. Where were his glasses? He managed to find a 10p coin and pressed it into the slot. It was a relief to hear Madge's familiar voice reciting their number as she always did. He interrupted her saying, 'Madge, it's me.' But she carried on until she had finished the number.

'Madge it's me. I've only got 10p so just listen.'

'Hello.'

'Look Madge could you come and pick me up?'

'Hello who's speaking please?'

'It's me Madge. You'd better take down...'

'Robin? Is that you? I was beginning to get worried.'

'Madge? Listen. I...Hello. Hello.'

The phone droned. Uselessly he said 'hello' three more times and then replaced the phone in its cradle. Searching carefully through all his pockets he found only pennies and 5p coins. He leaned his head against the door. The feeling began to rise in him that he might never escape from this place. The high buildings, the isolation, the unheeding traffic oppressed him with a mild sense of panic. Could he walk it? What alternative was there? Better than staying in this awful place. What was walking speed? Four miles per hour? No, probably less. Glancing at his watch he began to calculate. He'd be home by quarter to twelve at the latest. Madge would worry of course. Especially after that interrupted telephone call. Perhaps she would trace the call and ring him back. But then he thought, *She'll probably think I'm on my mobile*. He had a vague memory that even if it was discharged it would continue to operate for emergencies, especially for incoming calls. He searched in his jacket pocket and then all his other pockets. He realised that in his anxiety he must have left it on the seat of his car.

He decided to walk. If, on the way, he passed a bar he could nip in and phone home from there.

Yes he would walk.

He looked about him. Where was he? Strange how you could lose your bearings in an area so familiar. The rain had stopped but the wind was remorseless. From the North. 'We shall have snow,' he muttered to himself. 'And what will poor Robin do then poor thing?' He decided to take the underpass. That's what he'd do. There was the old fire station. He turned himself round orientating himself. His way lay South; South and a little East. He made his way towards the mouth of the underpass and descended the steps. There was hardly any light. At the bottom of the steps he put down the flowers and his briefcase and he wiped the rain off his glasses and polished them. The walls were tiled in a dreary yellow. Torn hoardings had been scribbled over with obscenities. There was a large poster of a girl sitting at a typewriter. She was advertising a deodorant. Down one side someone had scribbled obsessively over and over again, *I'll get you. I'll get you...* Ten times.

He walked on slowly. The incessant choiring of the wind made him think of a cold uncharitable chapel. On the wall at the bottom of the steps was printed a list of street names. The one he was looking for wasn't mentioned. An arrow pointed towards the city centre. His route lay away from that area. He set out determinedly. The underpass was longer than he imagined. At one point some steps rose sharply to the left but he suppressed an urge to climb into the fresh air and continued on his way. There was a patter of feet: the pack of stray dogs he had seen earlier appeared. He'd always liked dogs; and they'd liked him. Idiotically, he had a sense that these dogs would be aware of this. But they growled at him, lips drawn back against their teeth, their heads thrown back and to one side. They threatened him with a diffident, skulking aggression. He drew into the shadows, holding his briefcase before him. But a fight broke out between two members of the pack and the remainder turned their attention to watch. They panted and their red tongues lolled. Occasionally they approached the combatants sniffing them with nervous curiosity. The fight became a chase and the pack set off in baying pursuit. The sound of barking diminished and then there was silence.

The underpass curved gently to the right. It was darker. He heard the sound of dragging footsteps accompanied by an incoherent growling. At first, he thought one of the dogs was returning. Then he saw the tramp he had seen earlier in the phone-booth. He held a bottle to his lips. He walked as he drank; dragging his feet and sliding his right shoulder along the wall for support. Then he stopped and leaned his back on to the wall. He gazed upwards vacantly, muttering to himself. A yellow stream trickled from the bottom of his ragged trousers over his shoes and across the floor. Suddenly the dogs could be heard once more. Mr. Urban broke into a shambling run, not daring to look back. He was relieved to see steps rising before him. He felt the cold increase as he ascended. The paper about the flowers was now sodden and torn. One of the stalks slipped to the floor but he didn't stop to pick it up. At the top of the steps black, plastic refuse bags were piled high, one on top of another, their contents leaking across the ground. A large piece of corrugated cardboard, whipped by the wind, wrapped itself about his chest and face. His eyes watered and he had to stop in order to wipe them. Finally with a sigh of relief he emerged into the night air. He found himself on a crumbling pathway bordering a highway that was lined with hurdles, piles of cinders and aggregate. Strange, he thought, to find such dishevelment so close to the city centre. He recognised no landmarks. How harsh and alien it all was. His nose was running with cold. He stopped to blow it, looking up and round as he did so. He walked cautiously. The unmade road seemed to be disappearing altogether. Looking up, he found himself beneath an iron, bridge-like structure. The mist and darkness pressed in upon him. He continued for some fifty yards until brought up short by a flotilla of rusty, abandoned cars, piled oil drums and heaps of tyres. Beyond them was a high wire fence. He looked down at his watch but there was insufficient light by which to read it. He raised it to his ear. It had stopped anyway. He cursed and turning, fell clumsily as he caught his ankle on the jagged wing of a car. He gave a cry of pain and fell to his knees. Putting his fingers to the source of the pain he felt the sticky warmth of blood upon them. His trousers were torn and the pain in his ankle forced him to limp. He felt sick.

He was determined not to go down into the underpass again. There must be a way out. Surely he would soon come upon a familiar landmark. He stopped and listened. He heard the hum of distant traffic. He climbed the bridge but after struggling up a few steps he found to his dismay that a network of scaffolding barred his way. There was nothing for it but to return the way he had come. As he reached the top of the steps once more, somewhere in the distance, he heard a thin, almost lilting, reedy laugh, utterly strange, high and without humour. He shivered at the sound of it. It wasn't just the cold that made him shiver. As he reached the bottom of the steps he was horrified to see the dogs once more. They were piled one on top of the other against the wall. From their throats came murmurs of concentrated intensity. They worked in the way that creatures will when the habit of their being has occupied their souls. Occasionally, one moved away from the pack with something in its mouth. It attacked the meat with savage lunges, wrenching its head to the side while holding the meat down with both paws. He could not see the carcass of the beggar at all, though part of his clothing lay close by, and an empty wine bottle was spilled in the guttering. As silently as he could, he crept by, his back to the wall. But the dogs were too preoccupied with their task to concern themselves with him. They did not even raise their heads. Had he wished he could have walked by quite boldly but he thought of the blood on his leg and was wary. When he was clear, he broke into a run until the underpass hooked to the left and the dogs could no longer see him. He thought about the scene he had just witnessed. His reaction was mild disquiet rather than horror. 'I have just seen a human being torn to pieces by dogs,' he said aloud. Yet he remained relatively unmoved. He was more disturbed by his own predicament; the thought of Madge waiting for him at home. He still carried the flowers. He sunk his face into the petals and inhaled deeply. There was solace in their scent.

He trudged onwards. The return journey seemed longer but he thought that might have been because of the pain in his leg.

Even so, and making all allowances for the cold and his fear, he must have walked a mile. At one point he bent down to inspect his leg. There was a deep gash just above the ankle. A thin tongue of flesh hung down, and there was blood on his trousers. He bound the wound clumsily in his handkerchief and limped slowly on. The thought came to him once more that he might never escape from this dreadful place. Thus it was, with a kind of resignation, that he discovered his way barred by a heavy iron gate. He slumped there for some minutes, his hand hooked through the bars, gazing into the darkness. His mind was blank and he realised he was crying. But there were no tears. After an interval of gazing dully thus, he turned and limped back the way he had come, with the vague intention of turning up the steps he had passed some time earlier. The flowers had by now completely lost their wrapping paper; some of the stalks slipped from his hand. He made no attempt to collect them but trudged on unheeding. His fatigue was a weight in him. He had lost all track of time. How long was it since he had left the office? He tried to compute but his mind was too fatigued to sustain the attempt. His feet dragged. He closed his eyes wearily and walked on using his hand to support himself against the wall.

When the stick struck him, it came almost as a relief and he slumped to the floor. He saw the face of a boy of fourteen staring down at him, his eyes wide with a kind of desperate joy. A second blow crashed down across his face. He lost consciousness. When he came to, his overcoat and jacket were gone. The contents of his briefcase lay scattered about the floor. He raised his right hand to his head and tenderly touched the huge bump and torn flesh across his nose and forehead. He smelled blood on his fingers. There was a terrible pain in his abdomen and groin. His left arm ached unbearably when he tried to raise it and would not move. He presumed it was broken. There was something on his face. Something wet over his eye and cheek. He lifted his right hand frantically and clumsily brushed it away. It was the damp remains of one of the flowers. The remainder lay scattered about him. His head roared. He tried to shout but there was too much pain in his belly and chest. A thin, mechanical groan emerged from deep within him. Through the noises his body was making, he heard something else. Someone approaching. Many people; but softly as if on slippered feet. He tried to cry out once more but only a feeble groan emerged from his throat. He did not seem to be able to move his lips properly. He wondered if he was paralysed. The sound was nearer. These people, they would find him. Someone would call an ambulance. He must remember to tell them to phone Madge. He was hurt but he would survive. Laboriously he hauled himself to his feet. His pain made dribbles of sound in his throat and chest.

The first of the dog pack did not blink. His jaws were open and he was panting slightly. His breath hung on the dank air. The others massed behind him, shifting and merging. Their jaws too were open.

They appeared to be smiling.

South to that Dark Sun

As Constable Reddy clambered down the bank he heard a voice coming from the crashed car.

'We got a woman still alive in here,' he shouted back up the bank. 'Looks like she turned left instead of right. Get that ambulance here fast.'

The car lay capsized in the early morning wheat field. A stray hen stood clucking nervously on one of the battered doors that now stared up at the cold, January sky. It fluttered away squawking as the constable approached. When he flashed his torch through the crazed window, his experience told him right away that the driver was dead. He was slumped hard against the steering wheel, the head twisted beyond a point where heads are supposed to go. The flesh beside the right ear was torn open exposing a pink jaw bone and broken teeth. There was little blood. The eyes stared dull and unblinking into the yellow beam of the constable's flashlight; dead eyes. He was the only occupant. Yet the woman's voice still rang calm and clear from the speakers: a husky voice; rich dark and seductive as chocolate.

'Listen up honey. Next turnin' y'all going South off the turnpike, hear? Going to be home real soon.'

The soft voice continued to repeat the phrase to the lightening, morning sky, as the ambulance carried the driver's body away to the nearest hospital.

Even though his face was so savagely broken as to be almost unrecognisable, one of the older nurses at the hospital knew him immediately. 'It's Terry Arkari,' she whispered.

'Who?'

'He used to be somebody.'

'Well now he's nobody, just like the rest of us,' a young doctor muttered.

'At least we're alive,' said another.

'Speak for yourself,' said the young doctor.

The nurse was dabbing her eyes. She shook her head with embarrassment. 'It was just that he was part of my youth,' she sobbed. It was the first time she had cried over a patient. She didn't cry for long. It was she who embraced and kissed the singer's wife, Laura, when she came to identify the body.

That night the television news carried a brief item on his death. Another former rock star had hit the buffers. His name was added to the pantheon of others who had shared a similar fate; fallen from the skies in tumbling aeroplanes; overdosed on drugs; wrapped their cars, like T.A., round telegraph poles or trees.

The next day, few of the national papers thought the story important enough to cover at any length; after all he was yesterday's star; a has-been. By the end of the week, apart from his wife, his son, his former band members and a few die-hard fans, he was forgotten. In the popular music encyclopaedias of the future, the entry against his name would be cruelly brief:

Arkari, Terry. Lead singer with blues based band 'Nemesis'. Three albums mid seventies. 'Nemesis 1' reached number 5 in the National Charts. Top 3 single 1978. Killed in car crash.

That was it; a life in two-and-a-half lines.

*

Terry was ten years old when he fell in love with the Blues; it was a love affair that lasted a lifetime. His mother and father had separated when he was seven and, after his mother had died three years later, he had been brought up by his grandparents. It was his grandfather who imbued him with a love for the Blues. In his youth he had been a steward on a Blue Funnel boat out of Liverpool and had built up a large collection of obscure blues records that he'd brought back with him from the States: Robert Johnson, Leadbelly, Ma Rainey, Sister Rosetta, Bessie Smith: performers none of the other kids at Terry's school had even heard of. He was considered something of an oddity and had enjoyed being one. He became an encyclopaedia of information on the South and its music. Where his contemporaries pinned up shots of the current sports or pop stars, the walls of Terry's tiny bedroom were plastered with faded black and white photographs culled from magazines and newspapers: pictures of old black men from long ago crouching dolefully over battered six string guitars. From the wall above his bed Bessie Smith, in her looped pearls and long white dress, stared down imperiously over the young Terry as he slept; a Blues Madonna. Scattered amongst these 'heroes' were other pictures: shadowy, atmospheric depictions of Southern shanty towns; of rusting Chevrolets and Studebakers, abandoned besides fading finger posts and deserted railroad crossings on the fringes of Montgomery, Baton Rouge or Shreveport. On the back of his door he pinned a map of the South. He loved to repeat to himself the strange, beguiling names of those small, far-away townships. He would mutter them to himself like a litany before he slept: Evangeline, Vermilion, Lafayette, Pearl River, Tishomingo. So in love was he with that region, that era - that for a time he even cultivated a vaguely Mississippi accent that sat oddly with his native Northern inflections. For his fourteenth birthday, his granddad bought him a second-hand guitar. From then on, like Mary and her little lamb, they were never apart. Wearing a moody, discontented expression, he would carry it carelessly by the neck, slung loosely over his shoulder. When he had his photograph taken, he posed like his hero, Robert Johnson: his fingers spread along the frets; a cigarette dangling from the left corner of his mouth; staring out at the world, an expression of hope and detachment on his young face.

By the time he was fifteen he had put together a band of sorts who would rehearse in the School hall after the dining tables had been cleared. In a surprisingly raw, husky voice, pale– faced, bespectacled and acne-sprinkled, he would bellow forth strings of songs that spoke of what it was like to be poor, lonesome, black and living in America. The songs rose to the rafters of the high-ceilinged dining hall, mingling their forlorn heartache with the sickly fragrance of English school dinners, whose savour still hung on the air. As time went on, it became a normal thing, each Tuesday dinner time, for a small crowd of pupils to gather at these rehearsals. A few of the girls started dancing; others stood swaying at the foot of the stage, gazing up at Terry. And Terry, his eyes closed in rapture, utterly immersed in the imagery and landscape of his music, studiously ignored them all.

The road from obscurity to fame was surprisingly smooth. Two years after leaving school, the band was signed up by a small, local record company, run by a plump, moustachioed entrepreneur called Steve Fisher, who kept advising them to - *Trust him.* Hell bent on commercial success, he coerced them into forgetting about the Blues, encouraging them to write and play their own songs.

That's where the money is, guys, Steve would intone. *Trust me.*

And Terry, not without a certain sense of betrayal, went along with it, because there was no real alternative. But he trusted nobody; least of all Mr Steve Fisher. And Steve knew it. And Terry knew that he knew. So it astonished them all when their first single somehow made it to thirty in the charts. A larger record company came in and weaned them away from Steve who, slipping the compensatory cheque into his drawer, asked them sadly: *What ever happened to loyalty, guys?*

Their first album made the top five. They were on the crest of a wave. Terry had his photograph on the cover of *Melody Maker. The New Musical Express* ran a special feature on his songs and his unique guitar style. They starred on Top of the Pops; did interviews; they toured the Continent but never alas America.

Terry spent a large part of his advance on a three bedroom house with a garden and some assorted statuary, on the edge of town, sharing it with Dave Metheny, his sometime co-writer and keyboard player. Despite their evident good fortune, they still, from time to time, expressed discontent: comparing their lot unfavourably, as young men always will, with others whom they considered to be, undeservedly, more successful, more fortunate than themselves. In addition they were deluded into thinking that their hold on fame would somehow last forever; or at least until they were thirty, which, when you are eighteen, is what *for ever*, tends to look like. But fame in the poplar music industry, is often measured in months; sometimes even in weeks.

A number of their fans attributed the start of the band's decline to the appearance of Laura. But this would be unfair; *post hoc propter hoc* - rather than causality. A social secretary at Leicester University, Laura had booked the band for a New Year's Eve gig. She was beautiful, capable and intelligent and both Dave and Terry had fallen for her. But it was Terry's melancholy contrariness, his odd charisma that had won her. Dave considered she'd made a mistake. After all he had two 'A' levels and, as *wordman* and resident intellectual of the band, penned the lyrics of the songs that he and Terry wrote together. However, not wishing to appear a loser, he concealed his feelings under a cloak of indifference; successfully he thought.

After graduating, Laura's influence grew. It began innocently enough with her taking over the organisation of the gigs and keeping the books. But then, after she had moved in with Terry, it emerged that she could not only play piano with some competence but also manage harmonies. Terry thought her voice and presence added something; an opinion not shared by the rest of the band. She was featured on gigs, singing a song that she and Terry had written together. Dave was not impressed. Most of the other band members were uncertain about this new development but they could see how things were between Laura and Terry and so sat on their doubts. Terry had a ferocious temper when crossed, and his drinking was beginning to make his behaviour even more unpredictable. From behind his piano, Dave observed all this and wondered to himself how he could ever have found Laura attractive. He felt himself being pushed aside. Even so, it came as an unpleasant shock, when an A&R man from the Record Company called him one afternoon and told him that his services were no longer required. His rankling resentment overflowed and he savagely dialled Terry's number.

'What's this about Laura playing piano instead of me?'

'Aw Dave man, it's not me, it's the record company.'

'Your band, man. You could have said no.'

'Yeah, that's right, Dave. No was an option.'

'So why didn't you?'

'Why didn't I? Because I didn't want to.'

'Thought we was mates.'

'Us being mates doesn't make you a good player.'

'Could have told me yourself, Terry. Least you could have done.'

'What would you want me to tell you, Dave? That we've got someone better?'

'Why not?'

'Okay! We got somebody better. Does that make it all right? Can we get on with our lives now?'

'No,' Dave snapped. 'No it isn't all right. It's anything but all right.'

There was a silence. Terry sighed. 'You know what this about, Dave? It's not about the band. It's about Laura isn't it?'

In his heart, Dave knew Terry was right; *especially* in his heart. He hated him knowing. Maybe Terry was smarter than he thought. He stared at the wall before striking it hard with his fist. Then he put the phone down. For a year after that, whenever the phone rang and he heard Terry's voice on the other end, he put the phone down without speaking.

Perhaps he was lucky to get out when he did. At least he could watch from afar with a certain measure of detachment, as the band's fortunes went into meltdown. And *he* knew it wasn't Laura's fault. Not really. It was simply that they had had their moment; and now it was over. Their second album managed to scrape into the lower reaches of the charts only because a hefty chunk of the Record Company's publicity budget forced it there. And when the 3rd album bombed, the Company exercised its option and foreclosed on the deal. Terry fuelled with anger and vodka stormed into the office and shouted and hammered on the table: *There were plenty of other companies only too happy to sign them up.* The executives smiled distantly and told him he was welcome to try. And so he did. But all the doors he knocked on remained obdurately shut.

And that was it. Fortune having beckoned them with a seductive crook of her finger, now had little compunction in

head-butting them back into the oblivion from whence they had
so recently emerged.

*

And so, in a little over two years, they were back where they
started: playing in pubs, social clubs and holiday camps. In the
mid eighties they had a brief revival, when an international
manufacturer of power tools featured one of their old hits in
on a T.V. advertising campaign. But it didn't last. Terry went
back to playing the Blues. He insisted on it, even against the
wishes of the band and the boos of such fans as remained, who
wished only to hear the old familiar hits. Evading the insults and
the occasional hurled bottle, Terry stood centre stage, roaring
out the songs that nurtured his soul; blasting them out in that
characteristic hoarse voice of his, with a defiance that was
almost heroic in its recklessness. But the defiance required
something more than heroism to sustain it. What sustained it
was three bottles of vodka a day, a flirtation with hallucinogenics
and more funny cigarettes than were strictly good for him. One
night at a small social club in Birmingham, he suddenly stopped
in the middle of a number. The words were hidden somewhere
in the dark passages of his brain but the messengers he sent out
couldn't locate them. The band looked at one another uncertainly
and stuttered to a silence. Terry stared out at the screaming
audience. His face contorted with contempt and anger. He
spoke into the microphone: 'That was for Robert Johnson.' The
crowd was oddly silent. 'Robert Johnson, Robert Johnson…'

Over and over he repeated the revered name. There was screaming feedback on the mic. He hurled his guitar into the bemused audience and would have stormed off, if he hadn't fallen headlong from the stage onto a hostile bed of red, yelling faces and upraised fists.

It was a breakdown that had been waiting to happen for some years. The recuperation, as such, took three years. If it hadn't been for Laura, most of his friends believed, he would have been institutionalised. Or dead. Back home he lived life like a pensioner: pottering about the house; spending long hours in the small summer house staring at nothing in particular and, generally speaking, not even seeing that. But then, the urge grew in him to play once more. After all, it was the only life he knew. Against Laura's wishes he went back on the road with a new band, playing the music he loved. His experience had changed him. He was quieter, more affable. But his amiability was strangely unsettling. Instead of vodka, he consumed, endless mugs of tea and smiled a great deal. Yet the alcohol and the drugs had buried a legacy in his thickening body. He found it difficult to make decisions; to keep appointments. He was habitually dilatory. And worst of all for Laura, lying awake in the early hours, waiting for the grate of his key in the front door, he seemed to have lost his sense of direction; literally. At four or five o'clock in the morning the phone would ring, jerking her into bleary wakefulness. 'Yes?' she would mumble fearfully into the mouthpiece, her heart thumping with dread; expecting the voice of some stranger; some anonymous policeman to say with a hesitant sympathy: *Is that Mrs Arkari.*

Mrs Laura Arkari? I'm afraid we have bad news. It's about your husband.

But always, thankfully, it was Terry's familiar voice, ringing from Dumfries or Plymouth or Norwich; telling her he had driven three times round some sleeping suburb and was unable to find his way out; or had found himself inexplicably on the wrong motorway driving in a direction that was taking him even further away from his destination. *Can't understand it, babe. What they keep moving these roads about for?*

And yet the anxiety she felt was somehow more akin to what she might feel for an errant child than for a husband; a sexual partner. On an impulse, she rang Dave one evening and told him her worries. They were friends once more by this time and after all he knew Terry better than anybody. She was surprised to hear herself saying: 'It's like having *two* children. Only one can drive, get lost, and play in a band. What's more I have to sleep with him.'

Hearing the weary anxiety in her voice Dave felt an overwhelming compulsion to tell her that he loved her; that he had always loved her.

'I…' He hesitated.

Into the lengthy silence she said, 'Dave? You there?'

'Yeah. Yeah I'm here. I just wanted to say. Laura I…' He hesitated again. 'I…I'll have a word.' He laughed. 'Not that it will do much good. You know Terry.'

Yes, she knew Terry.

The anxiety, the lack of sleep, the draining away of her love was beginning to affect her life, her work. She had begun to make something of a name for herself: interpreting statistics at the University Institute of Occupational and Environmental Medicine. She was now the real bread-winner of the family. There was really no need for Terry to drive continuously from one end of the country to the other, being paid a pittance. And yet, on the other hand, she feared what might become of his state of mind, without the music; the camaraderie of musicians on the road.

When she was invited to deliver a paper at the University of Mississippi she asked Terry if he would like to come with her. 'It's the South Terry. Mississippi. It's what you've always dreamed of.'

But Terry, with a shake of his head had, tapped his forehead. 'It's up here see, darlin'. Dreamland. And that's where I want it to stay.'

And so she had travelled on her own. Their young son went to Laura's grandparents, while Terry moved into a local hotel, with instructions to the staff to keep an eye on him.

One afternoon Laura found herself hurrying for shelter from a sudden downpour into a tin-roofed store called *The Voodoo Shack*. Looking about her, she discovered she was the only white person in the place; the only *white woman*. But the staff were courteous and friendly. Their languid, musical voices telling her – *I just love the way you talk*.

It was mutual.

She took in the interior, thinking it would make a good story when she got home. The rain drummed on the corrugated roof. The thunder cracks sounded as if they had found their way inside. Surprisingly - among the tawdry voodoo bric-a-brac, the potions and oils, the painted dolls on sticks, the spells, the magic candles and incense; the juju's and the gris gris – was an incongruous motoring boutique, displaying monstrously oversized, heavily-sculpted, whitewall tyres, zebra-striped seat covers featuring the larger than life countenances of Marvin Gaye and Sam Cooke; garishly blinking side mirrors and even a Martin Luther King bouncing effigy that could be attached to the rear view mirror.

And then, as she was inspecting this odd assortment of merchandise, a velvety voice behind her said: 'Where y'all going to take me today, sugar?' It was a soft honey–flavoured voice that hovered on that divide where human speech melts into melody. But when she looked round, there was nobody. Her consternation must have shown on her face. The large assistant in the flowered dress hurried over. 'Soul Sister Betty Satellite Navigation,' she announced turning up the volume on the device. 'You ever hear anythin' pretty as that? You just take Soul Sister Betty in the car with you - she gonna make damn sure you ain't never gonna git lost while she's around.' She was instantly grave. 'An' just supposin' you was to git lost, ain't no big deal, seeing how you got Soul Sister Betty here to comfort your solitude.' She laughed uproariously, bending double, her hands slapping her knees, her skin taking on a purplish hue.

Laura was thinking about Terry and his early morning peregrinations; the sleepless nights; the alarming phone calls. 'I'll take it,' she said decisively.

'Mmh Mmh!' the assistant shook her head. 'Nice lookin'

lady like you. What you need is Soul Brother Marvin. That's what most the sisters here pick up on.'

'No,' Laura replied firmly, unconsciously aping something of the large assistant's cadences, 'This is for my man. Soul Sister Betty will do just fine.'

*

It was while Terry was driving back during the early hours, from a gig in Derbyshire some six months later, that Soul Sister Betty spoke to him. Of course in a general way, ever since Laura had unwrapped his gift, Soul Sister Betty had always done this; after all that was her function. He'd loved her from the day he'd first activated the device. There had been a burst of scudding sax, wailing over the heavy bass line and then Soul Sister Betty's entrancing, languid voice emerging from the speakers:

Hi. Another day. Another journey. Soul Sister Betty is here to help you make it safe and sound to your chosen destination. I'm cool, I'm real relaxed and I'm ready. I sure hope you are too. So, where we going this time, my man?

'I love it,' he'd said hugging Laura, before tapping in the details of his journey.

He loved the *we* in that sentence: wher*e we* going? He had the impression that this dulcet-toned, easy-going *ghost in the machine* was going to be travelling with him. Everywhere. His compadre. His honey-tongued navigator: Soul Sister Betty, who would ease the tedious rigours of the journey with her softly humorous injunctions to – make a right or left or to go straight ahead.

'Show me the way,' he would get into the habit of singing out to her.

And that is what she always did.

And driving along through the night, her voice served to evoke for him something of the topography of the Old South. A South that in truth, had no real existence, since it was a dream landscape that had tenanted his thoughts, like a faded daguerreotype, ever since he had been a boy. In the far reaches of his mind, that's where the South had always lived. And her voice, with its mundane directions, somehow opened a door onto that dream kingdom: evoking for him long dusty, shimmering roads between cotton fields; the shanty towns; the honky tonks; and over it all the sound of plangent guitars and black plaintive voices. It was a world made of shadows and yet stubbornly indestructible, since the dreamer instinctively understood that the vision could only survive if uncorrupted by any confrontation with reality.

At first he accepted her instructions in silence, enjoying her infallibility. But then gradually, as his familiarity with the device grew, he found himself responding to her instructions with tiny comments:

Whatever you say sugar, he would mutter. Or - *You're the boss, Betty.*

And as they approached a road sign, knowing she was primed to instruct him, he learned to anticipate her response with an appropriate question: 'Where to now, babe?'

And she would reply instantly and reassuringly: *We all gonna make a left here.*

'Left it is, sugar.'

It was a conversation. Of sorts. It amused him and helped pass the time. Then gradually, with familiarity, his part in the 'conversation' increased. What the hell, he thought. There was just him, the road, the darkness and Soul Sister Betty. And she didn't care what he said. It was how he wanted it. Over the months, his brief questions, his arch responses - lengthened into monologues. He began to tell her how much he enjoyed having her along for the ride; what great company she was; that he loved her. He would share his private thoughts about the band; of how his voice was standing up; of incidents from his past; of his doubts about his current bass player or drummer: whether he should replace them or not. Sometimes he'd sing to her or join in with a song he'd picked up on a Country radio station as the headlights sliced through the darkness:

Driving with my baby, driving South to that dark sun
Driving with my baby, yeah South to that dark sun
See Robert Johnson at the crossroads
With a guitar and a gun.

The Blues is a highway and the Blues can set you free
Yeah the Blues is a highway and the Blues can set you free
See Robert Johnson at the crossroads
And he's awaiting there for me.

And returning from Derbyshire, that early morning, he began, for the first time, to talk about himself and Laura:

'You see Betty I can talk to you about these things. Because, you know, they're important. Laura's not too interested. Well not that I blame her. She's got a heavy job and everything. Well it's even stevens. I don't talk about *her* work. Well that's because I can't understand what she's on about half the time. Not that I'm being disloyal or anything. It's just a fact. What you think of that?'

And after a moment, as if pausing for thought, Soul Sister Betty replied: *You gonna make a right off the turnpike real soon. You ready for this?*

''Course I'm ready Betty. You know I'm always ready. Ready for anything.'

Here it comes honey. Hook right nice and easy.

'How's that Soul Sister?'

You got it, boy. Now you keep on doin' what you're doin'. You don't have to worry about a thing for five long, sweet miles now. Y'all wanna know when you gonna git home?

'You tell me Sister.'

'Way I see it, honey. Gonna be home by half past three.'

And as Betty fell silent, he would leave a message on his mobile for Laura.

'Me and Betty are making good time. I'll be home just after three this morning. I love you.' He paused, then added on an impulse, 'But do you still love me? I hope so.'

He switched off the phone and feeling the grit of sleep in his eyes opened a window to let a rush of cold air strike his face. Then he began to muse aloud once more to Soul Sister Betty.

'Of course Laura's a terrific person. Beautiful too. And you know she saved me. Wasn't for her I don't know where I'd be. Dead I guess. No two ways about it. But, I don't know, we don't talk like we used to. You know what I mean. Really talk. I mean maybe it's my fault. I get the feeling she doesn't love me any more. What d'you think, Betty?'

Gonna have to make a change real soon, my man. Change down and make a right at the traffic circle that's coming up.

He did as he was instructed. As he always did.

Atta boy.

'Yeah thanks. What was I saying? Oh yeah - about Laura. You know, her work, well it's her life now. I think it's her main thing. Don't get me wrong, Betty. She looks after me. But I get a feeling it's a duty for her now. I sort of come second. We used to be terrific in bed. But now she comes home and she has work to do. And then she's tired. You know how it is. And I'm not what I was. And what am I? I'm only fifty something. That's nothing. These days. But you know, I'm not up for it like I used to be. You should have known me in my prime. All that booze and the drugs did for my libido. But don't get me wrong. I don't regret it. I had a great time. I wouldn't change anything. But you pay for it in the end. Like you pay for everything. But the way I see it, Betty, the paying was worth it. I'm not going to bad-mouth on my past. You know what I mean. It was really worth it.'

And Soul Sister Betty seductively intoned, *Got a crossroad comin' up. And you know what you gonna do here. We gonna make a left onto the Highway at the Intersection.*

And Terry, as always, did as he was instructed. Safely on the motorway, he once more took up the conversation. 'You know Betty, I haven't told this to anybody. I think I'm a different person. I'm steadier. I'm what she always wanted me to be. Isn't that funny? But I've lost something. I know that. An edge if you like. That's the worst thing. But there's nothing I can do about it. Nothing. That's the price I pay for not being dead or rotting away in some loony bin. The funny thing is - though Laura would never say it - I think she misses it too. You know that edge. Of course, she worries about me. But she worries like she worries about the kid; about little Robert. And you know, sometimes I'm lying in bed at night thinking about these things. And I sneak a look at her sleeping, you know. And I feel...I feel...'

You gonna go down hill here for a piece. Then straighten out.

'Alone. That's what I feel. And you know what I do then. I'm lying in bed looking at the ceiling and she's breathing there beside me. So, I take my head for a walk. I imagine I'm down there in...Mississippi. Don't laugh. I've always been able to do that. Mississippi and it's...I don't know- 1935. Well I've never been there, Never been to Mississippi. Never been to the States even. And I come to a crossroads. And there's a man sitting there under a sign post with 'Hazelhurst, Mississippi' written on it: little man in a dark suit with a guitar case on his lap; as if he's waiting for a bus to come along. And I know straight off who it is. It's him. It's Robert Leroy Johnson. You know how it is in a dream. You just know. So I go up to him. There's no one else about. Just dust and four roads running on forever. Maybe a broken down General Store. And I know that somehow he

275

knows me. He's expecting me to come along. It's me who he's sitting there waiting for. I go up to him and I say, "Hi, my name's Terry, Terry Arkari. I sing and play guitar." He looks up at me. And you know what he says? He says, "I know that, man." He says: "You don't have to tell me that. I know who you are." And you know, I'm crying. I'm lying next to my Laura and I'm crying. But she doesn't know anything about this cos she's sleeping. Like she's always sleeping or working when I need her. Always. I want to tell her how I met Robert Johnson in this dream. But she's sleeping hard. And you know what I do.

Watch out now boy, there's a turn coming up.

'I see it. I see it. Yeah. What I do is, I creep out of bed; go down to the garage just as I am. And I get in the car. Switch on the ignition and I dial in the place I want to go. Know where that is? Hazelhurst, Mississippi. That's where he was born. And it's like a dream, Betty. It's like a dream. And there I am, sitting in the garage in my car watching this monitor. Riding through Mississippi. But what am I telling you this for. You know all this, Betty. You're there with me.'

And he smiled softly at the reminiscence and his eyes blinked slowly into sleep. When the near-side tyre struck the kerb, he was jolted into sudden wakefulness. The car weaved crazily about the road but eventually he was able to correct the slide.

'Close, Betty. That was really close.' There was no fear in his voice.

And she was laughing too. *What you tryin' to do? Kill the both of us?*

And he laughed too. 'You live you die. What does it matter? What does anything matter?'

Maybe you should stop and have a sleep. Maybe you're still sleepin'. But you remember now, I'm gonna be lying right alongside o' you, boy.

'No. Can't sleep.'

You can't.

'No I want to get home. Want to get home and lie in my own bed.'

Home to Laura? That what you're tellin' me?

'Just home.'

Uh huh! You know something. Let me tell you something. That woman. She ain't right for you.

'What you mean, not right?'

I just know she ain't. Believe me. You know who you need?

'Who do I need Betty?'

Me, is who you need. Ain't that a surprise? Let me tell you something. I know about dreamers. And that's what you are, boy. You are a dreamer. And you know how I know that?

'Why's that, Betty?'

Because me, I'm a dreamer too. Ain't that something now?

'You are?'

Sure I am. And when two dreamers like me and you git to meet up, well there ain't but one thing you gotta do. You gonna a make a guess at what that might be? I mean you ain't riding alongside o' me all these long nights and days for nuthin' are you? You listenin' to me boy?

''Course I'm listening. I always listen to you Betty.'

What you gotta do boy is - you gotta make a choice now.

'I'm no good at choosing, Betty. Hate choosing.'

I know that. You think I don't know that? I know everythin' about you. Everythin'. You think I can't ride in this car with you six months in the middle of the night and not know where you coming from? Shit!

'Betty!'

Shut up, boy. Don't talk to me. You see these two roads coming up.

'I see them.'

That's what you call a divide. It's a divide in the road. And there are divides in your life just like there's divides in the road. And when you come to a divide, you gotta make a choice, boy. You like it or not, you gotta make a choice. You listenin' to me? This ain't no time for no compromisin'. And I know you hate that – you hate choosing. It gives you pain. But you gonna have do it, boy. You gonna have to ask yourself - Am I goin' North or am I goin' South? You hear what I'm saying?

'You tell me which way to go Betty. You always choose right. I never get lost with you.'

What is this shit you talkin'? You bin lost all your life, boy. You hear what I'm sayin'? You know why you lost? You lost because you're with the wrong woman. But I can't choose for you. I can't do that. Because it ain't just like any other road. It's about somethin' else entirely. And you know what that is?

'I think you're going to tell me. You decide. I'm lost Betty.'

Don't you go telling me you lost. You got me here 'longside o' you, boy. Hear what I'm saying? You got me. Don't that mean nuthin' to you?

'Means everything, Betty. Everything.'

I don't believe you.

'I mean it.'

Right. So, what's it going to be? You gonna ride with me down that old road to the South? The old, dusty road into that dark Mississippi sun. Into

your dreams, with Soul Sister Betty by your side. You gonna do that boy?
Or you gonna take that cold, hard road to the North; to lie in a cold, cold
bed beside this woman of yours who's cold as ice? Now you tell me, boy.
What's it gonna be?

And he screamed into the night. 'I don't know. I don't
know. I don't know.'

But he didn't have to make a choice. Of its own accord, the
steering wheel seemed to turn through his hands. And to his
delight, he found himself driving down a long dusty road
burned white by a dark sun that drained everything of its
colour. Driving between spreading fields, white with cotton; a
woman's soft voice whispering in his ear. Driving towards the
General Store beside the crossroads, where he knew the small
dark man with the guitar across his knee would be patiently
waiting for him.

How I met my wife

I t was on a damp Tuesday morning that Mr Arthur Beavis suddenly decided to give up the struggle with his unruly pupils. He had tried everything. But now he was sixty. He suddenly felt old and tired. More importantly, he decided that he simply didn't like them any more; any of them. Not just the bored, restive adolescents who sat facing him, but the whole generation. In his twenties, as a young, enthusiastic teacher with a first class degree from Cambridge, fired with enthusiasm, he had worked conscientiously and with some idealism to devise imaginative lessons that he felt would capture the interests and enthusiasms of his charges. He believed he could somehow change their lives. But now, his time seemed to be taken up entirely with generally fruitless attempts to keep some semblance of order. For the last ten years his exchanges with his English classes seemed to consist entirely of ineffectual reprimands on his part and casual insubordination on theirs. Sometimes, he felt that he might just as well not have been there; indeed, it often crossed his mind that they would probably have behaved *better* in his absence. He began to think of himself more as a sort of pedagogic policeman, than a teacher. What was the point of it all? So habitual had this embattled mode become that when, some three years earlier, he had done a week's supply-teaching in a reputable, local primary school and been faced by eager-eyed, attentive pupils, it had come as something of a shock to him to realise that he was actually expected to teach them something. From that moment the behaviour of his present pupils; their scorn for everything he believed important, everything that he held dear, began to gnaw at him. Gradually this disaffection mutated into something like loathing; not just for the particular pupils who faced him each day, but for youth in general. A lifelong Labour voter, he felt he was betraying something deep in his spirit but he could not help himself. He would have liked to have discussed the matter with someone but since his wife had died suddenly two years earlier, there was nobody he could open his heart to. Grace had so sympathised with his growling disaffection; been so understanding. And it was only now that she was dead, that he began to regret what he had done; how tedious and wearing it must have been for her. And now, thinking back on their relatively contented life together, he deeply regretted that he had so persistently unburdened onto her frail though understanding shoulders, the despair and disaffection he felt with his work; indeed with teaching in general. It occurred to him that the children he taught may well have indirectly contributed to her death. Travelling home by bus to his empty terraced house, he found some solace in carrying on an angry conversation with her. It was of necessity a one-sided conversation:

They murdered you, my darling. Yes they did. They might just as well have stuck a knife in your heart. Oh wouldn't I love to see them up before the judge. I'd love it. I'd have them all locked up for ten years. And as they walked out, heads bowed and lamenting to the cells, d'you know what I'd do? I'd stand up. I'd stand up in front of their crying, sanctimonious parents and hangers-on and criminal relations and I'd clap. I'd cheer. I'd shout out loud. Thank you Judge. Thank you so much. Justice has been served at last. Justice! Pearls before swine. My God! I try to feed them something that's precious to me, what I believe in: the humanising literature that's sustained and ameliorated civilisation over the last two and a half thousand years and what do they do? They sneer and shit on it. It's quite hard to sneer and shit at the same time but they manage it effortlessly. If there were PhDs in sneering and shitting they'd all get double firsts. And I'm supposed to take it all in good part. Shelley-shit! Hardy-shit! Keats-shit! Shakespeare-shit! And what do those ignorant cardinals in their ivory-towered educational altars say about all this. Make it relevant. So we have Keats on Big Brother. Macbeth is the leader of a rebel motorcycle gang. Let's make papier-mâché models of La Belle Dame sans Merci. Oh Education what crimes are committed in thy name!

Quite often when he arrived home, this internal diatribe left him utterly exhausted.

So, on that Tuesday, in the face of the habitual wave of contempt, boredom and derision, he quite suddenly stopped his usual stream of ineffectual reprimands - and became silent. He seemed to hear a soft soothing music in his head. He was still vaguely aware of the tumultuous mayhem the class was creating but it was all far off; something that echoed in the distant reaches of his consciousness. He switched off his hearing aid and retired into a haven of seraphic content deep within himself. A beatific smile illuminated his worn but still handsome face. For a short while the disorder continued unabated but then as the class gradually became aware that something had changed, that the habitual battle of words was no longer there, they subsided into a bemused discontent that teetered on the edge of silence. For the first time in almost a year Mr Beavis had their attention. They even began to ask him questions. Insolent they may have been, but they were still questions.

'What's up sir?

'What we gonna do?'

'Ain't you speaking to us sir?'

'You gone mad sir?'

Then one of the boys stood up and turning to the rest of the class, pointing, shouted, 'He's fuckin' bonkers.'

And the whole class had laughed.

But Mr Beavis ignored them all.

One or two of the boys began to circle him, laughing and jeering but when there was no reaction, they swiftly lost interest and began milling about the classroom in a desultory, dissatisfied fashion, as though Mr Beavis were no longer there. And in a way this was true. At heart they were conservative; happy under the old embattled dispensation; the daily battle of wills was what they came to school for. Now it was no longer there, they became edgily resentful; dangerous. Mr Beavis repaired to his desk and sat down. Reaching into his bag, he searched blindly for some book or other with which he might occupy himself.

Somewhere in the back of his mind was the thought that the simple act of reading might irritate them. He took out the first book that came to hand. As he read the title, he caressed the cover affectionately and leafed through the well-thumbed, familiar pages with something like love in his eyes. He turned to the first page, an old friend, and began to read aloud in a soft, measured voice, as though to a small group of attentive, eager students. He knew practically the whole of the first page by heart:

For a long time I used to go to bed early.

His French wasn't good but he'd memorised the whole of the first page in the original language.

Long temps, je suis couché de bonne heure.

It gave him a frisson of pleasure to repeat it to himself: to think of Proust, lying in his cork-lined room one day, picking up his pen and writing on a hitherto blank sheet, the words he was now reading. For something like the same reason, he had got the first page of *The Agamemnon* by heart in Greek, in order that he could repeat to himself the very words that Aeschylus had written over two thousand years earlier. He knew well enough why he was reading from a book that was so alien to all his pupils. It was the nearest he could get to an act of benign revenge. Ineffectual of course, but it rendered him some kind of satisfaction. He couldn't quite analyse his motives clearly but they went something like this: Here is something I believe in. You will loathe it. And I'm glad, because that is the whole point.

So there!

And indeed, there was something about his utter yet

contented disdain for them that irritated them beyond measure. He saw that and was pleased. The discontent increased until it attained a state of near mayhem; chairs were thrown across the classroom, desks over-turned, and the spilled books hurled through the air till they crashed against the walls. Fights broke out. One of the girls put both hands over her ears and began to scream piercingly and then to weep. A number of them conducted loud conversations on their mobile phones.

Another teacher, from a nearby classroom, alerted by the tumult, left his class and hurried down the corridor. His anxious, horrified face peered through the glass partition for a moment, before he ran down the corridor in the direction of the Headmaster's study. And in the midst of all this tumult, Mr Beavis continued to read the tale of the hypersensitive boy and his longing for his mother's goodnight kiss.

They hated it. And Mr Beavis was content.

The mayhem increased and became unbridled anarchy.

When the Headmaster finally entered the classroom and attempted to restore order, he was under the impression that Mr Beavis had left the classroom; that he had suddenly been taken ill and had had to abandon the class. But when, with the help of his backup staff: Mr Dorian, the P.E. Teacher and the caretaker, a bluff burly man in blue overalls, he managed to restore some semblance of order, he suddenly became aware of the tall, bearded figure of Mr Beavis seated behind his desk, reading aloud in a soft, well-modulated voice, as though totally unaware of the chaos that surrounded him. He read on: *Sometimes too a woman would be born during my sleep from some misplacing of my thigh.*

'Mr Beavis,' the Headmaster said.

Mr Beavis read on.

Conceived from the pleasure I was on the point of enjoying, she it was, I imagined, who offered me that pleasure. My body conscious...

'Mr Beavis!' the Head shouted striding across the classroom and snatching the volume from Mr Beavis's hand. The class was silent now, watching the unfolding drama with wrapt attention.

'Ah Headmaster,' Mr Beavis said. He switched on his hearing aid.

The Headmaster's face was red. He put both hands on his hips. 'Can you tell me what's going on here?'

'Going on,' said Mr Beavis amiably, 'Reading lesson.'

'Reading?' The Headmaster snapped. 'You're reading!' He held the book up. 'From this!' He turned the pages.

'That's right,' said Mr Beavis nodding.

The Headmaster snapped the book shut and turning to Mr Dorian, an eager, muscular, rather red-faced young man, wearing shorts and yellow sweat shirt, said: 'Mr Dorian would you be so kind as to take the class until break time. Mr Beavis,' the Headmaster said, taking him by the arm, 'be so good as to come to my office.'

'Of course Headmaster,' replied Mr Beavis smiling.

The class cheered derisively.

In his office, the Head had no idea what he should say. To give himself time for thought, he slowly removed his jacket, before carefully hanging it on a hook on the wall. Mr Beavis watched him with something like complacency. The Head seated himself behind his desk and began with some care, picking at his finger nails. He strongly suspected that Mr Beavis was suffering some kind of mental breakdown. It was a tricky area that he was unsure how to venture into. In addition, he felt at something of a disadvantage since he was aware that Mr Beavis had a vastly superior degree and was old enough to be his father. He turned the pages of the book he had taken from Mr Beavis then decisively snapped it shut and placed it on the desk. He leaned forward, his elbows on the table; a studied gesture.

'Proust?' he said.

'Proust. Indeed,' said Mr Beavis. 'Have you… er…read him?'

'No,' the Headmaster said; by a subtle inflexion somehow managing to convey the impression that he had somehow managed to acquire a working knowledge of the author without actually having to resort to the laborious task of actually reading him.

'Ah well, not every one's cup of tea. Some people do find it difficult. Indeed it positively exasperates others, who find the persona of the protagonist utterly uncongenial. And I can understand that.'

The Headmaster, despite his disinclination to engage in a literary discussion of the qualities of an author of whom he knew practically nothing, nevertheless felt a need to keep his end up.

'Wasn't he homosexual; and French?' he said, somehow managing to make both conditions sound equally disreputable.

'Oh yes. First came across him when I was at Cambridge. Wrote a thesis about him in fact. 'The Stream of Memory'.

Pretentious title. Someone published it though. But then I was only nineteen. I'm sure I still have a copy somewhere if you're interested.'

'No, no,' the Head said hurriedly. 'That won't be necessary.'

He wondered how he might best shift the conversation to bear on the subject of Mr Beavis's mental state.

'Probably wise,' said Mr Beavis. 'I'm sure it would read as something very naïve now. I've read him through twice since then, so my views have, of necessity, changed. But I still read a little every day, dipping in here and there and...

'Mr Beavis,' the Head interrupted him.

'Headmaster.'

'Arthur. I was wondering.'

'Yes Headmaster.'

'I hope you don't mind me asking. Knowing the boys we have at this school; the kind of backgrounds they come from; their social problems; their cultural background, would you say that this...,' He held the book up before him '...Proust, was appropriate reading? I mean, for a start do you think they'd understand it?'

'Well I read it in the English translation of course. I can manage in French but with some difficulty...'

The Head thumped his desk in exasperation. 'English or French what's the difference. It probably sounded Chinese to them. What were you thinking of? You saw how they re-acted. There was a riot going on in your classroom; a riot, Mr Beavis. Even in this school I've never seen such a thing. And it can spread you know. That kind of thing can spread. Anarchy is catching. And what were *you* doing as this riot was going on all round you. You were reading Proust to them. Proust! Are you mad?'

There he'd said it. It wasn't how he had meant it to come out but the matter was in the open now; and he was glad. To be on the safe side, he apologised immediately. 'I'm sorry, Mr Beavis. I shouldn't have said that.'

But Mr Beavis wasn't in the least offended. 'Mad?' he considered the word a trifle dolefully. 'Well of course it's possible. Although if I were mad of course, I should probably be the last to be aware of it.'

'I didn't mean it in that way. When I said mad, I was using the word loosely.'

'No that's perfectly all right. Although if I may say so there are two sides to the question. On the one hand, we have a group of adolescents, who scream, swear and shout, overturn their desks and appear to have no conspicuous talent whatsoever apart from a desire to enlarge their ignorance and a taste for mindless violence, and on the other hand a teacher who is reading from a novel widely believed by most fair-minded critics to be a beacon of 20th century literature. And yet I am the one who is concluded to be mad. It's an interesting question, Headmaster.'

The Head decided to change tack. In two days time there was to be a general inspection. He was anxious to get Mr Beavis out of the school for the remainder of the week; possibly for good. He needed younger staff who would be more in tune with these particular pupils. It had been in his mind for some months.

He put the book down and leaned back. 'Arthur, tell me. Your wife died not so long ago didn't she?'

'Yes indeed. Two years ago.'

'And you miss her naturally.'

'Of course.'

''Not my place to say this and please tell me if you think this is out of order but I was just wondering, have you considered marrying again.'

Mr Beavis sat back, his eyebrows raised. 'I must confess I'm somewhat taken aback.'

'I'm sorry, Arthur, I didn't mean to pry into your private affairs.'

'No, no Headmaster. Marry again? I can't really say I've thought about it.' He leaned forward. 'Am I to understand that you have a likely candidate in mind?'

The Headmaster shook his head. 'No, no of course not.'

'Ah, I see. Well you know, as I say, I've never really thought about it. But really I don't think so, Headmaster; although thank you for the suggestion. I was sixty last month. I never considered myself to be particularly prepossessing even when a young man so the likelihood of any woman finding me acceptable, would appear to be rather remote. And anyway I so rarely go out. And I'm aware that I'm a rather dry, scholarly sort of person, not really husband material.'

'Sixty?' The Headmaster said. 'Really.' It was the word he had been looking to bring up and now Mr Beavis had conveniently introduced it. 'You don't look it.'

'I may not look it, Headmaster. But at times I feel it.'

The Headmaster sat back in his chair and clasped both hands behind his head. He stared at the ceiling as if all the answers to their problems were written there. 'Mr Beavis, I just wondered if you'd ever thought about taking early retirement.'

'Retirement?'

'Yes. It would allow you time to pursue your, as you call them, scholarly pursuits. And you know the terms can be quite favourable and I'd be more than happy to make out a very good case for you. Of course we'd be sorry to lose you. That goes without saying. It's rare to have teachers of your academic calibre these days. You're the best qualified teacher on the staff. And, well perhaps you'd like to mull it over. Think about it. In the mean time I'd like to suggest that you take the rest of the week off. You look as if you could do with a rest and then there's half-term. We could discuss the matter further when school begins again. There's no need to make a decision now. As I said, go home, rest and have a good think about it and then we can talk further.'

The Head watched Mr Beavis, as he crossed the grey tarmac playground towards the school gates, his gabardine raincoat flapping about his knees; listing to the right slightly with the effort of carrying his bag. Then he picked up the phone and called the school secretary. 'Ah Margaret,' he said, 'It's me. I wonder if you could look out details concerning early retirement on medical grounds.'

*

At home at the unaccustomed hour of twelve o'clock Mr Beavis made himself a cup of tea and carried it into the small lean-to summer house at the back of his terraced house. Looking at the garden through the rain-glazed windows he rehearsed again the conversation in the Headmaster's study. Retirement, he whispered to himself. The word had always had a grey, fusty, sound to it. He repeated it to himself, easing the word languorously about his mouth; then louder, over and over. The thought of it had never crossed his mind before. He had somehow seen himself going on teaching for ever. But now, the more he thought about it, the more attractive it sounded. And it required little effort. It meant, in fact, not doing things: no more getting up in the morning, no catching the bus, no marking asinine pieces of fairly illegible writing, no staff meetings - and best of all, no more standing up in front of 3W.

Mr Beavis smiled to himself and sipped his tea.

Marriage though, was a different matter altogether. It required effort; an effort he was not much inclined to make at this stage of his life. And then, as he stared dreamily out at the rain-soaked garden, a vision drifted into his head of a smartly dressed woman with the scent of perfume about her, pouring tea into his cup and offering him a large slice of the simnel cake that she had herself baked that morning. Somehow her face remained shadowy but he had a sense that she was intelligent and good looking. The general vision struck him as being attractive.

He needed advice on the matter.

He picked up the phone and dialled his married daughter, Hazel's number in Hastings. He asked her what she thought of his getting married.

'Dad, are you all right?'

'Perfectly.'

'You're sure you're not ill.'

'Why should I be ill?'

'Well calling me at midday and suddenly asking me about getting married. It's … well I don't know what to say. '

'It's just that the Headmaster brought the matter up.'

'The Headmaster? The Headmaster said you should get married! What's it got to do with him?'

'Well it just came up. Amongst other things.'

'You always do what people tell you?'

'Well, I always give it serious consideration. It was he who brought up the retirement notion as well. And I'm rather taken with that. So I thought he might well be right as well about the marriage question.'

'Is it the asking bit that worries you?'

'Well sort of, yes.'

'Well think. How did you come to marry Mum?'

He thought about it, taking another sip at his tea. 'She proposed to me at the end of the pier at Clacton.'

'It was her idea?'

'Yes. Well no not entirely. I'd thought about it of course, but didn't really know how to go about it. So I was quite grateful when your mother brought it up.'

'So you married out of gratitude?'

'No of course not but you know your mother made all the important decisions. And that's one of the things I wanted to ask you about. I was worried it might make you angry.'

'What on earth should I be angry about?'

'Well I was thinking about your mother.'

'Mother?'

'That you'd think I was being unfaithful somehow.'

'Dad you can't be unfaithful to someone who's dead.'

'Well you can in a way. I thought you might think I was being unfaithful to her memory and so forth.'

There was a pause. Then Hazel said. 'Dad, if it helps at all, you don't have to worry at all about what I think. I mean even if I disapproved, it's not really any of my business. In fact, I think it would be a jolly good idea. Who is she?'

'Sorry?'

'The woman.'

'What woman?'

'The woman you're going to marry.'

'Oh I've no idea. It's just an idea at the moment and I wanted your approval. And I thought you might have some idea about how I could go about it.'

'Do you know any women?'

Mr Beavis considered the question. 'Well, no not really. There are some teachers at school. But they're a great deal younger than me and they believe in social progress, the innate goodness of all human life, and soap operas. So...' he left the sentence hanging.

'Well,' said Hazel slowly, 'I can only give you the usual advice. You could buy some new clothes and join an amateur dramatic society.'

'I loathe amateur dramatics. I don't like going to plays at all. The acting's better when I read them at home.'

'Dad you asked me for help.'

'Yes, I'm sorry.'

'You could go on a dating agency.'

'Oh no. Thank you for the suggestion. But the thought of these unknown women! It would horrify me. And suppose they got to know me and I couldn't get rid of them.' He poured himself another cup of tea. 'Perhaps I should give up the whole idea.'

'Just a thought. But wasn't there a lady you used to talk to when you walked the dog round Dinham?'

'Was there?'

'Yes. You used to stop and talk about hard pad and dog food and things. You seemed to like her. You met all sorts of people walking the dog.'

'Oh yes but Blanco died a year ago. I don't walk any more.'

'Daddy, you're being very negative if I may say so. I'm trying to help you. You don't need a dog to go walking. You can just walk. Apart from anything else the exercise will do you good. And you could just stop and talk.'

'Stop and talk?'

'Yes.'

'What would I talk about? I haven't got a dog, Hazel.'

'Anything. The weather.'

'The weather?'

'I'm only suggesting. Look I have to go, Dad. The boys have just come in. Let me know how you get on.'

He heard the boisterous noise of children shouting in the background. Between shouts to the children, Hazel said, 'Now you're retired, what are you going to do with the rest of your day?'

The rain had stopped. He smiled to himself.

'I think I'll go for a walk,' he said.

'Atta boy,' Hazel said and put the phone down.

*

On the Thursday, a letter arrived from the Headmaster with instructions about how, should he feel so inclined, he should go about arranging his early retirement. The whole procedure was accomplished much more painlessly than he had imagined. It didn't even entail him in meeting his headmaster. It was all conducted by a short interview at the Department of Education Offices in Penn Lane and afterwards the matter was concluded through letters and a series of phone calls. 'Almost as though they were anxious to see the back of me,' he confessed to Hazel during one of their weekly conversations. He understood that his pension would be somewhat reduced as a result of his claiming it early. But that didn't bother him a jot. The mortgage had been paid off a number of years ago and his needs were simple.

His walks became almost daily events and he even considered buying another dog. But then he thought how he might take a holiday abroad and the dog would be an unnecessary tie. Of the lady in question, however, there was no sign. And he did wonder, even if their paths were to cross, would he recognise her. He'd always had a poor memory for faces. Quite often people greeted him warmly in the street, on trains or in shops and he would carry on a fairly lengthy conversation with them, without having the slightest idea who they might be. Now he searched his memory but he could only conjure up the vaguest impression of the lady's appearance; the little dog, on the other hand, he remembered quite clearly. He had a feeling this did not augur well. And then again, suppose her dog had died and she had acquired a new one. Would he recognise her, if she were accompanied by a Labrador or a schnauzer and not the familiar Westie? And supposing he did recognise her, or at least her dog, what on earth was he supposed to say? The very idea made him nervous. He began rehearsing the sort of appropriate opening remarks he might make. He got into the habit of carrying a school exercise book with him on his walks and began entering into it what he considered to be his best overtures. But some inventive compulsion seized him and he began adding her possible replies. Half way through his walk he sat on a fallen tree, writing pages of fictive dialogue which ended with their marriage and taking a honeymoon on the coast of Normandy. He'd never been to Normandy; but then it had associations with Proust and that attracted him. He wondered if the hotel where the young Marcel had stayed with his grandmother still existed. There was little that was libidinous about these musings of his. It grew out of the nature of the task that he had set himself and he had always been the sort of person who liked to see things through.

In addition, he found himself enjoying these walks for their own sake. And, if the weather were inclement and the going hard, he would comfort himself with the thought that anything was better than facing an unruly class of adolescents with whom he had absolutely nothing in common. To keep his brain active he began learning some of his favourite poems as he walked along. He would scribble them down amongst the imagined exchanges with the unknown lady and repeat them aloud as he walked along; cantos from Don Juan; poems by Hardy and Sir Thomas Wyatt. His memory was still sound. He declaimed them aloud, while the chewing sheep gazed at him with complacent indifference. After a fortnight or so he had some fifteen poems by heart.

On the third week he was sheltering from the rain in a deserted barn, when he was joined by a short, morose looking man in his late forties who looked vaguely familiar. Mr Beavis stared out at the rain without saying anything for a few minutes and then glancing sideways, he noted that the short man's nose was peeling and pink with sunburn. A line from a book he had once read, unaccountably floated into his head. *He had a nose like a badly scraped carrot.* He tried to place the quotation but neither the book nor the author would come to mind. He took out his exercise book and covertly scribbled down the line beneath his proposal to the unknown lady.

The man with the peeling nose glanced at the pencil moving across the paper. 'Writing?' he said.

Mr Beavis nodded and surreptitiously slipped the exercise book into his pocket for fear the man should read the description of his peeling nose.

'Words eh,' said the man the man philosophically.

Ah, thought Mr Beavis, the sort of man who puts words to the blindingly obvious.

'Words,' repeated Mr Beavis who was beginning to find this statement of the obvious rather beguiling. They leaned side by side, both arms on a broken wooden gate staring out in silence as the rain hammered down on the lane and the distant grey hills.

'Rain,' said the man and then after a pause said 'rain' again, nodding his head in the direction of the downpour for fear Mr Beavis might be incapable of making the connection.

'Rain indeed,' said Mr Beavis.

There was something attractively philosophical about these exchanges. He decided to continue the game. 'Wet rain,' he said.

'You're right there.'

'Coming down.'

'True.'

'Not in here though.'

'No not in here. It's the shelter see.'

'Keeps you dry.'

'Looks set.'

'Till it stops.'

'True.'

'Very true.' said Mr Beavis nodding sagely. He wondered to what extremes this conversation might be carried. And Mr Beavis came to a sudden realisation that he was happy. What could be better than sheltering in this dishevelled barn with a passing stranger, staring out at the interminable rain? It was, at the same time, delightful and utterly pointless. He wished almost, that it might go on for ever. How many men throughout the long history of the universe, he wondered, had done what they were now doing: sheltering in a shed from the rain, staring out and exchanging banal commonplaces; putting names to the things of the world. And yet the things themselves had no idea that they had names. Rain did not know it was rain. Nor wind, wind. Thus mankind invented the universe. In his heart, Mr Beavis prayed that the rain might continue so as to prolong this epiphanic moment for ever. He had a sensation within him that was almost religious.

'Caned me,' the man said smiling.

'I'm sorry,' said Mr Beavis.

'In school. You caned me.'

Mr Beavis turned to look at the man. His profile was to the rain. He was smiling with gentle pleasure at the recollection of once being caned.

'I caned you?'

'You did that.'

'You mean I was your teacher?'

'You were that. Just come out of college. Didn't know what you was doing. I was a bad un. I tried it on. You caned me.' He laughed and banged his fist on the top beam of the gate.

Mr Beavis inspected the man leaning at his side. The face of a thirteen year old from forty years ago began slowly to assert itself.

'Blenkinsopp!'

'That's me. You didn't half lay it on, I can tell you.'

Now it all came back. This little man with the pudgy, unlined face was the only boy he had ever caned in his life. For a week after, he had vowed, no matter what happened, that he would never cane a boy again. The regret had remained with him all his life. He turned to the boy, who was now the man,

Blenkinsopp and whispered with utter contrition, 'I'm so sorry. So sorry. Please forgive me.'

And Blenkinsopp continued to smile. 'Don't give it a thought. I deserved it.'

Mr Beavis extended his hand and Blenkinsopp shook it warmly. 'You've taken a weight off my mind,' Mr Beavis said with utter sincerity.

'Pity you can't do it anymore. All these kids nowadays. Only thing they understand.'

'Oh I don't know,' muttered Mr Beavis voicing a liberal reflex.

'Don't you? Well I do. Only thing they understand. Shooting and stabbing innocent folk. Raping old ladies. What's happened to this country? I'd bring back the cat.' He turned and pinched at his left trouser leg. It was drenched and stained with mud. 'Look at that! Two of them went past me in their car, music pounding, shouting and swearing. Through a puddle. Did it a purpose. Look at that! Ruined. Floggings too good for 'em, I say.'

'Well perhaps there's something in what you say.'

'No perhaps about it. I know there is. I bloody well know there is.'

Mr Beavis felt himself reprimanded. They relapsed into silence and once more inspected the rain.

'How long you been walking?'.

'Mr Beavis was relieved the line of conversation had changed. He entertained a certain nostalgic longing for the old banalities. 'Today you mean?'

'No not today,' the man said with some irritability. 'In your life, like.'

'My life? Well, I used to do a great deal.'

'Oh ah!'

'Walking that is. With my dog. Our dog,' he corrected himself. 'My wife died,' he added, without quite knowing why. 'It was really our dog. But I was the one who used to walk it.'

'Dog?'

'Yes.'

'Big brown dog wasn't it? With a bushy tail.'

Mr Beavis shook his head. 'Small, white Westie.' He lowered his palm demonstrating the diminutive nature of the dog.

'You're right,' the man said emphatically as though it were Mr Beavis's opinion that was open to doubt. He looked about him suddenly. 'Where he gone?'

'Where's who gone?'

'Dog.'

'Ah,' said Mr Beavis. 'Heaven.'

'Heaven?'

'He died.'

'Ah!' said the man and turned his attention once more to the rain.

To his surprise Mr Beavis found his eyes filling with tears.

'Yeah. Small white Westie. Remember you talking to that lady. She had one.'

'Had one?'

'Westie. That's why you was talking. About your Westies.'

'You're probably right.' Mr Beavis blew his nose. This was the second time in a few days that the lady had cropped up. There was a prolonged silence then Mr Beavis said, 'That lady.

Do you ever see her now?'

'See her? Not now. Used to see her before.'

'Before what?'

'That car thing.'

'Car?'

'Was in the paper?'

'What was?'

'This lad ran into her. Not far from here. Hooligan. Took her to hospital. That was what? Three weeks ago now.'

'Good God. How is she? Is she going to be all right?'

He shrugged. 'Couldn't tell you, mate.' Then as an afterthought, 'Dog was okay though.'

The rain dwindled and then gradually stopped. Huge rain drops cascaded into the roadway from the eves of the barn and the trees.

'Looks like it's stopped.'

'Indeed.'

'Well,' the man said as though with reluctance, 'I'll be on my merry way then.' He put out his hand and shook Mr Beavis's firmly once more. Mr Beavis felt a sudden surge of unaccountable affection for this little man with the red and peeling nose with whom he had spent almost half an hour staring out at the rain.

They set off in opposite directions. Then Mr Beavis remembered. He turned and shouted. 'Do you remember what hospital she went to?'

'What?'

'Hospital? Which one?'

The man shrugged, spreading his arms wide.

A pale sun emerged slowly from behind the rags of cloud.

'Sun,' Blenkinsopp shouted pointing skyward.

'Sun,' shouted Mr Beavis and they both turned and walked away from one another.

Like duellists in that novel, thought Mr Beavis. Now who was it? Out of the arching blue that was now his memory, it suddenly came to him: Conrad! The great and one and only Joseph. He must read it again. Perhaps write a piece on it. That's what he should be doing to eke out his retirement. He made a note to that effect in his dog-eared exercise book. But the carrot? Who had said that about the carrot? He wracked his brain but nothing would come.

*

'Have I to buy a hat?' Hazel asked on her regular Tuesday night phone call to her father.

'Hat?'

'For the wedding?'

'Whose wedding?'

'Yours of course.'

He laughed. 'Good Lord no.'

'Shame. Was looking forward to it.'

'What?"

'Was looking…Dad have you got your hearing aid in?'

He shifted the receiver to his left, his better ear.

'Again.'

'I said I WAS LOOKING FORWARD TO IT.'

'No need to shout dear.'

Hazel sighed.

'Or sigh.'

'Have your paths crossed.'

'Sorry?'

'You and the lady with the dog. Have you met up with her yet?'

'Ah no. She's had an accident.'

'Oh dear. How do you know?'

'Blenkinsopp told me.'

'Blenkinsopp?'

'Taught him years ago. Now middle-aged little man with a penchant for the obvious and a peeling nose. I caned him.'

'You what!'

'Not now dear. Years ago. My first year in teaching.'

'Was he out for revenge?'

'On the contrary. He shook my hand. In fact he believes all young men under twenty should be birched regularly.'

'Oh a Guardian reader.'

'Two of them nearly ran me down. On purpose I think.'

'What?'

'Day before yesterday. Hooligans. Probably the same lot as did for the lady. I've remarked a difference in morality between men and women, where cars are concerned. The men drive past without slowing down. The women generally slow to almost a stop and wave. Youths in red cars do their best to run you down.

'Oh Dad! Come on!'

'Well these two did. If I hadn't leapt into the bushes I shouldn't be talking to you now.'

*

In fact a week prior to this encounter he had noticed the same little red Astra, untidily parked on the grass verge of the lane. The youths, both wearing grey hoods that gave them a malignantly monkish aspect, were busy hurling a series of bin bags and other debris down a slope at the lane's edge. Outraged, he had run forward to remonstrate with them but by the time he was within earshot they had driven off shouting, banging their fists on the outside of the doors, horn blaring. Mr Beavis had stopped, panting desperately, his heart pounding, as much with anger as with the effort of running. He was of the opinion that hanging should be reintroduced for litter louts. He sat down on a log at the lane's side, breathing slowly and deeply, waiting for his thumping heart to return to something like its normal rhythm. His mouth was dry and there were coloured spots dancing before his eyes. He took a series of deep breaths then took out his exercise book and jotted down the make and colour of the car and its registration number. With some difficulty he hauled himself to his feet and walked down to where the car had been parked. To the left of the road was a slope that ran down to a brook, beyond which was a wilderness of bushes and tangled undergrowth. He stared with disgust at the piled rubbish: black garbage bags, bald tyres, a kettle, a rusting fridge, piles of empty lager cans, a large galvanised bucket with a jagged hole in the side and a length of washing line with two or three pegs idiotically still pinned to it. The stripped carcass of a wrecked motorbike straddled the brook and protruding from it, was a pair of legs clad in worn black boots. Mr Beavis drew back and leaned against a tree for support. He looked about him but the lane was deserted. Slowly and tentatively, fearful of what he might find, he descended the slope. He stared at the legs for a few moments. He stretched out his hand gingerly towards the boots and then withdrew it. He lifted his leg and gently prodded one of the boots with his foot. He watched with a mixture of horror and fascination as the boot, as if of its own volition, slowly detached itself from the leg and tumbled into the brook with the faintest of splashes. The wooden leg stuck up in the air trembling slightly. Mr Beavis straddled the brook, leaning on the carcass of the motorbike for support. The grotesquely painted, flat face, stared up at him with something like surprise in its huge painted eyes. He couldn't forebear laughing at his own fear; a farmer's scarecrow. Or perhaps one of those effigies created by parishioners for some village fete. He crouched beside the brook and splashed handfuls of water on his face, before laboriously climbing back up the slope to the lane. There was a number one rang to complain about illegal dumping. They would know at the library. He saw himself and Blenkinsopp in an otherwise empty prison yard, thrashing the two youths with enormous birch branches till they wept and begged for mercy. Their mouths wide open.

Then it came to him. 'Mouth,' he suddenly shouted aloud. 'The Horses Mouth. Of course. Of course.'

Smiling he opened his exercise book and underneath *nose like a badly scraped carrot* he triumphantly scribbled in the title and underlined it twice. He returned the exercise book to his pocket and continued on his way humming softly to himself.

It had been six days later that the same little red Astra had roared past him, brushing his coat and forcing him to leap for safety. Lying amongst the nettles and damp bushes he heard the youths' cries of delight; saw their jeering faces leering back at him. He shook his fist and swore at them with a fury that astonished even himself. His anger was immense. The youths merely laughed the louder. He watched with some apprehension, as the car slid to a halt. The driver, a red-haired youth, opened the door and leaned out, staring back at him. Mr Beavis, still shouting, struggled to his knees. His trouser leg was torn and there was blood. He didn't seem to be able to bend his right knee.

'You fucking stay there mate. We're coming back for you. I'll get you next time.'

And laughing, the youth slammed the door, floored the accelerator and the car swept crazily down the lane and out of sight.

Mr Beavis's fury was overwhelming. He almost fainted so powerful was the emotion that gripped him. But his fear was greater than his anger. Slowly and painfully he hauled himself to his feet. He could still hear their shouts of laughter and the music pounding from the car radio. Now it was fainter. How long would it take them to complete the circuit and return? And what should he do when they did? Pointless to confront them; they were young and accustomed no doubt to violence. The phrase concerning discretion and valour came to his mind. In fifteen or so minutes they would be back; long before he had time to arrive at the sanctuary of the first houses. He looked about him and elected to hide amongst the bushes and undergrowth on the slope to his left. He staggered on some fifty yards and then began to half crawl down the slope searching for a secure hiding place. He winced as his right hand closed over a crushed lager can. The sharp key caused a deep cut in his palm. There were five or so other cans amongst piles of empty crisp packets. Then he realised he was back at the improvised, illicit rubbish dump he had seen a week earlier. The scarecrow was still there, its broom stick leg sticking jauntily and idiotically into the air.

Then it came to him. He knew as clearly as he had ever known anything, what he must do. Nemesis, he whispered to himself. Nemesis. And he meant all of them; the whole rotten generation. He glanced at his watch. How long would it take? Ten minutes? Possibly less. Time enough, he calculated, for what he had to do. But he must hurry. He scrambled painfully down the bank. He decided not to tug the scarecrow free by the leg for fear the whole thing fell apart. Crossing the now almost dry brook, he bent down over the scarecrow. The label attached to its chest still bore the name, *Archie* in fading letters. 'Come on Archie,' he said and lifted the scarecrow almost affectionately with both arms. But it refused to come free. He glanced at his watch once more. The skirt of the ludicrously striped blazer was jammed beneath the tyreless front wheel of the bike. With

some difficulty he managed to lift the bike and pull it clear.
Cradling the scarecrow and panting hoarsely, he struggled once
more up the bank. He stood for a moment looking up and
down the lane. 'Now then Archie let's find a good branch for
you.' Some ten meters up the lane he spotted a thick, leafless
branch that stretched from one side of the lane to the other. He
picked up Archie once more and laid him carefully, as though he
were an injured patient, beneath the branch. For a moment he
stood there panting, listening for the sound of the approaching
car. But there was nothing; just the soft soughing of the westerly
breeze amongst the trees. Blood seeped thickly from the wound
across his palm. He took a rather dirty handkerchief from his
trouser pocket and wrapped it clumsily round the wound. 'You
wait here Archie,' he said, patting the scarecrow. He limped
down the lane and half crawled down the slope once more. The
length of washing line lay half-covered by a pile of bags. He
pulled it free. He must have straightened himself too quickly. A
wave of dizziness swept through him. He would have toppled
over if he had not leaned on a tree trunk. He took a series of
deep breaths and shook his head vigorously. Slowly, his head
cleared but left a sharp ache about his temples. He looped the
rope over his right shoulder and crawled once more back up the
slope.

'Now then Archie,' he said.

As he had seen sailors do, he curled the line and flung it
upwards and over the tree. But he was hopelessly short of the
mark and the rope toppled down uselessly on top of him. It
wasn't as easy as in all those films he'd seen. He studied the

branch and the end of the rope, realizing that even if he succeeded in getting it up and over the branch, he wouldn't be able to reach it in order to haul it down again. He remembered the rusting galvanised bucket he had seen amongst the pile of rubbish and ran back and fetched it. He knotted the end of the rope about the bucket's handle and began slowly to swing it in a series of slow circles. And then he heard it; the unmistakable purr of a car's engine. He looked about him desperately, then lurched towards the screening bushes at the right side of the lane. Then he remembered Archie. He couldn't leave him lying in the middle of the lane. The sound of the car was nearer now. He picked up Archie in both arms but tripped over the rusting bucket and fell full length into the long grass of the verge, winding himself. Turning his head, he saw the glint of the approaching car through the screening branches of the trees.

'Sweet God almighty,' he murmured to himself and attempted to push himself unavailingly to his feet. The car appeared to be moving more slowly than he had imagined. Probably they were looking for him. With difficulty he hauled himself to his knees, breathing heavily, but then sensed the heat of the motor and its bulk as it stopped opposite him. He was too afraid to look up. He hung his head, ready to submit himself to his fate.

A voice said, 'Are you all right?'

He lifted his head. A white-haired couple gazed down at him with concerned curiosity from the window of their Rover. At the open back window, a large Labrador panted, its tongue lolling. It gave vent to a deep baying bark, lifting its head.

'You behave yourself Dolly,' the woman said. There was a southern inflexion to their voices, Mr Beavis thought.

Laboriously he hauled himself his feet and brushed himself down. He swayed slightly and leaned his right hand on the body of the car.

'I'm fine,' he said.

The man nodded. 'You sure?' he said. His eyes shifted away from Mr Beavis's face. Mr Beavis followed his gaze until they lighted on the crumpled figure of Archie.

'Ah, yes,' Mr Beavis said. He really wasn't quite sure how to explain the matter. He improvised unthinkingly. 'It's for my son.' He pointed down the slope. 'Found it with all the rest of the rubbish.'

'I see,' said the man.

In his mind, his invented son began to take on a reality of its own. 'Funny lad. He'd always wanted a scarecrow.'

What on earth are you talking about? Mr Beavis wondered. You haven't got a son for God's sake. And if you had; at your age he would be in his forties. What would a forty year old man be wanting with a scarecrow for God's sake? Unless he was mad. Like his father.

'For your son?'

'That's right.'

The man nodded sceptically. 'I see. Well, can we give you a lift somewhere?'

'Oh no. No, no,' Mr Beavis said. He gave a sweeping gesture with his hand. 'Walking,' he explained.

He was now concerned that the other car would come upon

them. 'You be on your merry way,' he said smiling. It was Blenkinsopp's line.

'You're sure?' the man said.

'Absolutely sure. But thank you for the offer.'

'Oh Gerald let's be moving on,' the plump wife said settling back.

Essex again, Mr Beavis judged. He wondered how they had met.

'Well enjoy your walk,' the man said. He slipped the car into gear and pulled carefully away. Mr Beavis followed it until it was out of sight. In the sudden silence, he stood listening for the note of the other car: the red Astra. He glanced at his watch. Twenty minutes had passed. Perhaps the youth had forgotten him and gone home. Perhaps he was intent on driving down other pensioners. But then, he would be back tomorrow. Or the day after. Mr Beavis wondered if his anger would sustain itself after a night's sleep; probably not. Once more he began to swing the rope with the bucket at its end in larger and larger circles. And then he let it fly. It looped clanging through the air and to Mr Beavis's great surprise and delight arced its way over the branch where it swung lazily back and forth creaking slightly. But it was out of reach. Once or twice Mr Beavis leapt as high as he could into the air but no matter how hard he tried, he was unable to reach the bucket. He swung the other end of the rope in snaking loops, but to no avail. Oh damn it all to hell, Mr Beavis swore. He was beginning to feel quite exhausted by the whole procedure. He thought to himself, I'm not cut out for this kind of thing. But it wasn't in his nature to give up. He looked about him and picked up a fallen branch at the side of the lane. He managed to curl one of its twigs over the rim of the bucket and slowly and carefully hauled it down until he could touch it with his hand, then hauled on the rope, until Archie dangled ludicrously in the air, just beneath the overhanging branch, swaying slightly in the wind. Mr Beavis untied the bucket and still holding the byte of the rope, withdrew into a hiding place amongst the undergrowth. From here he would be unseen from the road but could see enough of the curve in the lane down which the Astra would come. It was time for a practice. He counted aloud to three and with a little whoop released the rope. But to his dismay, Archie remained circling slowly in the air. There was insufficient weight in Archie to make him drop. And the drop needed to be sudden and instant. Oh this is all too much for me, Mr Beavis said crossly. Then he slowly lowered Archie to the ground and tied the bucket about his waist. He hauled him up once more until he hung over the centre of the lane, the broken bucket attached to his waist. Mr Beavis once more took up his position in the undergrowth. Time enough for a practice drop, he thought. But then he heard a persistent pounding. At first he couldn't make out what it could be but then he heard the approaching hum of the car's engine. No time for a practice. He took a deep breath and licked his lips. It was now or never. He felt strangely exultant. His heart beat fast so that he could feel the persistent drum of it in both his ears. He whispered instructions to himself. No good dropping it too late. It'll merely hit the windscreen and he'll drive through it. Then they'll stop and come back and kill me. Have to drop it just far enough ahead so that he sees it at the last moment and instinctively jerks the steering wheel one way

or the other in order to avoid it. The question of the youths'
morality crossed Mr Beavis's mind. In that flashing instant
when Archie dropped unaccountably from the skies in front of
him, would the youth merely smash through him heedlessly or
would some atavistic sense of human concern re-assert itself,
causing him to turn the wheel in an attempt to avoid him.

We'll soon find out, thought Mr Beavis.

The roar of the over-stressed engine and the pounding
music were louder now. Through the screen of trees to his left
he suddenly caught sight of a flash of red bodywork; the grey-
hooded figure of the driver bent over the steering wheel. He
appeared to be on his own. Sweat dripped from Mr Beavis's
forehead. His grip on the worn length of rope tightened. And
then the car was there. With a whoop that was something
between joy and abject terror, Mr Beavis released the rope,
throwing his arms wide. Archie and his attendant bucket
dropped an instant before the bonnet of the car struck it with
a resounding clang. The bucket detached itself and crashed
into the windscreen. Mr Beavis had time to see the youth's
mouth open; saw him wrench the wheel savagely to the left and
then he was sliding and snaking crazily down the lane in a
squeal of protesting tyres before plunging off down the slope,
cutting a violent swathe through splintering trees and bushes.
The galvanised bucket bounced noisily down the lane and was
still.

Then silence.

Mr Beavis for some reason expected to hear the sound of
running feet; the excited cries of rescuers. But there was nothing.

Nothing. He tried to move but was quite unable. For what must have been minutes, he crouched amongst the silent trees, staring before him, his hand to his mouth; seeing nothing. It was all much more violent than he had imagined. Something like regret began to seep into his consciousness. Finally, he managed to struggle to his feet and on to the lane. Of the little red Astra there was no sign. The battered bucket lay on its side completely crushed. Black skid marks snaked down the lane. Slowly and reluctantly, Mr Beavis followed them until he came to a point where the trees had been torn aside. The exposed wood gleamed damp and flesh-like. At the bottom of the slope the car lay, facing the wrong way. The driver's arm hung uselessly out of the open window. From within came a faint groan. Mr Beavis gazed up and down the lane, his hand to his mouth. There was no one. He scrambled down to where the car lay, straddling the brook. There was oil turning to rainbow colours in the shallow water. He crouched behind the boot where the driver couldn't see him.

He said, 'Are you all right?'

The moaning was louder.

'Are you all right?' he called now.

'My fucking leg,' the youth groaned. 'I done me fucking leg.'

Mr Beavis said, 'But you're alive.'

'Of course I'm fucking alive. Help me.' He began to cry. 'Do something. Fuckin' do something you pratt.'

Mr Beavis looked about him. 'Where is he?'

'What you fuckin' on about?'

'The other one.'

'What other one?'

'Your friend. I can't see him.'

'I dropped him off.'

'You dropped him off.'

'I fuckin' dropped him off. What you want you stupid cunt? Never mind about him. Help me. Do some fuckin' thing.'

'All right, said Mr Beavis. 'I'm going to do something all right. And what I'm going to do is to leave you.'

'Don't fuckin' leave me you cunt. You old fuckin' cunt. Help me.'

'I'm off now,' said Mr Beavis. 'Goodbye.'

Mr Beavis scrambled back up the bank, the curses of the youth ringing in his ears. He was oddly relieved at the vehemence of the boy's swearing. It reassured him the youth was likely to survive. It had never been his intention to kill him; merely to teach him some kind of lesson. Not even that: more to punish him in the name of all of them. And supposing he had died? I'd be a murderer, Mr Beavis said aloud. A murderer. Murderer. He repeated the word over and over, chanting it rhythmically in time with his hurrying footsteps. Murderer. That would all he'd be remembered for. Not for his acts of generosity; his teaching; or his odd pieces of writing. If ever people happened to mention him after he'd been committed to prison; or was dead even, they'd say automatically, *Oh you mean him? The murderer. Killed that young man.* Whatever he did with the remainder of his life, the memory of what he had done this day would be always in him, too; spreading like an ink stain across his conscience; not to speak of its effect on Hazel and her offspring. Having a grandfather who had murdered a young man in cold blood was not something those two young boys would be proud of. Although, given the way society was moving, one could be certain of nothing these days. But the boy would survive, he was sure of that. But what he had done was still a crime. How would the Justice System name it, should he, by some chance, be found out and arraigned for his actions? Grievous bodily harm most probably. To Mr Beavis that sounded apt; even satisfactory; although, on reflection, he'd prefer the 'grievous' part to be omitted. The sound of it however appealed to him. He walked down the lane turning the word over on his tongue as though it were chocolate. At the corner of the river bridge stood a phone box; to Mr Beavis's satisfaction still painted in the traditional red. The windows had been smashed but the earpiece still purred when he put it to his ear. He dialled the emergency number.

A woman's voice said, 'Which service do you require?'

The sing-song calmness of her voice irritated Mr Beavis.

'Well emergency of course that's why I called you.'

'Yes but you have to specify.'

'Specify what?'

'Well, do you want police, fire or the ambulance service?'

'Well all three I should think.'

'You need to state which service before we can help you.'

'It's actually not me who needs help. It's the young man in the car. So I'm not going to do that if it's all the same to you. I merely want to say that if you send someone down Oak Tree Lane…..'

*

That night Mr Beavis found himself trudging through a sloping, endless, ploughed field filled with scarecrows. They began to shift and move towards him almost imperceptibly. Their mouths, rather like children playing, made the sound of car engines as they moved towards him until finally he was surrounded. From their ill-fitting boots, blood oozed until it formed a vast lake covering the brown earth.

He awoke with a start and went down stairs to make himself a cup of tea. Back in his bed he sat upright watching the curtains lighten. He wondered if the youth and his crashed car had been found. It worried him. He picked up the phone beside his bed and was about to call the emergency services but half way through dialling the number, it struck him that they would probably be able to trace his number.

Hurriedly he replaced the phone.

You're behaving like a criminal, he thought. He took a sip of the hot sugary tea and concluded: But that's what you are. You are a criminal. It's just that nobody knows about it except you. And who was there who could denounce him? Certainly not Blenkinsopp. Even if he had discovered the truth he would be more likely to congratulate than to denounce him. Then he remembered the man and his Essex wife in their Rover with the Labrador in the back. The man had a busy-bodying air to him. Mr Beavis knew the type: someone who would enjoy phoning the police and giving his name in full. *Look there's probably nothing to this but I thought I'd let you know. It concerns the boy they found crashed, off Oak Tree Lane. Well...*

But remembering their accents, Mr Beavis felt fairly confident that they would be back in Southend, or wherever it was they came from, by now; it was unlikely that the news of a road accident in which nobody had been killed, would make the national papers.

But one never knew.

On an impulse he went to the bathroom and began to chop at his hair and beard with a pair of curved nail scissors. He lathered his face, stropped the open razor that he hadn't used for years and carefully shaved off his beard and moustache. When he'd finished, he studied the pink, naked stranger who stared back at him from the bathroom mirror. He didn't much care for him. Hello, he thought. That's you, Arthur. That's who you really are. He stroked the pouched, unfamiliar softness of his face. Well, at least Essex man won't recognise you.

He began to pull absurd faces: he wrinkled his nose; wiggled his ears and stuck his tongue out as far as it would go; he snarled at himself like a beast in pain. Then he clenched his upper teeth down hard over his lower lip and, rolling his eyes, began to smile insanely. The smile became a laugh. He couldn't stop. He laughed uncontrollably as he had laughed when a child; with a sort of hysterical joy that was on the edge of pain. His stomach ached with the effort of it. Supporting himself with his hand against the wall, wheezing with laughter, he staggered to his bedroom and collapsed on the bed still laughing. When the laughter finally subsided, he fell into a deep and dreamless sleep.

The next day Mr Beavis did not go for his usual walk. He felt the beginning of a cold in his nose and chest and merely went out of the house in order to buy the local paper at the corner shop near his house. To avoid arousing suspicion he refrained from opening it until he was back home in his untidy summer house eating his breakfast. But there was nothing in it about the boy or the crashed car. For the rest of the day he read his Proust; dipping into it at random, reading of Marcel's walk through Paris during the war and his observation of Charlus's sado-masochistic pleasuring in the Paris bordello.

The next morning, curiosity got the better of him and he pulled on his familiar walking boots and set out. As the black, snaking smear of the skid marks came into sight he slowed. When he reached the violently torn passage through the undergrowth, he found himself unable to turn his head in the direction of the car. When he finally forced his head to turn, he was dismayed to see the car was still there, exactly as he had last seen it. He considered the consequences of this for a few moments, gazing back and forth up the lane. What if the Emergency Services had ignored his call and the boy was still there - Dead from his all night exposure and his untreated injuries? After a further nervous glance up and down the empty lane, he clambered down between the smashed and splintered trees to where the wreck of the car lay. He stationed himself behind a tree and peered into the interior. What he dreaded, was discovering the body of the youth still slumped over the steering wheel. His body began to shiver uncontrollably. He felt cold. But to his relief the car appeared to be empty. Hesitantly he crept down and rested his hand on the bodywork. Yes, empty. The door on the far side had been opened. Heavy footmarks were printed in the mud. There was the taste of bile in the back of Mr Beavis's throat. He vomited violently into the brook. After, he splashed his face with water and felt better. A strange impulse seized him, to sit where the young driver had sat, crashing crazily through undergrowth. He eased himself in and sat back in the driver's seat, his eyes closed, gripping the wheel tightly. Above him in the lane he heard the sound of a car approaching. It stopped. A door opened. Voices. Fearfully, he hauled himself, stumbling from the car and crouched among the bushes on the far side of the brook. The voices were too far away for him to make out what they were saying. Peering, with infinite caution, through the leaves and branches, he could make out the outline of two men staring down at the car. They were both dressed in dark overcoats. He did not think they were policemen; unless of course they were plain clothes officers. He closed his eyes. If he was to be apprehended, then he was resigned to the fact. He would tell the truth of it. But then there was the sound of doors slamming and to his immense relief, he heard the car pull away. Merely curious observers, Mr Beavis presumed. For a further quarter of an hour he remained crouched in the tiny wilderness beside the crashed car. For fear of meeting someone on the lane, he decided make his way through the denser undergrowth alongside the far side of the brook, until well clear of the site of the accident. To regain the lane once more, he had to force his body through a thick hedge, scratching his face and hands. A small girl with a doll in her hand was standing in front of a row of cottages. She stared at him curiously, her finger in her mouth.

On his way home Mr Beavis bought a local paper but again did not open it until he reached home. And even then he left it unread until he had showered and daubed the scratches on his arm and hand with a dilution of Dettol.

The article was on the second page.

Mysterious car crash in Oak Tree Lane,

ran the headline.

On Tuesday, the police and ambulance services answering an anonymous call, discovered a car turned on it's side on Oak Hill Lane. Inside the driver, Nigel Drewitt of Maple Grove (19) had sustained a broken thigh and superficial bruises to his head and ribs. He informed the police that some unknown person had leapt directly in front of his car and in attempting to avoid them he had pulled off the road and ended up in a stream at the side of the road. The police searched the area but found no sign of any other injured person. A spokesman said: 'We did find a man's clothing scattered about the place but they appeared to belong to a scarecrow. There was also an old-type galvanised bucket. At the moment the matter is still under investigation and we would appeal to whoever it was who made the phone call or any other eye witnesses, to contact us a soon as possible so that the matter may be cleared up.'

Mr Drewitt was taken to St Mary's Hospital where he will remain for some weeks though a spokesman revealed that he is likely to make a full recovery.

Mr Beavis read the article several times. Then he cut it out carefully with a pair of kitchen scissors and hid it in a drawer in his bedroom amongst his socks and underpants. In the afternoon, for no reason that was apparent to him, he took a bus into town. Gazing out from the top deck onto the gardens of small terraced houses and workshops, he thought he should do something with his life. Begin to smoke cigars; perhaps go to live in Nice for a few months; buy a word processor and finish that book on Balzac that he'd begun and abandoned so many years ago.

Perhaps he could do all three. The thought cheered him.

The bus jolted to a stop outside the Hospital: St Mary's. He stared at it for some time, then as the bus was about to pull out he rushed down the steps and leaped out onto the pavement.

The lady behind the oval reception desk gazed at him over her spectacles with an instant smile that disappeared almost as soon as soon as it had appeared. The overbite of her upper teeth was smeared with lipstick.

Mr Beavis coughed. 'I wonder if you would be so kind as to tell me which ward Mr Drewitt is in?'

The receptionist brushed back a stray wisp of hair and consulted the computer screen in front of her.

'Mr Drewitt with a D?' she said in a sing-song voice.

'Yes.'

'Are you a relative?'

'Relative? I'm his uncle,' he said without thinking. Then after a pause: 'On his mother's side.'

'Ah here it is,' said the receptionist,' running the point of a biro down the screen. 'Yes he's in a mixed ward. It's Palmer. Here look.' She pencilled in a cross on a map and pushed it across the desk to Mr Beavis.

Palmer Ward was on the ground floor at the end of a long corridor. At the entrance to the ward, the pretty staff nurse walked towards him. Mr Beavis turned his back and began to read with simulated interest a list of instructions concerning the distribution of medicines. But the nurse walked past him and became engaged in an intense, whispered conversation with a young couple and their small son. Mr Beavis slipped past them unobserved into the main body of the ward.

The sense of oppression that hospitals always gave him tightened his chest. The last time he had been in one was when he'd visited Grace. Hazel had been with him. As they had walked between the beds he had whispered to her, 'Avert your eyes, avert your eyes!' trying to protect her from the more unwholesome sights that greeted them on either side. But when they had arrived at her bed, Grace was already dead. And nobody had known it.

The thought made him shiver.

Now, walking down the centre of the ward, he glanced covertly from side to side, searching for the boy, Drewitt. Those patients who were awake observed his passage, but without interest. Of Drewitt he could see nothing. Then finally he spotted him, three beds from the end of the ward and to his right. He appeared to be asleep. His right leg was encased in what, seemed to Mr Beavis, to be a grotesquely large plaster casing, suspended on a sling; he couldn't help but be reminded of a scene from a Carry On film. Drewitt's face in sleep, took on a different aspect: the sardonic twist to his mouth and the small, narrow eyes, now had something strangely innocent about them that reminded Mr Beavis of a sleeping baby. Then, as he watched, the youth's eyes opened and stared straight into his. Mr Beavis dragged his eyes away and smiling walked down the aisle as though greeting some relative on the other side of the ward. Once he had started he had to keep up the act.

'Well how are you?' he whispered settling himself into a chair beside the last bed. The occupant, a handsome woman in her early fifties, sat propped high on a pile of pillows her eyes closed, breathing gently. Mr Beavis bent his head pretending to engage the sleeping woman in conversation, while all the time he secretly observed the figure of Drewitt opposite. To Mr Beavis's relief the youth appeared to have lost interest in him. He was reaching up for a pair of headphones hooked over the bedhead and was settling them on his ears. Covertly, Mr Beavis explored Drewitt's face as his head nodded idiotically up and down to the rhythm of some music only he could hear.

Mr Beavis began to wonder why he had come. Why was he sitting beside a sleeping woman he did not know, staring at a youth wearing headphones that he happened to have tricked into crashing his car? He wasn't at all sure. Could it be, he asked himself, so that he might reassure himself of his victim's recovery? He thought not - though it was now evident that, by the look of him, Drewitt would be out in the world again in a matter of weeks if not days. Was it that he was attempting to assuage a vague feeling of remorse? Again he thought not. In fact he felt very little, other than a kind of emptiness. Not for the first time in his life, he speculated on how difficult it was to make any kind of clear connection between his feelings and the possible events that might have provoked them. In the end, he explained his presence in the hospital to himself as, a species of extreme curiosity; an ultimately fruitless attempt to make some kind of connection with another disparate person who occupied the world beyond himself; to wonder what it must be like to be him. It was the old self, non-self conundrum that had preoccupied him since he was a boy of eight or nine: that moment when he had begun to wonder whether *his* was the only true reality, and that the remaining inhabitants of the great world, all those who lay outside himself: his parents, his sister, his friends, and all those uncountable individuals in other distant lands, unseen and utterly unknown - everybody - were merely some kind of odd emanation of his own consciousness. This still remained a mystery for him. Naturally this rather philosophically simplistic view had changed with time but an atavistic remnant remained to haunt and perplex him. Now he attempted to divine in the blunt, coarse features of this nodding youth opposite, whom chance had brought so violently into his life, some secret explanation to this perplexing question of the separateness; the complete otherness, of those human beings who happened to occupy a space in the world beyond the limits of one's own flesh.

'We are all alone,' he concluded. 'Utterly alone.'

'What's that?'

Idiotically he'd spoken aloud.

The woman had jerked into wakefulness and was staring at him.

'I er…'

'What did you say?'

'Nothing. I…

'Yes you did.'

'I thought you were asleep.'

'Even more reason not to shout.'

He attempted to think of something that might reasonably explain his presence beside this unknown woman whom he had so rudely awakened. But nothing came into his head. 'Did I shout?'

'Of course you did. I heard you distinctly. Well let me tell you that I am by no means alone.'

'Ah. Well, that's good,' Mr Beavis said rather weakly.

'It's neither good nor bad. It's merely a fact.'

The lady reached for a pair of spectacles from the bedside table and peered at Mr Beavis. 'Do I know you?'

'I don't think so.'

'Are you a doctor?'

'No. Certainly not.'

'What are you doing here?'

'I…'

'You were watching me weren't you?'

'No, no I was…

'Yes you were. I think I'd better call a nurse.' She sat up suddenly. 'Nurse, nurse!' she cried.

Mr Beavis was concerned that Drewitt might be alerted by the cry but his head still nodded to the music. His eyes were closed. 'No, there's no need to call a nurse. I mistook you for someone else. My eyes you see. They're not good. I'm so sorry. I…'

And he rose and hurried from the ward.

*

Four days later he returned to the hospital. He had an inbuilt desire to say something to Drewitt; not to reveal his identity, but to exchange some commonplace with him. Now he paused tentatively at the foot of his bed. He smiled at him.

'Feeling better today?'

Drewitt raised his head. 'What's it to you?'

'Just asking,' Mr Beavis said.

'Yeah well. Soon as I'm out of this I'll be laughing.'

'Laughing?'

'I'm out tomorrow whether they like it or not. Drives me fuckin' crazy in 'ere, know what I mean?'

'Well good luck.'

'Fuck off,' the boy said and turned on his side.

The woman in the end bed was still there. She was reading. But Mr Beavis by some intuition was aware that she had been observing him. When he turned towards her, her head disappeared swiftly behind the book she was holding. There was something about the cover of it that caught his attention. He put on his glasses. He could make out the white cover with the red printing.

He could see where the pages had been cut; a foreign text; and the name. He knew that name. His heart stirred. He walked slowly across and stood before her. She continued to hold the book before her face but Mr Beavis knew that she was aware of his presence. He coughed. Quietly and carefully he pronounced: 'Longtemps, je suis couché de bonne heure.' For a moment the book was still. Then it shifted to one side to disclose the woman's face looking up at him; a still remarkably pretty woman with dark eyes and a heart-shaped face. She frowned but not with irritation.

'Je *me* suis couché,' she corrected him softly. 'It's reflexive. Long temps je *me* suis couché de bonne heure.'

'Je me suis couché. You're absolutely right.'

'Of course I am. Look.' She leafed back through the volume to the first page and held the book up to him. 'You see. "Je me suis couché".'

Mr Beavis leaned forward reading the words. 'You read it in the original?'

She said, 'My mother was French. A Gascon.'

'Oh that's good. Is it your first time?'

'First time?'

'The Proust.'

'Oh I see. No. One and a half actually. You?'

'Third.'

'Gracious.'

'In English of course.'

'Even so. Three times!' She whistled.

'I wrote a little monograph on it.'

'You did?'

'Not worth mentioning really. Thirty years ago now. Sold about two copies. Though that may be a generous estimate.'

'What was it called?'

' "The Stream of Memory." '

She took off her glasses. 'You're not...' she clicked her fingers...what's his name?'

'Arthur Whatisname. Beavis.'

'Beavis. That's the one. I've read it?'

'You read my book?'

'Of course.'

'That makes three then.'

They looked at one another smiling. She was about to say something when the bell rang in the ward to signal the end of visiting time.

'Ah Shame,' said the woman. She stretched out her hand. 'Jacqueline,' she said. She pronounced it in French way.

'Arthur.'

He held her hand a little longer than might be considered judicious but she made no attempt to withdraw it. A card slipped from between the pages of the book onto the floor. He bent to pick it up. It was a photograph of Jacqueline. She wore a red beret and was smiling. She cradled a small white dog in her arms. He stared from the photograph and then back to Jacqueline's face, pale against the pillow. It was a good face. And he thought how apt the word was; that what was attractive about her had a moral dimension. That it was who she *was*, that had made that face; that face that now stared up at him curiously. He held up the photo and was about to ask her about the dog but before he could speak she said, 'Look why don't you come back tomorrow. Only if you want to that is. You could read to me. My eyes get tired since the accident.'

'Accident.'

'I had an unfortunate quarrel with a car. The car won.'

'Oak Tree Lane?'

'Yes. How did you know?'

'It was in the paper.' He shook his head. 'No, that's a lie. Blenkinsop told me.'

'Blenkinsop?'

'Just somebody I talk to in the rain from time to time.'

'That sounds nice.'

'Was it an accident?'

'Well in fact the car didn't touch me. In jumping aside to avoid it I fell and broke my leg. It was quite a simple break but then there was an infection. And I also scratched my eye on a sharp branch. There was a macular tear. If you don't mind I'd rather not talk about it.'

'Of course.' He frowned. 'Are you sure you'd like me to read to you? My French is execrable. If not worse.'

'There's the possibility I'd find it charming.'

'Anything's possible.'

A bell rang. The staff nurse said, 'I'm afraid visiting time is over.'

Mr Beavis experienced an odd febrile sensation somewhere between his oesophagus and his solar plexus as he rose and walked from the bed. Then he turned back. He said: 'You're dog. It's a Westie isn't it?'

'Yes he is. Why d'you ask?' Then her eyes suddenly widened as if in recognition. She stroked her face with the back of her hand then pointed at him with a crooked index finger. 'Wait a minute,' she said. 'You're the…

'Yes I am…'

'The walker. I thought there was something.'

The bell rang once more.

He leaned forward and shook her hand. He said, 'I do like shaking your hand.' He felt himself blushing.

'Tomorrow,' she said.

'Of course,' Mr Beavis said. He released her hand reluctantly. 'I'll see you tomorrow.'

As he walked past Drewitt's bed, Mr Beavis called out with unaccustomed joviality, 'See you tomorrow as well.'

'You'll be fuckin' lucky,' said the boy Drewitt.

'Let's hope so,' said Mr Beavis and walked out of the ward without looking back.

*

The next day Mr Beavis returned. Drewitt's bed was empty. Some impulse made him sit down beside the empty bed; put his hand on the mattress. A lady walked by pushing a tea trolley.

'Cup of tea?'

'No thank you.' He pointed at the bed. 'What happened to the boy here?'

'That boy. He went home. They couldn't keep him. Checked himself out. Should have heard the shouting. The language!

Never heard the like. His brother came for him. Good riddance I say. You his dad?'

Mr Beavis smiled and shook his head.

Even though he knew the answer, nobody better, he asked the woman what had happened to Drewitt. He wanted to hear it from other lips. 'What happened to him?'

'Car accident. Going too fast. Ended up in a ditch. The coppers was here. Lucky to be alive. It was in the paper.'

'Oh yes I think I might have read it. Wasn't there something about a scarecrow?'

'That was something he made up. They're all liars those kids. I've got two myself. Just as bad. No, he was going too fast. Maybe it'll teach him a lesson. Sure you won't have a cup of tea?'

'No thank you.'

'Please yourself.'

He glanced across the ward. Jacqueline raised her hand in an odd, constrained wave. She was smiling.

He crossed to her and stood beside the bed.

She looked at him holding out the book. 'You going to read?'

'If you like but I warn you.'

'I know. You said.'

Essentially a shy man, Mr Beavis read the unfamiliar French with some embarrassment; like a schoolboy. Jacqueline let him progress, saying little. She frowned with concentrated interest, sometimes offering a correction to his pronunciation; sometimes she laughed aloud, so that his confidence bloomed - until by the fourth day he found himself throwing himself into the task with an uncharacteristic assurance that teetered on the edge of abandon. He even made a not wholly successful attempt to simulate the voices of the different characters.

On the Sunday, a week later, as he walked down the ward, he became aware that another youth, his head shaved and bandaged, his left arm in a sling, was occupying what had been Drewitt's bed. He questioned Jacqueline about him.

'Silly boy,' Jacqueline said. 'Fell off his motorbike. His poor mother was in earlier; was in tears.'

For the first time, it occurred to Mr Beavis that Drewitt must have a mother also. He wondered if she too had cried.

He asked Jacqueline if she believed in forgiveness. He wasn't sure why. But then before she could answer, the staff nurse stopped at the foot of her bed. She studied her fever chart.

'Good book?' she said without looking up.

'It's Proust,' Jacqueline said.

'Oh I like a good thriller,' the nurse said. She re-clipped the chart to the base of the bed. 'You'll be glad to hear that if you behave we'll be letting you out of here next Wednesday.'

'In that case I'll behave,' Jacqueline said.

When the nurse had gone Mr Beavis continued with his reading. He voiced the text but what he was thinking was, that he wanted to tell Jacqueline many things: that he felt that he knew her; that he was sorry that shortly, she would be going home; that he wanted to come and read to her here for the rest of his life; that his coming to the hospital had become central to his days. He dearly longed to ask her if he might possibly come and visit her at her home and continue the readings, in order that he might finish the book. There were six long volumes to go. At his present rate of reading – he made a swift calculation - it would take three years. The prospect seemed immeasurably enticing to him. But he had no idea how to broach the topic; how to switch from the mechanical process of reading to other more heartfelt matters. He realised he didn't even know where she lived.

So he turned the pages and continued with his reading.

He came to a passage whose sense he couldn't fathom. He read it once more. He said, 'Is this right?' and attempted a translation:

If a little dreaming is dangerous, the cure for it is not to... not to...

But then a shadow fell across the page. He realised it was Jacqueline's hand. It lay palely, obscuring the text, the plump palm upturned. Mr Beavis did not look up but stared at the hand, transfixed. Then he found his own right hand, almost without volition, closing upon it and squeezing it gently.

The woman who was Jacqueline said, '...*the cure for it is not to dream less but to dream more, to dream all the time.*

'Of course,' Mr Beavis said. 'Not to dream less.'

He continued holding her hand until the end of visiting time. On his way out, he stopped at the foot of the bed that had been Drewitt's. He read the name: Dave. He felt he needed to tell somebody how he felt: that he was intensely happy.

The young man looked up at him with half-closed eyes.

'Dave?' Mr Beavis said.

'That's me,' the young man said. 'Or what's left of me.' He smiled ruefully.

'You're going to be fine,' Mr Beavis said.

'I am?'

'Definitely. You've got youth on your side. That's a good thing.' He began to say, 'If a little dreaming is dangerous…' but then stopped.

'What's that?' the youth asked.

'Nothing. Nothing,' said Mr Beavis shaking his head and smiling. 'I'm a bit dotty today. I'll see you tomorrow.'

'Yeah tomorrow,' the young man called Dave said.

When he got home, Mr Beavis made himself a ham sandwich and a cup of tea. He stood in his back garden thinking; it was time that he mowed the lawn. The rain petered out reluctantly and the roofs of the houses gleamed in the sun. He returned to the house and searched in a large cardboard box for the monograph on Balzac that he had begun so many years before. When he had found it, he sat at the kitchen table turning over the pages. He put down his pencil and raising his head gazed out of the window; then picked up the phone and dialled his daughter's number.

'Dad?'

'I wanted to tell you something,' Mr Beavis said. 'I wanted to tell you my dear lovely girl that I love you very much and…' he hesitated.

'Oh Dad. And what, Dad. And what?'

'I think you should start looking for a hat,' Mr Beavis said.

*